MYTHOLOGY OF
THE INCAS

MYTHOLOGY OF
THE INCAS

MYTHS AND LEGENDS OF THE ANCIENT ANDES, WESTERN VALLEYS, DESERTS AND AMAZONIA

DAVID M JONES

southwater

I dedicate this book to Megan and to Sam, two continuing sources of inspiration.

This edition is published by Southwater

Southwater is an imprint of Anness Publishing Limited
Hermes House, 88-89 Blackfriars Road, London SE1 8HA
tel 020 7401 2077; fax 020 7633 9499

www.southwaterbooks.com; info@anness.com

Anness Publishing has a new picture agency outlet for images for
publishing, promotions or advertising. Please visit our website
www.practicalpictures.com for more information.

UK agent: The Manning Partnership Ltd; tel. 01225 478444;
fax 01225 478440; sales@manning-partnership.co.uk
UK distributor: Grantham Book Services Ltd; tel. 01476 541080;
fax 01476 541061; orders@gbs.tbs-ltd.co.uk
North American agent/distributor: National Book Network;
tel. 301 459 3366; fax 301 429 5746; www.nbnbooks.com
Australian agent/distributor: Pan Macmillan Australia;
tel. 1300 135 113; fax 1300 135 103;
customer.service@macmillan.com.au
New Zealand agent/distributor: David Bateman Ltd;
tel. (09) 415 7664; fax (09) 415 8892

Publisher: Joanna Lorenz
Managing Editor: Helen Sudell
Project Editor: Sue Barraclough
Design: Mario Bettella, Artmedia
Map Illustrator: Stephen Sweet
Picture Researchers: Veneta Bullen (UK), Anita Dickhuth (US)
Editorial Reader: Richard McGinlay

ETHICAL TRADING POLICY
Because of our ongoing ecological investment programme, you, as our
customer, can have the pleasure and reassurance of knowing that a
tree is being cultivated on your behalf to naturally replace the materials
used to make the book you are holding. For further information about
this scheme, go to www.annesspublishing.com/trees

Previously published as part of a larger compendium *Mythology of the Americas*

Page 1: *ATAHUALPA INCA*
Frontispiece: *INCA TUPAC AMARU*
Title page: *CHIBCHA GOLD PECTORAL*
This page: *SACRIFICIAL TUMI KNIFE*
Opposite page: *A MODERN MURAL IN LIMA DEPICTS THE
HONOURING OF INTI WITH THE OFFER OF A HERD OF LLAMAS*
Page 8: *FANCIFUL RECONSTRUCTION OF AN INCA PROCESSION*
Page 16: *PURUNMACHAS CLAY SARCOPHAGI, PERU*

PUBLISHER'S NOTE: The entries in this encyclopedia are listed alphabetically.
Names in italic capital letters indicate the name has an individual entry. Special
feature spreads examine specific mythological themes in more detail. If a character
or subject is included in a special feature spread it is noted at the end of their
individual entry.

CONTENTS

PREFACE

his encyclopedia describes the religious beliefs developed by the Incas and contemporary peoples, and by predecessor cultures and civilizations. It describes the beliefs of the high civilizations of the Andes, high deserts and western coastal valleys, and of the peoples of Amazonia and the southern and south-eastern regions of the South American continent. Although focused on the final development, at the time of European conquest, it projects back to civilizations before the Incas and describes beliefs recorded by 19th- and 20th-century ethnographers and anthropologists.

People migrated into the New World from the far north-east of Asia from at least 15,000 years ago. Some evidence suggests that they came both by land, following an ice-free corridor between the great glacial sheets of Canada, and by sea, along the western coast. By about 9,000 years ago, at least, the descendants of these migrants had populated the continents of North and South America, right down to the tip of Tierra del Fuego.

The word myth is derived from the Greek word *mythos*. It originally meant "word" or "story", but later came to be juxtaposed to the word *logos*, meaning "truth", and came to mean "fiction", or even "falsehood". These meanings form a Western point of view, and are popularly, and often subconsciously, applied to what is called the "mythology" of an ancient, and especially pre-Christian and pre-Islamic, culture, and even more especially of a "non-Western" culture.

When considered from the point of view of the peoples and cultures who created the myths, however, the stories and their characters described here constitute, in fact, the religion of the ancient peoples of the Andes and elsewhere in South America.

Myths are about gods and goddesses, and about divine or semi-divine heroes. The mythology of a people or culture is part of a coherent system of beliefs.

The myths themselves are sacred to those telling them or recording them, and are almost always linked to ritual. The sacred stories are re-enacted – usually through a regular cycle of specified days or other time periods, in specially designated or constructed places, and involve elaborate preparations. A culture's mythology is usually intimately linked to and endorsed by the élite of society – rulers and priests, who might be one and the same group. In ancient cultures, the mythology usually forms part of the élite's reason for being and part of its power base. The myths give the élite their power by explaining how it has been given to them as part of the divine scheme of life.

Scholars have analysed the mythologies of cultures throughout the world in an attempt to discover universal themes and a single cause for myth-making. They have approached the subject as external, trying to find common themes in mythological stories – for example divine rulership, or the nature of an afterlife – and as internal, attempting to identify universal features of the human psyche – for example the reason for human existence, or a perceived universal nature in the relationship between children and their parents. Complex meanings in mythological themes are said to explain and resolve apparent contradictions in the human experience. Universality has even been sought by constructing elaborate checklists of functions common to all world myths.

Such scholarly pursuits continue to be a basis for debate. Returning to the point of view of the peoples who created the myths, however, it seems clear that their purpose when the culture and mythology were concurrently active was to explain their world and everything in it. Every culture has a need to explain the vastness and power of the cosmos and the natural world around it. All peoples need to explain not only how they came into being as a tribe, village, city, state or larger political entity, but also how the universe itself came into being, how the land in which they live was formed, and their own origins within it. The nature of human desires, fears, likes and dislikes, capacity for doing good and evil, and selfishness and altruism requires an explanation. Thus "mythology" enables a people and culture to find meaning, balance and a sense of place in the world they inhabit.

Mythology is not just a miscellaneous collection of old tales and legends. To the people and culture concerned myth embraces all of what we now call religion, science and philosophy (natural, moral and metaphysical). It asks fundamental questions – how the world began, how it will end, where humans fit in and how they can influence it, and how individuals and communities should interact on a variety of levels. As such general ideas have universal underpinning and application, the questions asked are the same.

Common threads run through the mythologies of different South American civilizations and peoples, and through successive archaeologically defined cultures. A modern division of religion and politics was unknown to the high civilizations. In these the entire basis of political power was derived from divine development and designation. In Inca society, and probably in Chimor and in Moche and other cultures before them, rulers and priests were often one and the same. The Inca ruler himself was regarded as the living divine representative. Although certain specializations prevailed, the two groups were intimately entwined in ruling and regulating every aspect of daily life. Ruler worship was carried beyond the grave by continuing ritual with the mummies of past Incas. Especially important in Andean, high desert and western coastal civilizations was the sacredness of the landscape itself. Numerous natural features were regarded as semi-divine, ceremonial centres were constructed to represent myth, and ritual pathways were made across long distances, for example the Nazca lines and the Inca *ceques* pathways.

There were long sequences of traditional development among Andean and western coastal

THIS GOLD AND COPPER *jaguar head was discovered in the Lambayeque Valley in Peru. The jaguar features prominently in South American art and mythology, and it represents power, fertility and an ambivalent force that needs to be kept in check.*

peoples and cultures, fostered by ancient symbiotic relationships between mountain and coast. Many deities were almost universal, although given different names by different cultures, but distinct deities were the patrons from early times of particular peoples and civilizations. Nevertheless, long-standing places of ritual pilgrimage linked areas and regions and persisted despite the rise and fall of kingdoms and civilizations. The site and oracle of coastal Pachacamac, for example, had such potency and precedence that even the Incas recognized and revered it, but felt compelled to establish their imperial authority by building a temple to the sun god Inti in its shadow. Among Amazonian and other non-Andean tribal peoples there are also common themes, of a more naturalistic and animalistic nature.

The appeal of "mythology" from all of the approaches outlined above seems self-evident. The popular appeal of story-telling as pure entertainment forms one end of a continuum of interest that progresses through the analysis of myth itself as a universal human product. At the same time it is the diversity, the imaginative invention and richness of expression and depiction, as well as "alien" appeal – at least to Western readers – that makes the religion/"mythology" of South American cultures so fascinating.

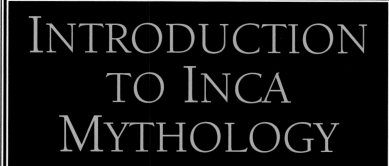

INTRODUCTION TO INCA MYTHOLOGY

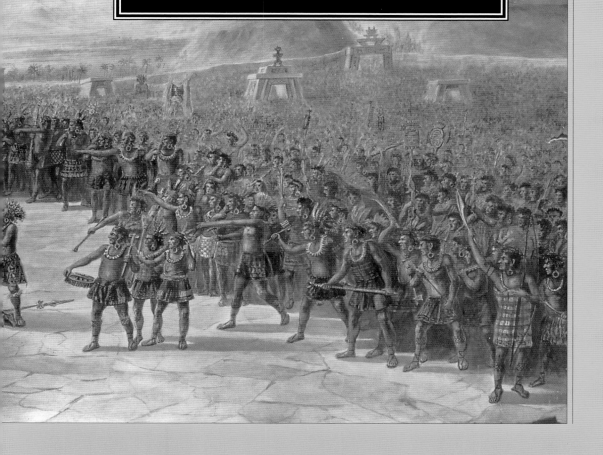

INTRODUCTION

THE ANCIENT PEOPLES OF the vast continent of South America never formed a coherent cultural unit. They cannot, therefore, be treated as such in describing their religions and mythologies.

Ancient urban-based societies were confined to the Andes mountains and adjacent western coastal valleys and deserts. Cultures with ceremonial centres, political organizations governing large areas, and advanced technology – including metallurgy – developed in present-day western Venezuela, Colombia, Peru, Bolivia, the northern half of Chile and the northwestern part of Argentina. Peoples elsewhere in South America developed sophisticated societies, but did not build monumental ceremonial centres or cities, or develop technology of quite the same complexity, or build kingdoms and empires. Mythologies varied throughout the continent, but seem less complex and had fewer deities in some areas.

The concentration of civilizations was in part due to geographic stimuli. Within a relatively small area, there is a range of contrasting landscapes, from Pacific coastal plains and deserts, to coastal and foothill valleys, to high mountain valleys and plateaux, to the eastern slopes on the edges of the rain forests and *pampas*.

A key factor in the development and endurance of these civilizations was control of water, which became important functionally, symbolically and religiously. Geographical contrasts fostered and nurtured the development of sophisticated agriculture based on complex irrigation technologies and a wide variety of crops within and between the lowland and highland regions. This development opened the way for economic specializations that enabled cultures to develop social hierarchies and complex divisions and distributions of labour and rulership, trading contacts across long distances, and sophisticated religious beliefs and structures, both theoretical and architectural.

THE INITIAL PERIOD *site of Cerro Sechín featured a distinctive style of low-relief carvings of grimacing warriors and severed heads on large stone slabs.*

South American cultures can be "classified" into three groups. First, the Northern, Central and Southern Andean Areas, where civilizations evolved in the mountains and adjacent foothills and coastal regions, north to south from the Colombian–Ecuadorian border to the northern half of Chile and east to west from the rain forests to the Pacific coast. Second, the Intermediate Area comprised the southern half of Central America, Colombia and western Venezuela, plus the Caribbean islands and adjacent South American mainland. Third, areas inhabited by tribal societies: the Amazonian–Orinoco drainages (Amazonian Area), the eastern highlands (East Brazilian Area), the *pampas* (Chaco and Pampean Areas) and Tierra del Fuego (Fuegian Area).

City-states, kingdoms and empires evolved within the Andean Areas, based on corn (maize) and potato agriculture and the herding of camel-family animals (llamas, alpacas and vicuñas). In the Intermediate Area, economies were based on maize/corn agriculture, but societal organization remained at the chiefdom level. Rain forest peoples thrived on manioc agriculture rather than maize/corn, plus hunting and gathering; and in some fringe groups, where agriculture was impossible, solely on hunting, gathering and fishing.

Within these simple frameworks of society, cultures developed on different timescales and at different paces, yet they interacted through trade, political alliance and conquest, and the diffusion of ideas.

Language and Sources

Thousands of languages and dialects were spoken throughout South America, but there were no writing systems before the Spanish conquest. The sources of ancient myths are therefore native oral records transcribed by Europeans or European-trained natives in Spanish, Portuguese and other European languages, or in a few cases, Quechua (the language of the Incas) or Aymará (in the Titicaca Basin) using the European alphabet, accounts by contemporary chroniclers and modern anthropological studies. Chronicles written during the century or so after the Spanish conquest were fraught with opportunities for misinterpretation, elision, embellishment, amendment and reinterpretation, and are therefore more difficult to interpret for their ancient mythological content.

These oral sources are supplemented by archaeological, artistic and architectural evidence, and much of the religious content of the transcribed oral sources can be projected back on earlier civilizations. Archaeological evidence shows how the deities were depicted and the physical spaces within which religion was practised. Gods, goddesses and ceremonial practices and rites were depicted in free-standing and architectural stone and wooden sculptures, on ceramics and in jewellery, in murals, featherwork, textiles and metalwork, and, by western

Peruvian coastal cultures, as geoglyphs – large-scale line drawings on the ground. Temples and ceremonial precincts tell us something about the nature of religious worship through their layout, divisions, and the use of spaces – open and enclosed, sunken and raised, between and within them.

The Incas were particularly enthusiastic about, and adept at, incorporating the religious practices and deities of subject peoples into their own religion in their attempt to create a cohesive empire. Knowing this Inca propensity – and the manifest continuity of many iconographic symbols, characters and themes – provides a sound basis on which to reconstruct Andean religion, beginning with the ancient civilization of Chavín.

Although not written, one recording device – the *quipu*, a system of tied bundles of string – served as an aide-mémoire to designated *quipucamayoqs* ("knot makers or keepers"). Many of the first records of Inca culture transcribed by Spanish priests were based on the memories of *quipucamayoqs* and the *amautas*, officially appointed Inca court poet-philosophers responsible for memorizing, recounting, interpreting, reinterpreting, amplifying, reciting and passing on the legends, history and genealogies of the Inca kings and queens.

About two dozen chroniclers' works provide information on the Incas and their contemporaries. Pedro Cieza de León's *Crónica del Peru* (1553 and 1554) contains much on Inca myth, as does Juan de Betanzos' *Narrative of the Incas* (1557), from the Inca nobility's point of view. Another record is Garcilasco de la Vega's (known as "El Inca") *Comentarios reales de los Incas* (1609–17), a complete history of the Inca Empire. A late pretender to the Inca throne, Melchior Carlos Inca, recorded the Inca origin myth, according to him, from interviews with four aged *quipucamayoqs* who had served the last emperor, in his *Relación de los Quipucamayoqs* (1608).

The exceptionally important Huarochirí Manuscript – written in Quechua – *Dioses y Hombres de Huarochirí* (c. 1608), records the myths of the central highlands of Peru. Accounts of the mythology of the peoples of the north Peruvian coast are Cabello de Balboa's *Miscelánea Antártica* (1586) and Antonio de la Calancha's *Crónica moralizada del Orden de San Augustínen el Perú* (1638). Accounts written by Spanish-trained native Quechua-speakers include Felipe Guaman Poma de Ayala and Juan de Santacruz Yamqui Salcamaygua. The former wrote his *Nueva Corónica y Buen Gobierno* between 1583 and 1613; the latter produced his *Relación de Antiguedades deste Reyno del Pirú* about 1613. Other documents, known as *idolatrías*, are records by Spanish priests attempting to stamp out idolatrous practices known to persist among local people under Spanish rule. These 17th-century documents are rich in information on local myth based on interrogations of local authorities, native curers, "witches" and other local diviners.

Lastly, the Jesuit priest Bernabé de Cobo, drawing principally from earlier chronicles, compiled the most balanced and comprehensive synthesis of Inca history and religion in his monumental work *Historia del Nuevo Mundo* (completed in 1653), books 13 and 14 of which are on Inca religion and customs.

Society and Religion

The term "mythology" reveals a cultural bias on the part of the user, for the legendary and

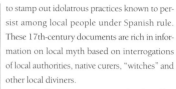

mythological accounts, together with deductions based on archaeological evidence, constituted the religions of South American societies.

Their religious beliefs and deities were those of the forces of nature. Like all peoples, they felt compelled to explain the important things in their universe, beginning with where they came from and their place in the larger scheme of things. They developed accounts of their observable cosmos to help them to understand what things were important, and

THE EARLY INTERMEDIATE
period north Peruvian coastal kingdom of the Moche was particularly rich in ceramic representations of warriors, such as this spouted bottle in the shape of a seated warrior wearing an eagle mask.

how and why things were the way they were. Explanations of these concepts were functional. They did for these ancient peoples what science and/or religion does for society today: they provided a conceptual framework for living and for comprehending and relating to the mysteries of their observable universe. Their myths sanctified the universe and humankind's place within it, at the same time educing or inciting direct experience of the sacred.

Common Beliefs

Despite the regional and cultural diversity of South America, there were common elements, some almost universal. In most regions, for example, there was a named creator god. Among the Late Intermediate Period and Late Horizon Andean civilizations Viracocha, with many variations, was the creator. Although his worship was prevalent among coastal civilizations, there was also confusion and/or rivalry with the supreme god Pachacamac. Viracocha prototypes appear in the imagery of earlier civilizations, for example Early Horizon Chavín and Middle Horizon Tiahuanaco. Among the Intermediate Area cultures, the Chibcha god Bochica, to name but one, fulfilled a similar role. In contrast, while most rain forest tribes acknowledge the existence of a creator deity, he was believed to have little interest in day-to-day human and earthly matters after creating the cosmos.

The religious iconography of cultures in the Andean and Intermediate areas, and therefore presumably their beliefs and mythology, was influenced from the earliest times by rain forest animals (jaguars, serpents, monkeys, birds) and composite anthropomorphic beings. In particular, both Andean civilizations and Amazonian cultures shared a fascination with the power and influence of jaguars. Iconographic motifs that persisted through the cultures of the Andes, in addition to the jaguar, were feline-human hybrids, staff deities (often with a composite feline face and human body), winged beings, and falcon-headed or other bird-headed warriors.

Andean Themes

The religions of Andean peoples share several common themes. As well as their creator Viracocha, almost all their rituals had a calendrical organization. There was a liturgical calendar based on the movements of heavenly bodies, including solar solstices and equinoxes, lunar phases, the synodical cycle of Venus, the rising and setting of the Pleiades, the rotational inclinations of the Milky Way, and the presence within the Milky Way of "dark cloud constellations" (stellar voids). Consultation of auguries concerning these movements were considered

THE EARLY INTERMEDIATE *Period Nazca culture, on the southern Peruvian coast , known for its textiles and the "Nazca lines" (geoglyphs), also produced highly painted pottery, in this example depicting a fierce-looking staring deity, perhaps in the tradition of the Paracas Oculate Being.*

vital at momentous times of the year, such as planting time, harvest time and the beginning of the ocean fishing season.

Sacrifice, both human and animal, and a variety of offerings were practised. Strangulation and beheading were early ritual practices, and were depicted in ceramics, murals, architectural sculpture, textile decoration and metalwork – and are also well attested from remains in burials and tombs.

Another theme, the recognition of special places as sacred, endured for centuries, regardless of the rise and fall of political powers. One of the most famous is the shrine and oracle of Pachacamac, but there were tens of thousands of others. Called *huacas*, such places could be springs (emphasizing the importance of water), caves (prominent in human origin mythology), mountains, rocks or stones, fields or towns where important events had taken place, lakes or islands in them, or artificial objects such as stone pillars erected at specific locations.

Hallucinogenic and other drugs were frequently used in ritual. *Coca (Erythroxylon coca)* leaves were chewed in a complex and many-staged ritual connected with war and sacrifice, and certain cacti were also employed. Tobacco was used in ritual by the cultures of the Intermediate Area.

Ancestor reverence and worship was widespread, and charged with its own special ritual. The mummified remains of ancestors – themselves considered *huacas* – were kept in special buildings, rooms or chambers, or in caves. They were brought out on ritual occasions to participate in the festivals and were offered delicacies of food and drink, as well as objects and prayers. Another Andean preoccupation concerned death and the underworld. Skeletal figures, depictions of priests imitating the dead in order to visit the underworld, skeletons with sexual organs and the dead embracing women were associated with beliefs in fertility.

Four common elements were associated with Andean accounts of cosmic origin and the creation of humankind. First was the belief that humanity originated at Lake Titicaca, and that Viracocha was the creator god. Second was the concept that each group recognized a particular place or feature in their landscape as the place from which they emerged. Third was a dual relationship between local people and a

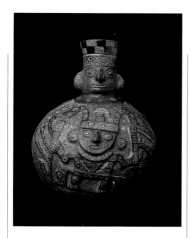

THE MIDDLE HORIZON *Huari Empire continued the tradition of the Staff Deity (depicted on this effigy bottle dated from 800 AD) after its highland predecessor, Chavín.*

group of outsiders; the relationship could be portrayed as one of co-operation or of conflict, but the relationship always defined the nature of the political arrangement that prevailed. Fourth was the conviction that there was a correct ordering of society and place in terms of rank.

Amazonia

Among Amazonian tribes, four almost universal themes can be recognized. First is the presence and power of shamans, and the associated use of hallucinogenic drugs to gain access into the spirit world for the wellbeing and guidance of humankind. Second is belief in the power and ancient divinity of jaguars. Third is the practice of cannibalism: both endocannibalism, to perpetuate the power and character of a dead relation, and exocannibalism, to entrap the power of an enemy and inflict insult and revenge on an enemy's relations. And fourth, less widespread, is headhunting, a practice steeped in supernatural and ritual significance for the purpose of capturing an enemy's soul.

Ancient Andean History

No single chronological scheme can be applied to the whole of ancient South America, for technology, social and political organization, and the pace of development varied greatly from region to region. Archaeologists employ several broad chronological schemes to define development within large areas of general cultural cohesion, and which can be used to compare the areas through time.

The earliest pottery was made by peoples in the Intermediate Area and Amazonian Area in the late sixth and fifth millennia BC. In the other areas – except the Fuegian, which remained aceramic until Europeans arrived – ceramics were developed from about 1500 BC or later. Corresponding roughly to the Andean Initial Period, the Intermediate Area chronology is divided into the Early Ceramic Period and the Formative (or Initial) Period; similarly, the far Southern Andean Area had Early Ceramic and Initial Periods from about 1500 BC.

Ancient Andean chronology is subdivided into eight major periods, each characterized primarily by emphases on technological development and political organization. Much of the artistic expression and iconography of these civilizations endured for long periods, through political changes, but distinctive styles arose and were copied, changed, embellished and interpreted by successive cultures.

People migrated into South America in the Archaic Period – hunter-gatherer, stone-, bone-, wood- and shell-tool-using cultures reaching the tip of Tierra del Fuego by at least 9000 BC. The term Preceramic Period (from c. 3500 BC to the development of ceramics, which varies by region), is applied to the first agricultural societies, which by 3000 BC had mastered the domestication of plants and animals – a process that had begun several millennia earlier – and constructed the first monumental architecture in the form of platform compounds. These cultures were initially aceramic, but during the third and second millennia BC, pottery technology spread throughout the Andes.

In the Initial Period (c. 1800–900 BC), irrigation agriculture was developed into a sophisticated technology. Constructions of monumental architecture included much more ambitious projects, such as a tradition of U-shaped ceremonial centres at Sechín Alto/Cerro Sechín, Garagay, Los Reyes and other sites on the northern Peruvian coast, and sunken courts and other constructions at Chiripa in the Titicaca Basin and at Kotosh and La Galgada in the sierras.

In the Early Horizon (c. 900–200 BC), the earliest civilization of the central Andes, Chavín, dominated much of the area, both artistically and religiously, if not politically. Chavín imagery was distributed (east–west) from the upper Amazon drainage across the Andes mountains to the north Pacific coastal valleys. Its iconography comprised animal and anthropomorphic figures with feline, serpentine, harpy eagle and falcon heads, and humanoid bodies. Canine teeth protrude menacingly from wide, grimacing mouths. The Staff Deity (male or female) was portrayed ubiquitously, and endured into the 16th century. He or she was shown frontally, with outstretched arms holding two staffs or corn stalks, and was depicted on architecture and portable objects of all kinds. The exact significance or meaning of the Staff Deity is unknown, but his/her importance is without doubt. It seems likely that the Staff Deity was a creator being, and that the principal city, Chavín de Huántar, was a place of cult pilgrimage.

The Paracas culture, contemporary with Chavín, flourished on the southern Peruvian coast, where the mainland population used the peninsula as a necropolis for burials rich in grave goods, especially textiles – both woven and embroidered – wrapped around mummified bodies. Paracas textiles and ceramics display a wealth of iconographic symbols and deities in rich colours. One deity, known as the Oculate Being, was particularly prominent.

The Early Intermediate Period (c. 200 BC–AD 500) followed the Early Horizon. The cohesion of Chavín disintegrated, and several regional chiefdoms developed in the coastal and mountain valleys. Despite this political fragmentation, some remarkable advances were achieved in urbanization and in political, social, economic and artistic expression. Prominent among the kingdoms that developed were the Moche in the north Peruvian coastal valleys, and the Nazca in the southern coastal valleys. Rich iconographies are displayed in both cultures on architecture, pottery and textiles, and as geoglyphs.

Moche iconography is rich in painted figures – humans, anthropomorphized animals, birds and marine animals – and in set scenes showing rituals and sacrifices. Archaeological evidence from élite burials of Moche Sipán lords bears out the real-life practices depicted. On the south coast, the Nazca and contemporary cultures practised an apparently common religious tradition focused on burials of mummified bodies wrapped in rich textiles, on sacred ceremonial and pilgrimage sites – such as Cahuachi – separate from urban settlements, and on ground drawings including lines, outlined areas, and geometric and animal figures representing supernatural images and sacred ritual pathways.

In the Intermediate Area, contemporary cultures developed ceremonial sites and rich and sophisticated traditions of metal technology in gold, silver and alloys – Tumaco, San Agustín, Tierradentro, Calima, Tolima – in the Regional Development Period (c. 200 BC–AD 900).

In the Andean Area, the Middle Horizon (c. AD 500–1000) followed the Early Intermediate. The wealth of cultures and political entities that had existed continued to develop but, during the course of the next 500 years, two political centres built empires that unified the northern and southern Andes and adjacent western coastal regions.

In the north was Huari (or Wari), in the south-central Peruvian highlands. Through military and economic conquest, Huari rulers built an empire that eventually extended to the Pacific coast and engulfed the Nazca and Moche areas. A powerful central Peruvian coastal kingdom, Pachacamac, although conquered by the Huari, remained a pre-eminent shrine and pilgrimage site throughout the Middle Horizon and after.

In the Titicaca Basin, the city of Tiahuanaco (or Tiwanaku) was built, and Tiahuanacan rulers expanded their state throughout the Basin and beyond. At their northwest border, they confronted the Huari Empire at the pass of La Raya near Cuzco. Tiahuanaco included a large ceremonial centre with monumental architecture, enclosed compounds and monumental freestanding stone sculpture.

Although distinct politically, Huari and Tiahuanaco shared numerous cultural features. Their rich iconographic traditions drew from earlier developments in their respective areas. Much of their religious imagery was shared: staff deities, winged figures, feline and serpentine beings, bird-headed figures and decapitated heads. The importance of the Staff Deity emphasized its almost certain role as a creator god and possible precursor to the gods Viracocha and Pachacamac. Tiahuanaco became an important religious shrine, and later cultures believed Lake Titicaca to be the place of creation.

Following the demise of Huari and Tiahuanaco, the Late Intermediate Period (c. AD 1000–1400) was a new era of political fragmentation. As before, numerous local and regional city-states were established, which, towards the end of the period, were being unified into larger kingdoms. The Kingdom of Chimor (or Chimú) arose in the valleys of the north Peruvian coast (the ancient Moche area). Its capital, Chan Chan, surrounded an imperial precinct of compounds dedicated to the perpetuation of the memory of the kings of Chimor. Chimú iconography had obvious roots right back to Chavín and yet the culture was distinctive for its monumental architecture, vast administrative quarters, carved *adobe* wall friezes depicting repeated birds and marine animals, and a distinctive arched, double-headed beast called a rainbow serpent.

In the Intermediate Area, in the Integration Period (c. AD 900–1450), the rich metallurgic traditions continued – in addition to those listed above, the Nariño, Popayán, Quimbaya, Tairona, Sinú and Chibcha (also known as Muisca).

IN THE TITICACA BASIN, the city of Tiahuanaco, Huari's Middle Horizon rival, specialized in monumental stone sculptures, such as the Ponce Stela depicting a noble figure holding a beaker and short sceptre.

In the final Andean period, the Late Horizon (c. AD 1400–1532), the Incas established their capital at Cuzco and built their immense empire – from Colombia to mid-Chile and from the rain forest to the Pacific – in a little over 130 years. They conquered and subjugated the peoples throughout this vast area. In an attempt to unify religious belief, Inca emperors and priests emphasized the supremacy of the sun god Inti and continued to honour the all-powerful creator god Viracocha/Pachacamac, while incorporating local beliefs, pantheons and *huacas*.

Perhaps inevitably, the strains and tensions of holding together such a vast and diverse empire led to rivalry over the throne. When the Spanish adventurer Francisco Pizarro landed on the north coast of the empire in 1532, a civil war had been raging for more than six years between the half-brothers Huascar and Atahualpa. Exploiting this situation, appearing to support one side, then the other, and recruiting native allies, Pizarro played the king-maker, and proceeded to conquer the Inca Empire and strip its wealth, both material and cultural.

SOUTH AMERICA

Caribbean Sea

Caracas

VENEZUELA

Georgetown

Paramaribo

Cayenne

R. Orinoco

Pacific
Ocean

Bogotá

COLOMBIA

Atlantic
Ocean

ECUADOR

GUYANA

SURINAM

FRENCH
GUIANA

Manta
Ingapirca
Sipán
Chot/Chotuna
El Brujo
Moche
Cerro Sechín/
Sechín Alto

Quito
Túcume
Batán Grande
Pampa Grande
Pacatnamú
Galindo
La Galgada
Cajamarca
Chavín de Huántar
Kotosh
Chan Chan

R. Amazon

BRAZIL

PERU

Pachacamác
Garagay
Huari

Ollantaytambo
Cúzco
Urcos
Cacha
Pukara

Lima
Ayacucho
Paracas
Ventilla
Cahuachi
Machu Picchu
Pikillaqta
Vilcas Waman
Llullaillaco

Misminay

La Paz
Tiahuanaco
Ampato

L. Titicaca

BOLIVIA

PARAGUAY

N

Asunción

0   Kilometres   1000
0   Miles   600

CHILE

Andes Mountains

INTERMEDIATE AREA

Atlantic
Ocean

NORTHERN
AND
CENTRAL
ANDEAN AREA

AMAZONIAN
AREA

EASTERN
AREA

Pacific
Ocean

SOUTHERN ANDEAN AREA

CHACO
AREA

PAMPEAN AREA

Archaeological
Regions

FUEGIAN
AREA

0   Kilometres   2000
0   Miles   1200

URUGUAY

Santiago

ARGENTINA

Patagonia

Buenos
Aires

Montevideo

Tierra
del
Fuego

CHAVÍN CULTURE
(c. 900–200 BC)

Chavín de
Huántar

Paracas

Lake
Titicaca

PARACAS CULTURE
(c. 700–200 BC)

MOCHE CULTURE
(c. AD 1–700)

Moche

Cahuachi

Lake
Titicaca

NAZCA CULTURE
(c. 200 BC–
AD 500)

HUARI EMPIRE
(c. AD 500–800)

Huari

Lake
Titicaca

Tiahuanaco

TIAHUANACO EMPIRE
(c. 100 BC–AD 1000)

Gold Cultures

TAIRONA

SINÚ

CHIBCHA

CALIMA
POPAYÁN
TUMACO
LA
TOLITA

QUIMBAYA

TOLIMA

TIERRA-
DENTRO
SAN
AGUSTÍN

NARIÑO

CHINCHASUYU

Chan Chan

KINGDOM OF CHIMÚ
(c. AD 1000–1470)

ANTISUYU

INCA EMPIRE
(c. AD 1438–1532)

Lake
Titicaca

CUNTISUYU

COLLASUYU

Cuzco

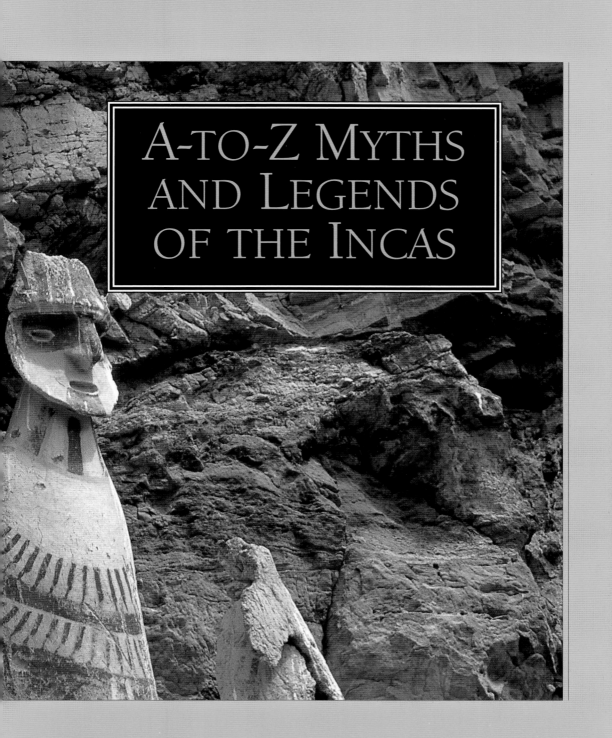

A-to-Z Myths and Legends of the Incas

A

ABE MANGO was the daughter of the *TUKANO* creator god *PAGE ABE*. After her father had created humans, she descended to the earth and personally taught humans how to use fire and to cook, how to build huts for shelter and how to weave cloth and make pottery.

ACLLAHUASI see under *ACLLAS*.

ACLLAS ("chosen women") were hand-picked *INCA* girls trained to serve in the cult of *INTI*, the sun god, and destined to become the concubines of the Inca ruler. They were sometimes referred to as the "Virgins of the Sun". The maidens were chosen at the age of eight, and kept in special cloisters called *acllahuasi* in the Inca capital at *CUZCO*, where they were super-

ACLLAS, the "chosen women" of the Inca emperor and sometimes referred to as "Virgins of the Sun", kept the sacred fires alight in the Temple of the Sun (Inti).

vised by elderly women called Mama Cunas. Here their tasks were to guard and keep the sacred fire of Inti burning, to weave and sew special clothing, and to prepare food and *CHICHA* (corn/maize beer) for state ceremonial occasions and the ceremony of *INTI RAYMI*. As concubines at the command of the emperor, they were also used by

him to bestow favours on high-ranking foreign officials and to secure arranged marriages with foreign rulers for political alliances.

AI APAEC was a *MOCHE* and later *CHIMÚ* sky god and creator god (or, alternatively, the son of the sky god) in the Early Intermediate Period. Fanged-being images depicted on *CHAVÍN* pottery of much earlier date might have been his prototype.

The archaeological evidence suggests that the Moche worshipped a creator god who was a remote and somewhat mysterious deity, a mountain god who paid little attention to the daily affairs of humankind. His throne was usually placed on a mountain top, beneath which Ai Apaec, perhaps a manifestation of the creator, was more active in terrestrial affairs. Moche military conquest and/or ritual combat provided prisoners for sacrifice to the gods, usually by slitting the victim's throat and offering his blood and body to the sky gods.

The image of Ai Apaec is conspicuous among a host of minor deities depicted on Moche pottery vessels. He is portrayed with a fanged mouth, wears snake-head earrings and sometimes a jaguar headdress, and snakes almost invariably form part of his belt. Sometimes he is shown in combat with a monster being, which he always overcomes. His role as a sky god appears to be implied by his association with a tableau of two scenes separated by a two-headed serpent. In the upper part appear

AI APAEC was the fanged creator god of the Moche and later Chimú cultures. A somewhat remote deity, his fanged nature stems from a long tradition going back to Chavín imagery.

gods, demonic beings and stars, while in the lower part there are musicians, lords or slaves; and rain falls from the serpent's body, implying a celestial/terrestrial division.

According to some authorities, Ai Apaec was also the principal god of the Chimú of the Late Intermediate Period, derived from the Moche cult. Others argue that Ai Apaec simply means "to make", and was therefore an invisible creator comparable to later Inca *VIRACOCHA*.

AKAPANA TEMPLE see under *TIAHUANACO*.

ALCAVICÇA was the pre-*INCA* Lord of the Valley of Cuzco. His existence establishes two links between Lake *TITICACA*, the place of origin of *VIRACOCHA*, and *CUZCO*, the Inca capital. From

URCOS, Viracocha travelled to the Cuzco Valley during his wanderings northwest from Lake Titicaca. At the site that would become the Inca capital he created, or summoned up from the earth, a great lord and named him Alcavicça. Alcavicça became the ruler of a people of the same name who occupied part of the valley when the Incas arrived. When Viracocha left the valley to continue northwest, his last act was to command that the *OREJONES*, a Spanish nickname for the Inca nobility, should rise out of the earth after his departure. This act gave Cuzco and the Incas a divine precedent for claiming rulership of the valley.

In another, more elaborate, version of Inca state origin, six of the four brothers and sisters/wives of "the ancestors", including *MANCO CAPAC* and *MAMA HUACO*, travelled from *HUANACAURI* into the Valley of Cuzco and to the town of Cuzco, where Alcavicça ruled. They went to Alcavicça and declared that they had been sent by their father, the sun, to take possession of the town. The Alcavicça people agreed to this and provided the six ancestors with accommodation. Manco Capac then took corn (maize) kernels, which he had brought with him from the cave of *TAMBO TOCO*,

ALCAVICÇA, according to legend, was taught to plant corn (maize) by Manco Capac. Corn and the potato were the staple crops that sustained ancient Andean populations.

and taught the Alcaviçças how to plant it, thus introducing the first corn crop into the valley. In yet another permutation of the story, it was Mama Huaco who planted the first corn field.

Thus, the takeover of Cuzco by divine command, after travelling from Titicaca (place of the world's birth) and teaching local people the art of agriculture, established the Incas' right to rule. Viracocha's very creation of Alcaviçça hints at a divine master plan; and these acts established and justified the pattern of Inca expansion and their hierarchical political relationships with the peoples they conquered: foreign invaders (the Incas) subordinating local peoples and taking control of their destinies. Nevertheless, things did not always work out as smoothly as was anticipated, for MAYTA CAPAC, the fourth legendary Inca emperor, was forced to put down a rebellion by the Alcaviçças, who were apparently dissatisfied with Inca overlordship.

ALUBERI, among the Orinoco River ARAWAK tribe, is a sort of supreme being – a "first cause". He/it is remote and indifferent towards humankind, and did not create men and women. Instead, humans were created by Aluberi's "agents" on Earth, KURURUMANY and Kulimina.

AMAUTAS were INCA court poet-philosophers – colleagues of the QUIPUCAMAYOQS – responsible for keeping the state histories alive through oral remembrance. In addition to recording in song the deeds of the present emperor, they had to remember the official histories of the founding and history of CUZCO, which inevitably were bound up with myth and the legendary exploits of former leaders and state heroes. They created songs to document royal genealogies and to chronicle the deeds of the Incas, their queens, coronations, battles, and important state events, per-

forming them for the emperor and his court at state ceremonies.

As the Inca Empire continued to expand, the *amautas* were tasked with reconciling (through recasting) the myths, legends, histories, dynastic ties and religious tenets of the conquered peoples, incorporating them into the official Inca version of events and state religion. For example, the reconciliation of the shared name and visionary connection between VIRACOCHA the man and the god, and the usurpation of Viracocha's throne by PACHACUTI INCA YUPANQUI must have occupied the talents of successive generations of *amautas*. The official account of the Inca conquest of the CHIMÚ is a classic example of how they recorded the defeat and incorporation of a people to the advantage of both the state and the conquered peoples (see MINCHANÇAMAN).

After the Spanish conquest, the *amautas* were a principal source for Spanish chroniclers, who recorded the myths, legends, histories and beliefs of the Incas and other peoples of the empire.

AMPATO is a mountain peak in the southern Peruvian Andes near Arequipa, the site of several ritual CAPACOCHA child sacrifices discovered in 1995 (see LLULLAILLACO). The victim, a young teenage girl who has come to be known as the "ice maiden", was found near the summit at about 6,300 m (20,670 ft). Her sacrifice was probably an offering to the sun god INTI or VIRACOCHA.

The frozen state of the body, hidden until volcanic ash from

nearby Mount Sabancaya and an earth tremor freed the body from its covering of snow, preserved a wealth of archaeological evidence. The girl was dressed in the style of a CUZCO noblewoman, in finely woven llama-wool garments, including a red and white shawl clasped about her with a silver *tupu* pin. A computer-tomography scan of her body showed a fracture, 5 cm (2 in) long, on her right temple, implying that she was clubbed to death, or had been finished off with a final blow. Accompanying her was a small female figurine, similarly dressed, made of shell. Also nearby were woven woollen bags containing corn (maize) kernels and a corn cob. Another bag contained *coca* (*Erythroxylon coca*) leaves and was covered with feathers. The bodies of two other child sacrifices were excavated below the summit.

At 4,890 m (16,040 ft) a camp, presumably used by the performers of the rituals, was excavated, included the bases of rectangular and round stone structures and a llama corral. Remains of a second camp were found at 5,670 m (18,900 ft) and, just below the summit, excavations revealed an area strewn with *ichu* grass, wooden tent posts and a stone-walled platform, suggesting that Mount Ampato was used repeatedly for sacrifices.

ANACONDA see YURUPARY.

APACHETAS, a special type of sacred huaca, were believed to be inhabited by local deities, whose protection travellers sought by leaving offerings on them.

ANTISUYU, the northeast quadrant of the Inca Empire, stretched from the Andes to their eastern foothills on the edge of the Amazon rainforests.

ANAN YAUYOS see HUAROCHIRÍ MANUSCRIPT.

THE ANCESTORS, INCA, see MANCO CAPAC.

THE ANDEAN TRIAD comprised the "three Viracochas" (see CON TICCI VIRACOCHA).

"ANGELS" were winged, running beings that accompanied the STAFF DEITY in the iconography of HUARI and TIAHUANACO.

ANTISUYU was the northeast quarter of the INCA Empire (see TAHUANTINSUYU). It comprised the Andes mountain regions north, east and southeast of CUZCO, as far as the foothills overlooking the Amazon forests.

APACHETA was the Inca name for a particular type of HUACA (sacred place), that comprised a pile of stones set at the top of a mountain pass or at a crossroads. *Apachetas* were believed to hold the spirits of local deities, and travellers would seek their favour by leaving offerings of *coca* (*Erythroxylon coca*) or clothing. Another method of obtaining their aid was to add a stone to the heap before continuing on a journey. (Compare APU, CEQUE and HUANCA)

APU was the Inca name for a type of *HUACA*, or sacred place. In a land dominated by the high peaks and volcanoes of the Andean cordillera, the mountains were believed to have supernatural spiritual powers. In particular, the mountain tops were regarded as the abodes of the gods – and long-standing tradition, which continues to the present day, regards especially prominent peaks as sacred and powerfully imbued. These were (and still are) venerated as *apu* (literally "lord") and were believed to have a direct influence on animal and crop fertility. Sacred pilgrimages, made to these mountain tops to seek the favour of the spirits of the *apus,* were a regular feature of Andean traditional religion. (Compare *APACHETA, CEQUE* and *HUANCA*)

AQLLA see *ACLLAS.*

AQLLA WASI see *ACLLAHUASI.*

ARAVATURA was the culture hero of the tribes of the *XINGU RIVER* region, and the discoverer of the fate of the spirit after death. Following the death of his best friend, Aravatura went to seek for his spirit in the forest. He eventually found it, along with many other spirits of the departed, all preparing to do battle against the birds. The ultimate fate of the spirit, if it were defeated, was to be devoured by a huge eagle. Because of his discovery, Aravatura was afflicted with the stench of death when he returned to his village, but he was cured through the intervention of the tribal *SHAMANS.*

THE ARAWAK were a rain forest tribe of the Orinoco River drainage in South America, and, before the arrival of the Spaniards, also the prehistoric culture/people of Haiti, Cuba and other islands of the Greater Antilles. (For their mythological concepts, see *ALUBERI, KURURUMANY, THREE-CORNERED IDOL, ZEMÍ*)

AROTEH and Tovapod are the creators of the Tupi of southeastern Brazil: two magicians who lived at the beginning of time, when humans lived beneath the earth and had little food to eat. The magicians jealously guarded the edible plants and animals on the surface so, when some humans climbed up through a tunnel one night, and stole food from them, Tovapod dug up the hole. Out tumbled hordes of ugly, web-footed people, with boars' tusks growing from their mouths. Undeterred, Aroteh and Tovapod reshaped these creatures into the humans of today by breaking off the tusks and remoulding their webbed feet into toes (see also *VALEJDAD*).

APUS, another aspect of ancient Andean sacred landscape, were mountains believed to be the abodes of the gods. Mount Ausangate in central Peru is a typical example.

ARUTAM see *HEADHUNTING.*

ATAHUALPA was the 14th and last pre-Spanish conquest *INCA* ruler (ruled AD 1532–3). When Francisco Pizarro and his followers landed on the Peruvian coast in 1532, a civil war between Atahualpa and his half-brother *HUASCAR* had been raging for more than six years since the death of their father, *HUAYNA CAPAC* and his chosen heir, in 1526. Different court factions had backed each of the rival brothers' claims to the succession, and Atahualpa had only recently captured his brother and secured the throne when Pizarro arrived.

Atahualpa's pivotal place in Inca legend rests with the fact that he was beheaded by Pizarro following his defeat and capture at Cajamarca in 1533. From that point onwards, the legend of the "future return of the king" developed – known as the *INKARRÍ* – in which the severed and buried head of Atahualpa was believed to be slowly growing a new body for the ruler's eventual return and overthrow of the Spaniards and the reinstatement of the Inca world order.

YOUNG GIRLS of the Wapisana, one of the Arawak tribes of Guyana, whose dress might indicate considerable acculturation away from ancient mythological beliefs.

ATUN-VIRACOCHA ("great creator") was the *INCA* name given to *VIRACOCHA* by the people of *URCOS*, and to the statue of him erected by them – described by the 16th-century Spanish chronicler Cristobal de Molina.

THE AUCA peoples of northern Chile were some of the fiercest opponents of the *INCAs'* expansion into the southern Andes (see *GUE-CUFU, GUINECHEN, PILLAN*).

AUCA see *AYAR AUCA.*

AUCA RUNA were the people of the *INCA* Fourth Sun (see *PACHA-CUTI*).

AYAHUASCA SNUFF see *SHAMAN.*

AYAR stems from the *QUECHUA* word *aya* ("corpse") (see *MANCO CAPAC* and *MALLQUIS*).

AYAR AUCA, also Cuzco Huanca, the brother/husband of *MAMA HUACO*, was one of the original eight *INCA* ancestors (see *MANCO CAPAC*). The name of the Inca capital, Cuzco, is derived from the alternative form of his name.

His alternate name reflects his importance in the Inca state foundation myth as the stone pillar (see *HUACA* and *HUANAYPATA*).

AYAR CACHI was the brother/husband of *MAMA IPACURA* (although one chronicler names *MAMA HUACO* as his wife) and one of the original eight *INCA* ancestors (see *MANCO CAPAC*).

AYAR MANCO see *MANCO CAPAC.*

AYAR UCHU, the brother/husband of *MAMA RAUA*, was one of the original eight *INCA* ancestors (see *HUACA* and *MANCO CAPAC*).

AYLLU ("family", "lineage" or "part") is the *QUECHUA* term for

ATAHUALPA Inca was one of two claimants to the Inca throne when Francisco Pizarro arrived and began the Spanish conquest. (PAINTING FROM THE 18TH-CENTURY "CUZCO SCHOOL".)

These became the ten groupings of commoners at Cuzco, to complement the ten royal *ayllus* called PANACAS. In addition, *ayllus* kept the mummified bodies of ancestors, to be venerated by all the members of the group on ceremonial occasions, and to provide a setting for the recital of the *ayllu* creation myth. Each *ayllu* also recognized and maintained one or more HUACAS, or sacred places, within their lands, at which regular offerings were made. A larger group, of several *ayllus*, was the MOIETY.

AYMARÁ was once a major ancient Andean language. It now survives mainly in northern Bolivia.

BACHUE ("large breasted") was the CHIBCHA earth goddess and mother goddess, symbol of fertility and protector of crops. According to Chibcha myth, shortly after the world had been created by CHIMINIGAGUA, she emerged from a sacred lake in the mountains bearing her three-year-old son with her. She waited for the boy to grow to manhood, then "married" him and proceeded to people the world with their offspring. Once the earth was populated, the two were transformed into serpents and returned to the sacred lake.

THE BARASANA were a rain forest tribe of the Colombian Amazon (see YURUPARY).

BATÁN GRANDE was the largest Middle Horizon religious centre of the SICÁN

culture in the LAMBAYEQUE Valley. The site had been occupied from the Early Horizon, from as early as 1500 BC, and was finally abandoned about AD 1100. The Sicán religious precinct comprised 17 *adobe* brick temple-mounds, surrounded by shaft tombs and multi-roomed enclosures filled with rich burials and furnishings reminiscent of Early Intermediate Period MOCHE burials. The mummy bundles and the iconography of the Sicán culture's metalwork, ceramics and architecture also drew on, and continued, those of CHAVÍN and Moche.

Batán Grande was abandoned, apparently owing to economic disaster accompanying an El Niño weather event. Piles of wood were deliberately placed against the temple walls and set alight. The survivors established a new religious centre at TÚCUME.

BENNETT STELA
see TIAHUANACO.

BIRD PRIEST
see DECAPITATOR GOD.

social and economic groupings within the INCA Empire. In pre-Inca times they were blood lineages, but in the time of the Inca Empire they could be blood lineages or local administrative groupings unrelated to actual kinship.

There were tens of thousands of *ayllus* throughout the empire, each discontinuously distributed across the land. Members of the same *ayllu* lived in different ecological zones, some up in the high montane *puna* (tundra), some at mid-altitudes, and some in intermontane valleys, coastal lowlands or tropical forest lowlands. This distribution of each socially and economically closely tied group ensured that there was a regular redistribution among the *ayllu* members of agricultural produce and man-made goods and commodities from each zone. Exchange occurred both through the regular movement of *ayllu* members

among the zones and at annual gatherings and festivals, at a central settlement.

In addition to this internal co-operation, each *ayllu* was obliged to render tribute to the Inca Empire – to the regional administrator sent out from CUZCO. This took the form of public labour called MIT'A (literally "turns of service"), which included working lands and herding the llama flocks in the region that belonged to the emperor and the gods, and performing a quota of work at a state installation, such as a redistribution warehouse.

As with so many Inca state institutions, this official organization was interwoven with mythical and ritual overtones. The origin of the *ayllu* concept was grounded in the creation myth of the empire and of the royal line of rulers. Upon their emergence from the cave of TAMBO TOCO in PACARITAMBO, the Inca ancestors conquered the locals and organized them into ten *ayllus*.

REMAINS of an ayllu field system are seen at Carangas, Bolivia. From such designated lands, members of the kinship group could supply crops for redistribution among ayllu members in other ecological zones.

BACHUE, who was the "large breasted" fertility goddess of the Chibcha peoples, is possibly represented in this handled effigy vessel from Ecuador.

BOCHICA was the legendary founder hero of the *CHIBCHA*. In Chibcha myth he arrived in Colombia from the east and travelled through their world as a bearded sage, teaching them civilization, moral laws and the sophisticated technology of metalworking.

Not all accepted his teaching, however. A woman named Chie challenged him by urging men and women to ignore Bochica and make merry, whereupon Bochica transformed her into an owl. Even so, she was able to help the god *CHIBCHACUM* to flood the earth. Bochica appeared as a rainbow then, as the sun, sent his rays to evaporate the waters and also created a channel by striking the rocks with his golden staff for the water to drain into the sea. For this role he is sometimes worshipped as the sun god Zue, while Chie is known as the moon goddess. When he disappeared into the west, he left his footprints, literally in stone.

(Compare *NEMTEREQUETEBA* and, for Central Andean cultures, *CONIRAYA VIRACOCHA*, *ROAL*, *THUNUPA VIRACOCHA* and *VIRACOCHA*)

BOIUNA, a fearsome goddess described by many tribes along the Amazon and its tributaries, takes the form of a snake. She will eat any living creature, and a mere glance from her flashing eyes can, it is believed, make a woman pregnant.

BORARO ("the white ones") are rather fearsome Amazonian *TUKANO* tribal forest spirits. They are tall, hairy creatures, with huge penises, ears that point forwards and feet that point backwards. Their legs are not jointed at the knee so, if one falls down, he has great difficulty in rising again. The Tukano believe that if a Boraro is seen carrying a stone hoe, he is searching for a human to eat!

BOTOQUE, the legendary culture hero of the Kayapo tribe of the central Brazilian rain forest, was

responsible for bringing knowledge to humankind. At the beginning of time, the people of the earth did not know how to use fire. The edible plants that they collected were eaten raw, and they only warmed their meat on rocks in the sun. Then one day the young man Botoque and his brother-in-law were in the forest and saw a macaw's nest high up on a cliffside. Botoque climbed up to the nest, using a crude ladder that he made on the spot, and threw down two eggs to his brother-in-law. On the way down, however, the eggs turned to stone and broke the brother-in-law's hand when he tried to catch them. Angered, the brother-in-law pushed the ladder away, so that Botoque was stranded on the cliff ledge, and left him.

After several days, Botoque spotted a *JAGUAR* walking through the forest, carrying all sorts of dead game as well as a bow and arrows. When the jaguar noticed Botoque's shadow, he pounced on it, but then realized his mistake. The jaguar spoke to Botoque, promising him that, if he would come

down, the jaguar would not kill and eat him. Instead, he said, he would adopt Botoque as his son and teach him to hunt. Botoque agreed, and the jaguar replaced the ladder for Botoque to climb down.

The jaguar's wife was not at all pleased with the idea of having to raise a human son, and feared that it would lead to trouble, but she was overruled by her husband. Botoque observed, and so learned, how it was that the jaguars made fire and cooked their meat. The next day, when the jaguar went out hunting and left Botoque with his wife, Botoque asked her for cooked tapir, but she refused him and bared her claws. The frightened Botoque took refuge up a tree. When the husband returned and heard about what had happened, he warned his wife to leave Botoque alone, but she was very reluctant to do so, so much did she resent Botoque's imposition.

Next, the jaguar taught Botoque how to make a bow and arrows. When the jaguar went off hunting again, his wife once more threatened Botoque, and so Botoque

THE REVERSAL of the rulership of the earth, taken from the jaguar by Botoque, is celebrated by the Kayapo of central Brazil after the killing of a jaguar.

fired an arrow from his bow and killed her. He knew he had to flee, so he gathered up some roasted meat, a burning ember and his bow and arrows, and found his way through the forest back to his village.

When his fellow humans saw these amazing things, and realized their meaning and use, they too went to the jaguar's house. From it they stole the fire, all the cooked meat, bows and arrows, and even the jaguar's cotton string. (In some versions of the story, they dropped some embers as they ran from the house, and birds caught them up to keep the forest from catching fire – those that were singed became the species with flame-coloured beaks, legs and feet.) When the jaguar returned, he was enraged at Botoque's ingratitude and disloyalty, but, now outnumbered and weaponless, was forced to begin eating his meat raw and to hunt with his claws and teeth, while

C

men could hunt with bows and arrows and cook their food on the fire. To this day, the jaguar's lost fire can be seen, especially at night, in the gleam of its eyes.

CABILLACA see CAVILLACA.

CACHA, a pre-INCA and Inca city/ceremonial centre about 100 km (62 miles) southeast of CUZCO, was the site of a temple to VIRACOCHA. Its religious significance was revealed when excavations, which uncovered dense occupation of the site from at least the late Middle Horizon, demonstrated the antiquity of belief in Viracocha. The temple itself, a massive building with interior columns, was unlike many other Inca constructions in being made of adobe bricks rather than stone.

Myth and legend form a significant part of the city's pre-Inca history. After the creation at TITICACA, Viracocha travelled widely, teaching and performing miracles, and soon came to Cacha. When they saw him approach, the people came out of the town in a hostile mood and threatened to stone him. Several of them rushed at him with weapons. Viracocha fell upon his knees and raised his arms to the skies as if in supplication. The skies were immediately filled with fire, and the people of Cacha, terrified and cowed, asked for Viracocha's forgiveness and begged him to save them. According to one source, he extinguished the fires with three strokes of his staff, but not before they had scorched the huge rocks of the area such that they became "light as cork".

The people of Cacha thereafter revered the stones and regarded them as HUACAS. They gave the god the name CONTITI VIRACOCHA PACHAYACHACHIC ("god, the maker of the world") and carved and erected a large stone sculpture on the spot where they had met him. They brought offerings of gold and silver both to the stones and to the representation of Viracocha.

The 16th-century chronicler, Juan de Betanzos, described his visit to the site, where he saw the statue (he also records having seen a similar one at URCOS). He questioned the people of the town, who described Viracocha's appearance: tall, dressed in a pure white robe that fell to his ankles, belted at the waist; he was bare-headed and had short-cropped hair, tonsured like a priest's; and in his hands he carried an object that was said to resemble a priest's breviary.

It is easy to suspect Christian influence and overtones in this description, particularly since the Inca had no writing system and were under heavy proselytizing pressure from Spanish priests. But what is mythology to Europeans was firm religious belief to Andean peoples, and their description was undoubtedly sincere, and might well have been accurate. It might be that the Spanish words and interpretations transform the Inca description into an image familiar to European understanding.

CACHI see AYAR CACHI.

CAHUACHI, in the NAZCA Valley of southern Peru, comprised a vast complex of ceremonial mounds and associated plazas scattered over 150 ha (360 acres). Its location was deliberately chosen in the middle section of the valley, where, for geological reasons, the Nazca River disappears underground (it re-emerges below Cahuachi). The mounds were built of adobe bricks to enhance the tops of a cluster of about 40 natural hills in the middle of the valley. The earliest mounds were constructed before AD 100, by which time Cahuachi was the most important site in the region, but later mound-building ceased rather abruptly, and by about AD 550 the site was abandoned – although it continued to be recognized as sacred, and remained a mortuary ground and place of votive offerings long after that date.

Cahuachi faced north, towards the desert of San José, and a virtually straight "road" leads from it across the desert to the site of Ventilla, thought to have been a Nazca "capital". Few architectural or artefactual elements found at Cahuachi indicate permanent residence. There was no domestic refuse, and storage buildings were mostly for ritual paraphernalia or workshops. Two-thirds of the ceramics are special wares for offerings, rather than Nazca household wares. The burials and artefacts associated with the mounds show conclusively that the entire site was a place of pilgrimage and ritual burial in family plots, each kin group building its own mound. The largest of the mound structures, known as the "Great Temple", was a 30 m (98 ft) high modified hillock made up of six or seven terraces formed by adobe-brick retaining walls. At its base, excavations have revealed small storage rooms filled with caches of clay panpipes used in Nazca ritual ceremonies.

As with so many other cultures in the Andean and adjacent western lowland regions, the focus appears to have been on ancestor worship alongside a pantheon of gods who are now nameless.

Although most of the burials have been looted over the past centuries, excavations of unlooted tombs in the 1980s and 1990s uncovered mummified burials accompanied by exquisitely decorated, multicoloured woven burial coats and pottery, and sometimes by animal sacrifices. By virtue of their treatment, some of the burials appear to be sacrificial victims – not captured enemies, but men, women and children of the Nazca themselves. Some of the skulls had excrement placed in their mouths; some had been perforated and a cord inserted for carrying; some had blocked eyes, cactus spines pinning the mouth, tongues removed and placed in pouches: all indicative of ritual practices.

On the textiles and pottery were images of the gods: half-human, half-animal figures – felines with long, ratcheted tails, spiders with human faces, birds, monkeys, lizards. The fringes of some of the textiles display rows of dangling heads/mummified skulls with staring eyes, and even lines of full figures wearing short tunics, dancing above round-eyed deities who appear to be flying. In general the figures resemble those depicted in the Nazca "lines", the geoglyphs on the pampa desert nearby.

As the coastal plains and lower valleys of southern Peru became more arid, through changes in the weather patterns in the mountains to the east (perhaps coupled with disastrous earthquakes), Cahuachi was abandoned – deliberately, for the mounds were systematically covered with layers of dirt, as the Cahuachi people believed that the power of the gods had abandoned them. At the same time, there was an increase in the number and elaboration of Nazca "lines" and ground markings on the desert between Cahuachi and Ventilla.

EXQUISITELY PRESERVED *textiles from Nazca burials in the ritual city of Cahuachi depict mythological symbols and figures in vivid colour.*

CAJATAMBO, an *INCA* and Spanish colonial town in the highlands of central Peru, was remarkable for the strength of *IDOLATRÍAS* recorded there by the Spanish "extirpator of idolatries" in the early 17th century. It serves as an exemplar of the intimate connections that persisted between Inca provincial communities and their local *HUACAS*, or sacred objects and places, in the countryside around them, both in Inca and post-Spanish-conquest times.

The peoples of Cajatambo, like most provincial inhabitants of the Inca Empire, were grouped into lineage *AYLLUS* and *MOIETIES*. Here they were divided into two perceived "types" of people, the Guari and the Llacuaz. The Guari, the original inhabitants of the region, had established the earliest towns throughout the lowland valleys, and their economy was based primarily on corn (maize) cultivation. The other group, the Llacuaz, were not indigenous, but had come from the *puna*, or highlands, and cultivated the potato, as well as herding flocks of llamas and alpacas; they were later arrivals, having migrated into or invaded the region probably shortly before it was conquered by the Incas in the 15th century, and had established dominance over the Guaris.

Each group had its own principal deity. The patron god of the Guaris was a giant referred to as "Huari" who lived among the caves. Another important Guari deity was the "night-time sun" (the sun after sunset, when it was believed to pass through a hidden, watery passage into the underworld until the next day's sunrise). Guari myth recounted how their ancestors came into the region in the distant past, either from the west, across the ocean, or from the south, from Lake *TITICACA*. The principal god of the Llacuazs was Llibiac, the god of thunder and lightning, and they also worshipped, in contrast to the Guaris,

the "daytime sun" (that is, the sun from sunrise to sunset), as well as the stars.

The religious ritual of the two groups celebrated the conquest and domination of the Guaris by the Llacuazs, and also their reconciliation and confederation into what might be termed a symbiotic relationship. Each group would perform rituals to commemorate the other moiety, and there were also certain rituals that were performed jointly. Both of the groups maintained and revered common *huacas* and sacred objects, and the Guaris worshipped special amulets called *canopas*, which they believed to control the fertility of their corn (maize) crops. Each group recognized sacred places throughout the region where *CAPACOCHA* sacrificial victims were buried. At the time that the Spaniards recorded the "idolatries" that the people of Cajatambo believed these sacrificial burials to be the link between themselves and the Inca overlords, and that the Incas were the rightful owners of the land.

In addition, each group maintained exclusive bonds with special *huacas* (mountain-tops, springs and caves in the surrounding countryside) and *HUANCAS* (particularly prominent boulders) that they believed held the spirits of one or more of the group's ancestors. Particular focus was given to the numerous caves in the region, called *machay*, for it was from these that the *ayllus* believed that their ancestors had come, and it was in these that they stored the mummified bodies (*MALLQUIS*) of the ancestors. They dressed the mummies in new clothes at ceremonies marking the agricultural turning-points of the year, especially planting and harvest times, and offered them food and drink so as to assure the prosperity of the community. The importance of the *mallquis* is shown by the *idolatría* accounts for 1656–8, which record 1,825 mummies among four towns

around Cajatambo alone. The beliefs of the Guaris and Llacuazs thus included myths recounting the events that led to the establishment of these sacred places and how the ancestors came to be incorporated into the landscape and to interact with it.

(For another source of comparable "idolatries" see *HUAROCHIRÍ MANUSCRIPT*.)

CANNIBALISM was a widespread feature of many cultures, both "civilized" and "primitive", throughout the ancient Americas. Among the Aztecs of Mesoamerica it was a regular ritual practice of the nobility and priests following human sacrifice, and in South America the practice was widespread among rain forest tribes, and was documented historically to recent times.

The practice was always associated with ritual, rather than with nourishment in the physical sense. It was bound up with sacrifice, warfare, death and regeneration, with social identity and kinship relations, and with the transference of

the soul or essence of being from the eaten to the eater. It was an act intended to transfer the power, prowess, accomplishments and skills of the dead person.

"Exocannibalism" was a form that involved the eating of the flesh of an enemy in order to prove one's power, to confirm and finalize martial triumph and the humiliation of the defeated foe, and to take revenge on his companions. Cannibalistic warriors were thought to have the spirits of *JAGUARS*, whose behaviour was seen as not dissimilar.

"Endocannibalism" had a more respectful motivation. The dead person's bones were ground to dust and then mixed into manioc "beer", to be drunk by the family and other relatives in order to preserve within the kinship groups the essence of the dead person. By this means, his or her qualities were believed to be perpetuated in the bodies and spirits of the cannibals.

CANOPAS see under *CAJATAMBO*.

CAPAC RAYMI was the December summer solstice, the occasion of one of the two most crucial, and, it was hoped, propitious ceremonies of the year in honour of the *INCA* sun god, *INTI*. It was a royal feast and a ceremony that focused

CANNIBALISM, when discovered by Europeans among Amazonian tribes, was abhorred and therefore depicted in an exaggerated fashion. (GOTTFRIED'S HISTORIA ANTIPODUM, 1665.)

HUANAYPATA PLAZA, in present-day Cuzco, is thought to be where Capac Usnu – "the navel of the universe" of the Inca world – stood, and from which astronomical observances took place.

on the initiation rituals for boys of royal lineage (see also *INTI RAYMI*). Plotting and confirmation of the date of the ritual was done by observations taken from the *CORICANCHA*.

CAPAC TOCO, *INCA*, literally "rich window", was one of the caves of *TAMBO TOCO*, the central "window" from which *MANCO CAPAC* and the Inca ancestors emerged.

CAPAC USNU, or Capac Ush-nuo, ("navel of the universe"), stood in the sacred *CORICANCHA* in *CUZCO*, at the centre of the *INCA* Empire (*TAHUANTINSUYU*). It was the first *HUACA* on a sacred *CEQUE* line that linked it to two stone pillars on the skyline west of the city, and to the *huaca* at *CATACHILLAY* spring.

The Capac Usnu comprised a multifaceted, finely carved stone dais with a carved seat and the vertical pillar of Usnu itself. The seat was the throne of the *SAPA INCA* ("Son of the Sun") from which he refreshed and maintained the order of the world. The emperor sat on this throne to review processions of the mummified ancestors – the *MALLQUIS* – and to placate them with offerings. From the dais, he toasted the gods, especially *INTI* and *VIRACOCHA*, with copious libations of *chicha* (corn/maize beer), which were poured down the "gullet of the sun": a stone basin, lined with sheet gold, that was set at the foot of the Usnu.

The Usnu pillar served as a sighting point for astronomical observations. From it, both the sunset on 26 April and the setting of the Pleiades on or about 15 April were observed through the distant pillars on the skyline. Astronomical observations of *MAYU* (the Milky Way) and other celestial groups, and of the southern constellations,

were made from this and other positions around the Coricancha plaza, including from a tower of finely fitted stone blocks. The time of the zenith could be predicted precisely from a window in the tower by viewing at sunrise a marker point set up on the skyline to the east of the city.

CAPAC YUPANQUI was the legendary fifth *INCA* ruler of *CUZCO*, probably ruling at some time in the first half of the 13th century. Like all Inca rulers, he was considered to be a direct descendant of the ancestors, *MANCO CAPAC* and *MAMA OCLLO*.

CAPACOCHA, or Qhapaq Hucha, were ritual practices that involved taking specially selected individuals, usually children, from among the high-ranking *AYLLU* kinship lineages of the provinces of the *INCA* Empire and bringing them to the capital at *CUZCO* to be trained and prepared for the ritual. The selection was made annually and those chosen were destined to become sacrificial victims following ritual ceremonies in the capital. Such sacrifices were offerings to the sun god *INTI*, to the creator god *VIRACOCHA*, or to both. Momentous events – war, pestilence, famine or other natural disasters – could also provoke such sacrifices.

Having been brought to Cuzco, the chosen ones were sanctified by the priests in the *CORICANCHA* precinct, who offered them up to the supreme god, Viracocha, and then marched back to their home provinces along the sacred *CEQUE* lines that linked those provinces to the capital. There, the victims were sacrificed by being clubbed to death, strangled with a cord or having the throat slit, before burial, or by being buried alive in a specially constructed shaft-tomb. Children were sometimes drugged with *chicha* (corn/maize beer). Votive offerings usually accompanied the victim in death, such as elaborate clothing, human figures made of gold, silver, bronze or shell and dressed in miniature garments, llama figurines and miniature sets of ceramic containers.

The victims were sometimes carried up and left on high mountain tops regarded as sacred *HUACAS*, where their bodies sometimes became preserved in the cold, dry conditions that prevailed in such places; some famous examples include Cerro el Plomo in the Chilean Andes, Mount Aconcagua on the Chilean–Argentinian border, Puná Island off the coast of Ecuador, the "ice maiden" at Mount *AMPATO* and

CAPAC YUPANQUI, the fifth Inca emperor, depicted in an imaginary sketch. (NUEVA CORÓNICA Y BUEN GOBIERNO BY FELIPE GUAMAN POMA DE AYALA, 1583–1613.)

the sacrifice of two girls and a boy on Mount *LLULLAILLACO*.

Such practices served two purposes: to renew or reconfirm the bond between the Inca state and the provincial peoples of the empire, and to reassert Inca overlordship and reaffirm the heirarchy between the Inca centre and the provincial *ayllus*.

CARANCHO see *CHACO*.

CARI and Zapana were legendary rulers of city-states in the *TITICACA* Basin in the Bolivian highlands. According to an *INCA* legend, Cari sought the help of the Incas in the valley of Cuzco to the northwest, against his rival Zapana. The Incas, however, saw this as an opportunity (or invitation) to invade the region and subjugate both cities. Although long after the civilization of *TIAHUANACO* had flourished, the Incas were conscious of the powerful empire that had obviously created the ruined city and its huge stone statues, and were keen to legitimize their own empire as its heir, as well as to justify their own incursions into other regions. This legend therefore seems to be another example of the Inca rewriting history to suit their own purposes.

25

CATACHILLAY was the name of an *INCA* sacred spring on a ritual *CEQUE* line radiating from the *CORICANCHA* in *CUZCO*. The line led west and linked the spring to the *HUACAS* of the *CAPAC USNU* and to two upright sighting stones on the horizon between the spring and the pillar.

Because the alignment was used for observations of the April setting of the Pleiades, Catachillay was also an alternative name for that star group (see *COLLCA*).

CAVILLACA, in pre-*INCA* and Inca legend, was a beautiful female virgin *HUACA* wooed by *CONIRAYA VIRACOCHA*. The tale is related in the *HUAROCHIRÍ MANUSCRIPT*.

CAYLLA VIRACOCHA, the *INCA* name of a creator worshipped by the *Wari Wiracocharuna* of the "first age" (see *PACHACUTI*), was one of many variations of *VIRACOCHA*.

THE CEQUE system was an *INCA* concept interwoven with myth, astronomical observation, architectural alignment, and the social and geographical divisions of the empire.

Ceques were sacred "lines" that radiated from the *CORICANCHA* precinct, *CUZCO*, each line linking numerous sacred locations (*HUACAS*) along its length. There were 41 *ceques* uniting 328 *huacas* and survey points within and around Cuzco. It is perhaps significant that the 328 *huacas* and stations equal the number of days in 12 sidereal lunar months (328 ÷ 12 = the 27.3-day period of the rotation of the moon around the earth–moon centre of mass). They were grouped according to *HANAN* (upper) and *HURIN* (lower) Cuzco and thus according to the four quarters (*TAHUANTINSUYU*) of the empire. Points along the lines also served to regulate landholdings, water distribution, labour divisions, and ritual and ceremonial activities. *Ceque* lines also served as processional paths to be followed by the *CAPA-*

COCHA victims before being sacrificed. Similarly, the combination of *ceques* and their *huacas* were used to distinguish the different *PANACA* kin-group landholdings. Sunset on 26 April and the setting of the Pleiades on or about 15 April were observed from the pillar in the *CAPAC USNU* between two stone pillars, together regarded as a *huaca*, erected on the skyline west of the city. Along the same *ceque*, beyond the horizon, was a further *huaca*, the spring of *CATACHILLAY* (a name for the Pleiades). The 16th-century chronicler Juan de Betanzos describes the sixth *ceque* of *ANTISUYU*, on which lay the sixth *huaca*, known as "the house of the puma". Here, the richly dressed and mummified body of the wife of the emperor *PACHACUTI INCA YUPANQUI* was kept, to whom child sacrifices were offered.

Similarly, the movements of *MAYU*, the Milky Way, were linked to the *ceque* system by a division separating the four quarters of the empire along the intercardinal axis of the Milky Way and the southernmost point of the Milky Way's movement in the night sky.

CETERNI was the wife of the *LAMBAYEQUE* ruler *NAYAMLAP*.

CEUCY was the virgin woman of the Brazilian *TUPI* tribe, instrumental in the domination of humans by men (see *JURUPARI*).

THE FANGED GOD, or stylized jaguar, along with the Staff Deity, was typical of Chavín imagery. Numerous representations adorned the Old Temple.

SACRED CEQUE LINES of Inca ritual and astronomical sighting radiated from the Temple of the Sun (Inti) in the Coricancha precinct in Cuzco, on the Inca base of which now stands the church of Santo Domingo.

CHACO and Chaco tribes were the region and peoples of the *pampas* of northern Argentina and Chile, Paraguay and southeastern Bolivia (see also *TOBA*). The hunting peoples of this area seem to have lacked a consistent cosmology or supreme being. Variations include Kasogonaga, the sky goddess who brought rain, and a red anteater and a giant beetle as the creators of the first man and woman. There were also ancestor deities referred to as the "grandfather" and the "grandmother", and various benevolent spirits who aided the hunt. Different tribes recounted stories of rival brothers to explain duality; of the rainbow that brought death by its tongue; of killer stars; and of a culture hero – "the hawk" – whom they called Carancho, who was confronted by a fox, but overcame him.

CHAN CHAN see *CHIMÚ*.

CHANCA was a powerful political unity west of the *INCA* capital, *CUZCO*. The Chancas attacked Cuzco in the early 15th century but were defeated by the tenth Inca ruler, *PACHACUTI INCA YUPANQUI*.

CHASCA see *CHASKA-QOYLOR*.

CHASKA-QOYLOR ("shaggy star") was the *INCA* goddess of Venus, one of the luminaries recognized within *MAYU*, the Milky Way. She was the guardian of young maidens and flowers.

CHAVÍN, the first great civilization of the central Andean region, defines the period known as the Early Horizon (900–200 BC). Its principal "city" and ceremonial centre was Chavín de Huántar.

Although not the largest ceremonial centre, Chavín de Huántar was one of the most elaborate sites, and the focus and source of a pan-Andean religious cult, together with its accompanying iconography. It also played a crucial role in the dissemination of technology. The site would appear to have been strategically located in the Andes roughly midway between the coast (west) and the tropical lowlands (east). Although not truly urban in layout and proportions, Chavín de Huantar's size and importance implies that it housed a resident population of priests, officials, artisans, servants and pilgrims to support and serve the cult.

At its greatest extent the site covered about 42 ha (104 acres) and had between 2,000 and 3,000

inhabitants. The Old Temple is a U-shaped platform wrapped around a circular sunken courtyard. Projecting from its four-storey high stone walls are scores of sculpted heads. Inside the temple itself there is a labyrinthine series of interconnecting narrow passages and chambers. The southern wing, later doubled in size as the site flourished, is known as the New Temple, although both temples were used simultaneously after the expansion.

In one of the interior galleries stands the stone idol known as the *Lanzón* (so called because of its lance-like shape) or Great Image, probably the earliest pan-Andean oracle: a carved granite monolith 4.55 m (15 ft) high. The idol faces east and portrays a humanoid, but overall monstrous visage. Its right hand is raised, its left lowered by its side, and both feet and hands end in claws. Its mouth is thick-lipped, drawn in a hideous snarl and punctuated by long, outward-curving canine teeth (see *FANGED GOD*). Its eyebrows and hair end in serpent-heads; its earlobes hang heavy with pendants. It wears a tunic and headdress, both decorated with feline heads. The notched top of the idol protrudes through the ceiling into the gallery above, where it is thought that priests sat in secrecy projecting their voices as the voice of the god.

That Chavín de Huántar was the site of a cult seems indisputable. In a gallery next to the sunken circular plaza, excavators found some 800 broken ceramic vessels decorated in a variety of styles from cultures spread as far apart as the northern coast and the central highlands. There were bowls and bottle-like containers and, scattered among them, the bones of llamas and other camelids, deer, guinea pigs and fish. The pots and bones are thought to have been either offerings or stored ritual trappings for ceremonies.

Chavín iconography drew its inspiration from the natural world – animals and plants – and from a

THE RUINS of Chavín de Huántar, the first great cult centre and pilgrimage site of ancient Andean religion.

gamut of ecological zones – the ocean, the coast, the mountains and the tropical lowlands. The Tello Obelisk, found buried at Chavín de Huántar, is a low-relief granite monolith, 2.52 m (99 in) high, carved in the shape of a supernatural crocodile. Notched at the top like the *Lanzón*, it probably also stood upright in a gallery. Additional carvings on and around the crocodile depict various plants and animals, including peanuts and manioc from the tropical lowlands and *Strombus* and *Spondylus* shells of species native to the Ecuadorian coast, attesting to the wide net spread by the Chavín cult. In addition there are *JAGUARS*, *SERPENTS* and harpy or crested eagles.

As the fame of the cult spread and the site was enlarged, ceramic styles and further exotic foods, plants, and animals continued to inspire the cult iconography. There is evidence from the domestic buildings for the development of social hierarchy among the citizenry, in the form of unequal distribution of goods, and for craft specialization. The religious cult supported artisans who applied its symbolism to portable artefacts as well as to monumental sculpture, and the distribution of these artefacts by exchange expanded and entrenched the spread of the cult.

With the expansion of the south wing of the temple complex, the iconography began to grow still more elaborate. The relief of a new supreme deity was set up in the patio of the New Temple. Like the *Lanzón*, this depicts a humanoid figure with a fanged mouth, who is shown wearing multiple bracelets, anklets and ear pendants. It is holding a *Strombus* shell in its right hand and a *Spondylus* shell in its left hand. This deity may be the precursor for the late *MOCHE/CHIMÚ* god *AI APAEC*.

Another huge carved stone slab, the Raimondi Stela (1.98m/6½ ft long), depicts a hallmark of the Chavín cult: the *STAFF DEITY*. This figure, ubiquitous in Chavín iconography, was portrayed with male or female attributes as a full-frontal, standing figure of composite animal and human characteristics. Like other Chavín deities, the hands and feet end in claws, the mouth displays huge, curved fangs, and the ears are bedecked with ornaments. The arms are outstretched to either side and clutch staffs in one form or another, themselves elaborately festooned with spikes and plume-like decorations.

The significance and meaning of the Staff Deity is uncertain. His/her importance is attested by the appli-

cation of the image all over Chavín de Huántar, and throughout the central Andes and coast. His/her potency is likewise demonstrated by the fact that the imagery of a full-frontal, staff-bearing deity endured from the Early Horizon to Late Horizon times. Given this exceptional importance, it seems certain that the Staff Deity was a supernatural being with a distinct "personality", possibly a primeval creator god (see also *HUARI*, *TIAHUANACO*).

A final aspect of the labyrinth of galleries and passages in the Chavín de Huántar temples is the ritual use of water. A system of conduits in the chambers could literally be made to roar when water was flushed rapidly through the drains and the sound vented around the chambers. What this sounded like, and what other-worldly feelings it evoked in the minds and hearts of worshippers, can only be imagined (see also *MACHU PICCHU*, *PARACAS*, and *SACSAHUAMAN*).

CHAVÍN DE HUÁNTAR
see *CHAVÍN*.

CHECA YAUYOS
see *HUAROCHIRÍ MANUSCRIPT*.

CHEQO HUASI (WASI)
see *HUARI*.

THE TELLO OBELISK, carved in the shape of a crocodile, is covered with images of animals and plants from mountains, coast and rain forest, attesting to the widespread influence of the Chavín cult.

CREATION MYTHS

CREATOR DEITIES AND CREATION myths feature in all the ancient South American cultures. Among the ancient civilizations of the Andes and the adjacent western coastal valleys, two supreme creator gods were particularly prominent: Viracocha and Pachacamac. The former had numerous manifestations and names, but most accounts portray him as a creator who once walked among the people and taught them. Pachacamac was somewhat more remote, more an oracle to be consulted than a missionary. Common features were the creation of the sun and moon, and the emergence of humankind from underground. Most myths name the Titicaca Basin as the place of creation; indeed, so all-pervading was its importance that the Inca sought to link their own origin to Tiahuanaco in Titicaca, and went to great lengths to embrace the accounts of all the peoples they conquered.

Among the rain forest tribes of the Amazon drainage, eastern coasts, *pampas* and Patagonia, accounts of creation are more discursive. All tribes have beliefs about where people came from and how they came into being, but there is less emphasis on detail, and wider variation in the place of origin. For example, humans came either from underground or from the sky. After creating the world, however, rain forest gods take little further interest in humankind's day-to-day existence. A prominent theme is that jaguars were the masters of the earth before humans, and that the jaguars' powers were acquired by humans after they had been adopted by jaguars and had betrayed them.

VIRACOCHA (above) was perhaps the most universally recognized Andean god. He was known by numerous additional names, and his character varied in detail from culture to culture. In general, he was described as a benevolent god who created the earth, sun, moon and humankind at Lake Titicaca and travelled throughout the land teaching the arts of civilization before departing across the ocean. Variously described in Inca accounts as wearing a white robe or in the rags of a beggar, and having a long beard, numerous stone statues – assumed from their contexts to represent him – present a different image, such as this angular Tiahuanaco stone idol.

LAKE TITICACA (above) was a place of reverence for most of the ancient cultures of the Andes, and almost universally believed to be the place where the world began. The sun and the moon were believed to have risen from islands named for them, created by the act of Viracocha. The islands became places of pilgrimage, and the nearby ancient site of Tiahuanaco was revered by the Incas, who recognized the power of the civilization that must have ruled there.

THE IMPORTANCE and power of the jaguar (above) was a prominent theme among rain forest tribes east of the Andes. The jaguar was believed to have originally been the possessor of fire and of hunting weapons, both of which were obtained by humans through trickery or theft. The roles were then reversed, and jaguars had to hunt by stealth, kill their prey with their fangs and claws and eat their meat raw. Nevertheless, reverence for the jaguar's power and ancient knowledge endured, for example through shamans.

THE EMERGENCE of humans from underground (left), usually from caves, was a common theme in Andean creation myths. The Incas identified the caves of their own origin in the mountain Tambo Toco ("window house") in Pacaritambo, about 26 km (16 miles) south of Cuzco. Acknowledging the importance and power of the ancient site of Tiahuanaco in the Titicaca Basin, however, they sought to link their origins – and right to rule – to Titicaca by claiming that the Inca ancestors were led by Manco Capac underground from the lake to emerge at Tambo Toco.

29

THE CHIBCHA, or Muisca, of the Colombian central highlands were one of several skilled metal-working peoples who developed distinctive cultures in the cordilleran and western coastal regions from about the 1st century AD to the Spanish conquest. They worked primarily with gold and copper (individually, or alloyed as *tumbaga*) but also with silver and platinum. The Chibcha were less interested than others in making finely finished objects, but focused on making multiple versions of an object. Other metal-working cultures included Tairona and Sinú (northern Columbia); Tolima, Tierradentro and San Agustín (in the eastern cordillera); Quimbaya, Calima, Popayán and Nariño (western cordillera); and Tumaco (coastal lowlands).

According to Chibcha myth, the sun and moon created the first man from clay and the first woman from reeds. All these cultures held the afterlife as an important realm, judging by the richness of their graves, in which intricately worked gold and alloyed metal diadems, pectorals, masks and pendants, as well as stone and ceramic items were placed beside the mummified bodies. It was from the Chibcha ritual of the gilded heir to the throne that the legend of EL DORADO was born. (See BACHUE, BOCHICA, CHIBCHACUM, CHIE, CHIMINIGAGUA, HUITACA, NEMTEREQUETEBA)

CHIBCHACUM, the CHIBCHA patron deity of workers and merchants, was important among a people whose metalworking skills were highly valued. That honour notwithstanding, in Chibcha myth he once attempted to destroy humankind with a flood, enlisting the help of a woman called CHIE, to spite the founder hero BOCHICA. The people appealed to Bochica for help, and Chibchacum was unsuccessful. He fled underground in fear, and from that day on was burdened with having to support the world on his shoulders.

CHICHA

was the fermented corn (maize) beer that was offered to the mummified bodies (MALLQUIS) of ancestors and drunk by priests and attendants in ritual worship and ceremony.

CHIE was the CHIBCHA moon goddess who helped CHIBCHACUM in an attempt to defy BOCHICA.

CHIMINIGAGUA was the CHIBCHA so-called creator god. He created the large black bird that carried the light (probably of the sun) over the mountains, but left the rest of creation up to others. The goddess BACHUE was responsible for the procreation of humans.

CHIMO CAPAC ("Lord Chimú") invaded the LAMBAYEQUE VALLEY following the death of FEMPELLEC of the NAYAMLAP dynasty. According to myth, he came from the south by sea. As with the earliest INCA kings, this myth appears to be an early account, handed down the generations, recording the early days of the CHIMÚ Kingdom. Chimo Capac probably came up from the MOCHE Valley, the centre of Chimor, in the 14th century, conquered the Lambayeque Valley and incorporated it into his kingdom. The account of this says that he appointed a man named Pongmassa as local CURACA, and that Pongmassa was succeeded by his son and then by his grandson. During the rulership of the grandson, the Incas conquered the valley, established their alliance with the Kingdom of Chimor and continued to administer the valley through five further *curacas*.

THIS PECTORAL
of hammered and repoussé gold is in the Calima style and depicts a deity. The cultures of Colombia probably shared similar beliefs and deities, although we know the names of only a few Chibcha gods.

CHIMOR see CHIMÚ.

CHIMÚ, or Kingdom of Chimor, emerging in the Late Intermediate Period, was a state-level society that established its dominance in the northern coastal valleys and adjacent Andean region of Peru, and later came into conflict with the INCA Empire. Like the MOCHE before them, the Chimú conquered north and south over a period of about 400 years. The Chimú are second only to the Incas in importance in the study of Andean mythology, as their culture is the only other one for which we have written accounts of the myths and cosmology, although these have reached us primarily through the Incas (see AMAUTAS and QUIPUCAMAYOQS). Much of Chimú religion appears to have been influenced by the Moche; certainly the Chimú were the inheritors of Moche

power in the region, although they seem to have come from outside, a possibility recorded in their mythology (see CHIMO CAPAC, TAYCANAMU).

Chan Chan, their capital, was founded *c.* AD 1000 and endured until the Inca conquest of the region in the 1470s by TUPAC INCA YUPANQUI, overcoming MINCHANÇAMAN. It comprised an extensive complex of individual compounds covering 6 sq km (1,480 acres), around which domestic and workshop suburbs spread over 20 sq km (4,940 acres). Each walled compound (known as a *ciudadela*) of the central core was rectangular, its long axis oriented north–south, and made of thick walls up to 9 m (30 ft) high of poured *adobe* mud. Most had only one entrance, on the north side, guarded by painted wooden human figures set in niches on each side. Each court contained the residences of the reigning Chimú king, and his officials. Around other courtyards within the compounds were storerooms, U-shaped structures (called *audiencias*) and burial platforms. Adjacent wings

CHICHA beer was drunk on ritual occasions in most ancient Andean cultures. This Moche stirrup-spouted vessel is in the shape of a noble holding a chicha cup.

contained rooms for service and maintenance retainers, and walled-in wells.

Burials were placed in and near the U-shaped structures, which were possibly meant to reflect reverence for the ancient U-shaped ceremonial complexes of the area (see *CHAVÍN*). They represented "cosmic niches", and served a ritual purpose. They were also centres for the redistribution of goods, part of a tightly controlled social structure for collection and distribution of wealth, foods and commodities, according to social rank. Along the

THE FUNERARY ciudadela compounds, each surrounded by massive adobe walls, form the core of the ruins of Chan Chan, the ancient capital of Chimú.

that might have housed the mummified dead body (see *MALLQUIS*) of the king. The Chimú king list, which was recorded by the Incas, names ten kings.

There are also five monumental *adobe* brick mounds at Chan Chan, possibly temple platforms, but they have been so destroyed by treasure-seekers that we cannot now be sure of their function.

THE WALLS of the Tschudi ciudadela at Chan Chan show characteristic Chimú carved friezes of repeated figures and geometric patterns, and storage niches.

south walls of the compounds, sloping ramps led to burial platforms for the royal family. There are ten compounds, nine of which have a truncated pyramid in the southeast corner. Entered from above through a court, each pyramid contains a suite of cells and a larger room

We know the names of only a few Chimú gods. Chief among them appear to have been *AI APAEC* (a sky/creator god), the moon goddess *SI*, and the sea god *NI*.

The walls and other aspects of the *ciudadelas*, however, and artefacts from these and other Chimú sites, give some insights into the nature of Chimú religion. The walls of the compound were carved and sculpted with repetitious friezes: of geometric patterns, images of birds and marine animals, and of the double-headed rainbow serpent (considered to be associated with the moon goddess Si).

CHIMÚ CERAMICS depicted everyday objects, as well as zoomorphic, anthropomorphic and ritual scenes. This stirrup-spout bottle of polished blackware (left) shows a small figure on a reed fishing raft (c. AD 1000).

More generally, Chimú iconography appears to be a merging of Moche and *HUARI* styles and mythological beings, and Chimú ritual architecture reveals Huari influence. The *FANGED GOD*, *JAGUARS* and *JAGUAR-HUMANS*, and *SERPENTS* (all elements that ultimately stem from Chavín) figure prominently. On the other hand, the Chimú repertoire seems more limited than Moche, and composed ritual scenes were rarely portrayed. In general, the Chimú religion and pantheon seem more remote.

The nature of Chimú ceremonies is uncertain, so filtered was their history by the Inca record keepers. A huge burial platform next to one of the *ciudadelas*, however, held more than 200 bodies, including those of young women who might have been sacrificed to accompany the Chimú king into the afterlife.

More informative is a painted wooden model excavated in a Chimú tomb inserted into the Moche Huaca de la Luna. It appears to represent an episode of the periodic

reopening of a Chimú tomb for the addition of bodies and/or replenishment of offerings. It is 410 x 480 mm (16 x 19 in) and comprises a rectangular, miniature *ciudadela*. On its diminutive walls is a painted frieze of fish in yellow, brown, black, and white ochre. The compound has just a single, narrow entrance, and wooden human figurines stand within, carved and inlaid with mother-of-pearl and *Spondylus*-shell ornament. The figures all face a ramped platform, some standing on benches along the sides of the enclosure, others serving *CHICHA* beer. At the rear, partly covered by a tiny gable supported by two columns, is a sunken chamber, within which were three miniature mummy bundles, two females and one male.

HUACA EL DRAGON, a funerary compound northwest of Chan Chan, includes well-preserved examples of Chimú images, including repeated staff-bearing figures, a variety of creatures and repeated arched, double-headed "rainbow serpents".

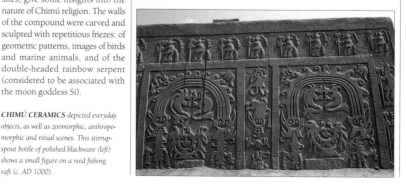

CHINCHASUYU, the northwest quarter of the *INCA* Empire, comprised the Andes mountain regions and the coast west and north of Cuzco, encompassing most of modern Ecuador and stretching as far north as southern Colombia. Its western limit was the Pacific Ocean (see *TAHUANTINSUYU*).

CHOCO is a region of the Colombian rain forest inhabited by tribes whose cosmological belief is typical of the cyclicity that imbues the religion of most peoples of South America in some form. Their myths tell the story of a first race of humans that was ultimately destroyed by the gods because the people practised cannibalism. A second race was transformed into the animals, while the present race of humans had been created by the gods from clay.

THE CHOCO tribes of the Colombian rain forest believe that the present-day human race was made by the gods from clay.

CHOT was the capital city that was established by *NAYAMLAP* in the *LAMBAYEQUE VALLEY*.

CIUM, the eldest son of *NAYAMLAP*, was the second legendary ruler of the *LAMBAYEQUE* dynasty in north coastal Peru. Unlike his father, who had invaded the valley with his wife, Cium married a local woman named Zolzoloñi – the myth refers to her by the Spanish

CHINCHASUYU, the northwest quadrant of the Inca Empire, stretched from the central Andes of modern Peru and Ecuador west to the fertile Pacific coastal plains.

word *moza*, "commoner" or "outsider" in a specified group, that is, the descendants of Nayamlap. They had 12 sons, each of whom married and also produced a large family. As the population grew, each son left the capital, Chot, and founded a new city within the valley.

COCA see *MAMA COCA*.

COLLARI was the first woman in a central Andean *Q'ERO/INCA* variation of the creation myth (see *ROAL*).

COLLASUYU, the southeast and largest quarter of the *INCA* Empire, encompassed the entire *TITICACA* Basin of modern Peru and Bolivia as well as the vast Atacama Desert of northern Chile. It stretched from *CUZCO* in the northwest, south as far as, or even beyond, modern Santiago in central Chile. Its eastern and western limits were the tropical forests of the southern Amazon drainage and high *pampas* of northern Argentina, and the Pacific Ocean (see *TAHUANTINSUYU*).

COLLCA ("granary"), or Catachillay, was one of the star groups the *INCA* saw within *MAYU*, the Milky Way, identified as the Pleiades. It was believed to be the guardian of stored seeds and of agriculture.

COLLASUYU, the southeast quadrant of the Inca Empire, encompassed the high Andes and alti-planos of modern southern Peru and Bolivia, including numerous rich, high-altitude valleys.

CON see *PACHACAMAC*.

CON TICCI VIRACOCHA (central Andean/pre-*INCA*/Inca) was, at the simplest, another of the many names for *VIRACOCHA*. He was the creator god of the peoples of the Colloa region of southern highland Peru, possibly predating the Inca supreme god Viracocha and later conflated within the mythology centring on Viracocha and his travels from the *TITICACA* Basin northwest towards *CUZCO*.

Among the Colloas, he was believed to have created the sun and then made stone figures of the various peoples of the Andes, which he placed throughout the valleys. Then he travelled around bringing the stone models to life and instructing them in his worship.

One version of the Inca creation myth, related by the 16th-century chronicler Cristobal de Molina, begins at a time when the world was already full of people. A great flood rose to the tops of the mountains, destroying all except one man and one woman, who were cast up on land at the ancient site of *TIAHUANACO*. Con Ticci Viracocha appeared to them and

ordered them to remain where they were as *MITIMAES*. He repopulated the land by making the Inca ancestors out of clay and painting them with the regional dress by which they were to become known, and also made a second race of people at Tiahuanaco. He also made the birds and animals (two of each, male and female) and spread them among their habitats, designated what each was to eat, and gave each bird its song.

In Inca mythology, this dispersal of the models of the new humans was crucial to their legitimization of conquest, state creation and empire-building. Scattering humans across the regions as distinctive peoples or "nations" was regarded as a "seeding" of the land in preparation for the "coming into being". They were ordered by Viracocha to descend into the ground and re-emerge out of caves, mountains and springs when called upon.

Con Ticci Viracocha kept two of his creations with him, naming them *IMAYMANA VIRACOCHA* and *TOCAPO VIRACOCHA*. The inclusion of "Viracocha" in their names imbued them with divinity and supernatural power, as well as identifying them with Viracocha himself. In some versions, they are said to be Con Ticci Viracocha's sons.

After these creations, Viracocha began his pilgrimage from Lake Titicaca. He commanded his elder son, Imaymana Viracocha, to travel northwestwards along a route bordering the forests and mountains,

THE RICH, intensive agriculture carried out on terraces in the Andes was believed to come under the protection of Collca, or the Pleiades, one of many star groups that were recognized in the Milky Way.

and his younger son, Tocapo Viracocha, to journey northwards along a coastal route, while he went along a route between them, northwestwards through the mountains. As they passed through the land, they called out the people created by Viracocha, named the trees and the plants, established the times when each would flower and bear fruit, and instructed the people on which were edible and which medicinal.

They continued to what would become the northwesternmost edge of the Inca Empire, in modern Ecuador, to the coastal site of MANTA, then continued across the sea, walking on water until they disappeared.

The trinity implied by the three Viracochas suggests that there was an element of Christian persuasion in the relations of the Spanish chroniclers, but it is an argument that cannot be concluded. The Incas had no writing system and were under heavy pressure from proselytizing Spanish priests. Their religion, written as mythology by the chroniclers, brought them favour if it could be shown to have an element of the "truth" by being a warped version of Christian belief. One 16th-century Inca chronicler, Juan de Santa Cruz Pachacuti Yamqui, even believed that the creator, known as THUNUPA VIRACOCHA to him, was the apostle St Thomas; and the Inca chronicler, Felipe Guaman Poma de Ayala, identified Viracocha with St Bartholomew.

On the other hand, triadism is a general concept, and was held by many ancient cultures throughout the world. The specific "Andean Triad" of a tripartite Viracocha had several variations, and only in some of them does the triad comprise a father and two sons – which in itself is not a configuration characteristic of Christian trinitarianism.

CONAPA see *TONAPA.*

CONCHA YAUYOS see *HUAROCHIRÍ MANUSCRIPT.*

CONIRAYA VIRACOCHA, a pre-INCA deity named in the early 17th-century HUAROCHIRÍ MANUSCRIPT, was described as a creator god by its compilers, but they reach no conclusion as to whether Coniraya Viracocha was the same deity as the pan-Andean VIRACOCHA, who created the world at Lake TITICACA. The significant point is that the adventures of Coniraya Viracocha, some of which parallel those of Viracocha, were recounted to the compilers by highland Andean dwellers even though the legendary events take place in the coastal lowlands. The reality of ancient coastal and Andean cultural interrelationships and interdependencies, and Inca efforts to integrate and reconcile the peoples and religious beliefs throughout its empire, appears to be reflected in the mythology.

The story in the Manuscript begins when the god HUALLALLO CARHUINCHO had ruled Huarochirí for some time. The authors are unclear as to whether Coniraya Viracocha lived before or after this time. Still he was a powerful deity who, by his word alone, could create towns and villages, agricultural lands, and terraces across the hillsides. To water the lands, he created irrigation canals by tossing the flower of the *pupuna* reed down into the ground to form channels.

Like Viracocha, Coniraya Viracocha was a wandering teacher. He travelled around dressed in the rags of a beggar and was often taken for one. Those who failed to recognize him often treated him with abuse.

During his journeys, Coniraya Viracocha learned of a beautiful female virgin HUACA, Cavillaca. He became enamoured and desperate to sleep with her, but she would have nothing to do with him. One day he observed Cavillaca weaving beneath a *lúcuma* tree (a coastal tree that bears yellow-orange fruit). Changing himself into a bird, he flew to the tree and put his semen into one of the ripened fruits, then caused it to fall beside Cavillaca. She ate the fruit, thus becoming impregnated. Nine months later she gave birth to a boy, still unaware of who had made her pregnant.

When the child was a year old, Cavillaca grew determined to discover the father. She called upon the aid of the VILCA and huaca male spirits of the surrounding landscape, who came, dressed in their finery, each hoping to "claim" the fatherhood and love of Cavillaca. Conspicuous among them stood Coniraya Viracocha, dressed in his usual rags. Cavillaca asked the assembled company which one of them was the father of her child, but none spoke. Cavillaca then placed her son on the ground to see which god the boy would crawl to; the child crawled along the line-up until he came to Coniraya Viracocha and promptly climbed into his true father's lap.

Cavillaca, furious at the idea of such a despicable-looking being as her husband, seized her son from his father's lap and raced for the western sea. There, near the site of PACHACAMAC (just south of present-day Lima), she continued straight into the water, where she and her son were turned into stones which, the manuscript claims, could still be seen offshore.

Coniraya Viracocha was so distressed by Cavillaca's disappearance that he set off to find her. He asked every creature he encountered after her whereabouts. Depending on whether the animal gave him encouraging or discouraging news, he gave it good or bad traits. Thus, for example, the condor told him that he would surely soon find Cavillaca, and so Coniraya Viracocha declared that the condor would enjoy long life and always have plenty to eat, and that anyone who killed a condor would also die. In contrast, the skunk told him that Cavillaca had gone far away and that he would never find her, so he gave the skunk its stink in order that people would hate it, and confined its activities to the night-time. (Clearly, this part of the myth resembles Viracocha's journeys from Lake Titicaca.)

Coniraya Viracocha continued his search for Cavillaca until he too reached Pachacamac. There he saw the two daughters of the god Pachacamac guarded by a snake, as their mother, URPAY HUACHAC, was away. He seduced the elder sister and tried to sleep with the younger as well but, before he could do so, she turned herself into a dove and flew off. Coniraya Viracocha was enraged at this rejection and, as a result, became the cause of the presence of fish in the ocean. At the time, the only fish in existence were those raised by Urpay Huachac in a special pond near Pachacamac, the site; he sabotaged her operation by smashing the pond and scattering her fish into the oceans.

He continued his search for Cavillaca and his son but never found them. The manuscript says that he travelled far up the coast, playing many more tricks on the peoples and huacas whom he met.

CONTITI VIRACOCHA PAC-HAYACHACHIC

CONTITI VIRACOCHA PAC-HAYACHACHIC (meaning "god, creator of the world") was the name given to the central Andean/INCA god VIRACOCHA by the people of CACHA, and recorded by the 16th-century Spanish chronicler Juan de Betanzos.

CORI OCLLO see MAMA OCLLO.

THE CORICANCHA

THE CORICANCHA ("golden enclosure" or "building of gold"), the main square of the INCA capital at CUZCO, was the perceived centre of the Inca world and cosmos on earth. Together with the royal palaces and shrines, it served a multitude of religious and official functions. It was the "centre" of the city itself – and, by extension, of TAHUANTINSUYU, the four quarters of the empire – and was the supreme sacred ceremonial precinct of the city. From the Coricancha, sacred CEQUE lines were projected from the capital to the provinces, partitioning the empire, as well as the capital; and the movements of the Milky Way (see MAYU) across the night sky were keenly observed and plotted from points within the precinct. (One such was the pillar of the CAPAC USNU, from which sightings of Mayu were taken between two pillars on the distant horizon.)

The complex itself was in the tail of the image of a puma, as seen in profile by linking with lines the various edifices of the Inca city, and lay at the confluence of Cuzco's two rivers, the Huantanay and the Tullamayo. The head of the puma was formed by SACSAHUAMAN, another sacred precinct. The Coricancha consisted of an enclosure known as a *cancha*, constructed of fitted stone blocks. Within this were six *wasi*, or covered chambers, arranged around a square courtyard. (In some cases the entire complex is referred to as the "Temple of the Sun". In fact, the temple to the sun god, where the sacred fires of INTI were guarded by the ACLLAS, was only one of the several temples making up the complex, although the increased emphasis on Inti by the later emperors led to a certain focus on that cult.)

The walls of the buildings were covered with sheet gold, referred to as "the sweat of the sun", and silver. Specific rooms within the group of buildings were designated for the six principal Inca state gods, guardians of the official religion. Each room housed the images and idols of its appropriate deity, plus lesser objects of worship. There were VIRACOCHA, the supreme creator, Inti the sun god, QUILLA the moon goddess, CHASKA-QOYLOR the god of Venus as the morning and evening "stars", ILLAPA the god of weather, and CUICHU the god of the rainbow, ranged hierarchically in that order, although the relative positions of Viracocha and Inti are thought to have been equivocal.

The intimate mythological connection between Inti and gold was

THE INTERIOR of the Temple of Inti (the sun) in the Coricancha includes the large niche in which was displayed the golden mask or image of the god.

THE SACRED CORICANCHA precinct in Cuzco comprised the temples of the principal Inca deities, including those of Inti (the sun) and Quilla (the moon).

further borne out by images in the temple garden. Here Inca goldsmiths and craftsmen created cast gold and silver models of all the creatures known to them. There were butterflies and other insects, JAGUARS, llamas, guinea pigs and many others.

One room of the complex was reserved for the storage and care of the mummies of past Inca emperors (see MALLQUIS). On special ritual days, these formed a focus for the sacred ceremonies (see, for example, CAPAC RAYMI and INTI RAYMI). The mummies were dressed in rich garments and placed upon royal litters, which were carried in procession around the capital. In the precinct, too, sanctification and incantations to the CAPACOCHAS – specially selected sacrificial victims – took place before their ritual journey along the *ceque* lines back to their provinces for sacrifice.

Other rooms within the complex were used to store sacred objects taken from the conquered provinces, including a sacred HUACA from each subjugated population. The *huaca* was required to remain in perpetual residence as a sort of "hostage", and selected members of the nobility of each subject population were forced to live in the capital for several months of each year.

The tenth emperor, PACHACUTI INCA YUPANQUI, reorganized the Coricancha into this final form in his rebuilding of the city. His actions, it is argued, were taken in order to formalize his defiance of his father, VIRACOCHA INCA, and brother, INCA URCO, from whom he had usurped the throne.

Alongside the oracle temple of PACHACAMAC and the ISLAND OF THE SUN in Lake TITICACA, the Coricancha was one of the most revered places in the Inca Empire. Something of its splendour is captured in the words of conquistador Pedro de Cieza de León, who recorded his experiences in his *Crónica del Peru* (Seville, 1550–3): "The temple was more than 400 paces in circuit. . . [and the finely hewn masonry was] a dusky or black colour. . . [with] many openings and doorways. . . very well carved. Around the wall, halfway up, there was a band of gold, two *palmos* wide and four *dedos* in thickness. The doorways and doors were covered with plates of the same metal. Within [there] were four houses, not very large, but with walls of the same kind and covered with plates of gold within and without. . .

"In one of these houses. . . there was the figure of the sun, very large and made of gold. . . enriched with many precious stones. . .

"They also had a garden, the

clods of which were made of pieces of gold; and it was artificially sown with golden corn [maize], the stalks, as well as the leaves and cobs, being of that metal. . . Besides all this, they had more than 20 golden sheep [llamas] with their lambs, and the shepherds with their slings and crooks to watch them, all made of the same metal. There was [also] a great quantity of jars of gold and silver, set with emeralds; vases, pots, and all sorts of utensils, all of fine gold."

The golden wealth of the Coricancha formed the basis of the ransom with which Inca ATAHUALPA attempted to secure his freedom from Francisco Pizarro at Cajamarca in 1533.

COYA see *MAMA OCLLO*.

CRYSTAL TABLET see under *PACHACUTI INCA YUPANQUI*.

CUICHU was the INCA god of the rainbow. His idol was one of the images of the gods kept in the sacred *CORICANCHA* in *CUZCO*.

CUNA see *MAMACUNA*.

CUNTISUYU, the southwest quadrant of the Inca Empire to the south of Cuzco, encompassed the dry desert regions bordering the Pacific Ocean.

CUNTISUYU, the southwest and smallest quarter of the INCA Empire, comprised a triangular region whose borders diverged from a point at the capital at *CUZCO* to points in the Pacific coast in

CUICHU, the Inca rainbow god, was among the deities honoured with a temple in the Coricancha precinct in Cuzco.

modern central and southwestern Peru; see *TAHUANTINSUYU*.

CURA see *MAMA CURA*.

CURACA was a member of the INCA provincial nobility (see also *HATUNRUNA*). In the first century after the Spanish conquest, the *curacas* became an important source of information on local belief and legend for Spanish and Spanish-trained native chroniclers, in their attempts to root out local idolatry (see *IDOLATRÍAS*). In the legend surrounding the foundation of the Inca state by *MANCO CAPAC*, he was said to have been the son of a local *curaca* of *PACARITAMBO*. Similarly, according to legendary histories which narrate the foundations of the *CHIMÚ* and *PACHACAMAC*, CHIMO CAPAC installed Pongmassa as his *curaca* in the former, and the god Pachacamac named several *curacas* to rule the local peoples of the coastal lowlands.

CUSCO see *CUZCO*.

CUZCO, the INCA capital in the Valley of Cuzco in central Andean

Peru, was the "navel" of the Inca world. From it radiated the highways and politico-religious tendrils of the vast Inca Empire (*TAHUANTINSUYU*). Within its *CORICANCHA* ceremonial precinct and élite residential structures were planned and executed the administration of the empire, through its extensive network of provincial capitals and local rulerships.

The final plan of the city was established by *PACHACUTI INCA YUPANQUI*, the tenth emperor, and, seemingly deliberately, forms the shape of a puma profile if viewed

from above. Principal compounds included the sacred Coricancha temples and the *SACSAHUAMAN* complex, the latter of which formed the shape of the puma's head. Precincts of the city were grouped into *HANAN* (upper) and *HURIN* (lower) Cuzco to reflect the hierarchical social divisions of the capital's citizens.

CUZCO HUANCA see *AYAR AUCA*.

THE "DARK CLOUD" CONSTELLATIONS see *MAYU* and *PACHATIRA*.

DAY-TIME SUN, that is, the sun as it passed across the sky from sunrise to sunset, was an object of worship of the *LLACUAZ* lineage of *CAJATAMBO*.

THE FINAL PLAN of the Inca capital, Cuzco, was established by the tenth emperor, Pachacuti Inca Yupanqui. His addition of the Sacsahuaman temple precinct completed the outline of a puma's profile.

D

35

E

DECAPITATOR GOD, a *MOCHE* deity, was a fearsome half-human, half-*JAGUAR* being depicted on ceramics, metalwork, friezes and murals at Moche (on the Huaca de la Luna and in temples), at *SIPÁN* in the *LAMBAYEQUE VALLEY*, and at other sites. He was frequently portrayed holding a crescent-shaped *tumi* ceremonial knife in one hand and a severed human head in the other, but appeared in several other guises as well. Elaborate plaster friezes at the Huaca de la Luna depict a fearful face framed in a diamond. In black, white, brown and shades of red and yellow ochre, a grimacing mouth bares four long fangs, eyes stare menacingly, and the face is embellished with double ear-ornaments and curling hair and beard.

He is shown in an elaborate bloodletting rite painted on pottery vessels and on temple and tomb walls. His role, acted out by priests, embodied a gruesome sacrificial ritual. It was once thought such scenes were merely representational imagery of a mythical event, but archaeological evidence at several sites attests to its reality.

At the Huaca de la Luna, an enclosure at the back of the platform contained the buried remains of 40 men, aged 15 to 30. They appear to have been pushed off a stone outcrop into the enclosure after having been ritually mutilated and killed. The structure, outcrop and enclosure seem to mirror nearby Cerro Blanco. Some skeletons were splayed out as if they had been stretched when tied to stakes; some had their femurs torn from the pelvis; skulls, ribs, finger-, arm- and leg-bones all have cut marks. Several severed heads, their lower jaws ripped off, were scattered among the bones.

The skeletons and scattered bones were covered in a layer of sediment that had been deposited during heavy rains, indicating that the ceremony took place in response to an El Niño weather event

THE FEARSOME DECAPITATOR GOD was depicted in every medium by Moche craftsmen – here as a gold disc showing the god with a fanged mouth and crescent-bladed ceremonial tumi knife.

that might have disrupted the economic stability of the realm – some victims being offered to the gods in a plea for them to stop the rains and flooding, others in gratitude when the rain did finally cease.

Detailed combat scenes were painted on Moche ceramics and walls. Friezes show opposing warriors in combat, usually both wearing Moche armour and bearing Moche arms. Pairs of combatants are shown in narrative sequences. Instead of being killed in battle, the loser is shown stripped and tied with a rope round the neck, being marched off for arraignment. Finally, the captives are shown naked, having their throats slit, and then their blood presented in goblets to four presiding figures. The most elaborate is the Warrior Priest, wearing a crescent-shaped metal plate to protect his back, and rattles suspended from his belt; to his right sits the Bird Priest, wearing a conical helmet bearing the image of an owl and a long beak-like nose-ornament. Next to the Bird Priest is a priestess, identified by her long, plaited tresses, dress-like costume, and plumed and tasselled headdress. The final figure wears a headdress with serrated border and long streamers, decorated with a *FELINE* or similar face.

The fact that most of the combatants in these scenes are Moche seems to indicate that they represent not battles but ritual combats among the fields near Moche cities for the purpose of "capturing" victims for sacrifice to the gods.

In keeping with these scenes, the Sipán tombs contained bodies and artefacts that verify the practices depicted. Several unlooted tombs (dated *c.* AD 300) contain rich burial goods – including gold, silver, turquoise and other jewellery, and textiles – and bodies dressed in costumes similar to those in the ritual scenes on pottery and murals. The principal body, possibly a noble, personified the Warrior Priest. He wore a crescent-shaped back plate and had rattles suspended from his belt. Both plate and rattles are decorated with the image of the Decapitator, in this case an anthropomorphized spider, with the characteristic Decapitator fangs and double ear-ornaments, perched on a golden web. The spider is thought to reflect the parallel between bloodletting and the spider's sucking of the life juices from its prey. Offerings to the Decapitator God consisted of three pairs of gold and turquoise ear-spools (one of which depicts a Moche warrior), a crescent-shaped gold headdress, a crescent-shaped nose-ornament, and one gold and one silver *tumi* knife. At the Warrior Priest's side lay a box-like sceptre of gold, embossed with combat scenes.

Near this tomb was another, not quite as rich, containing the body of a noble with a gilded copper headdress decorated with an owl with outspread wings – clearly the Bird Priest of the friezes. Sealed rectangular rooms near the tombs contained other offerings – ceramic vessels, copper goblets, miniature war gear – and, tellingly, the skeletal remains of severed human hands and feet, probably from sacrificed victims.

Further confirmation of the accuracy of the Moche friezes was discovered at San José de Moro in the Jequetepeque Valley, where the tombs (dated *c.* AD 500–600) of two women were found to contain silver-alloyed copper headdresses with plume-like tassels and other accoutrements of the Priestess. Finally, at El Brujo in the Chicama Valley, a terrace frieze shows a life-size warrior leading a procession of ten life-size nude prisoners tied by a rope around their necks. On a terrace above this (later destroyed by looters) a huge spider or crab with fanged mouth and double ear-ornaments was depicted, identifying it as the Decapitator. It had segmented legs, one of which was brandishing a *tumi* knife.

EKKEKO, the household god, is a traditional Andean deity still honoured today. This silver example has a pre-Spanish conquest "feel" while displaying a modern guitar and umbrella.

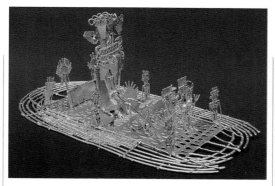

EKKEKO, a Late Horizon, central Andean deity, was a household god, thought to bring good fortune if looked after properly. Like a good-luck charm, he was portrayed as a little man with a round stomach, festooned with tiny household utensils. He was thought to rule a miniature city. Ekkeko figurines are still bought today in the Andes as good-luck charms.

EL DORADO ("Gilded Man" in Spanish) was the legendary king of the chiefdom of the *CHIBCHA* or Muisca of the far northern Andes in Colombia. El Dorado was a person, city, entire kingdom and in time, a myth. The Spanish myth or legend is a product of their lust for gold. Once tales of untold wealth from the northern "kingdoms" reached their ears, the Spaniards began to associate the legend with the entire region of central Colombia. In reality, the quest for gold and riches beyond belief turned out to be a chimera: El Dorado was always just one more range of mountains away, but was never found.

The most reliable sources of the legend focus on the Chibcha/Muisca and their chiefdom around Lake Guatavita in central Colombia. Gold was extremely important to the chiefdoms of the far northern Andes, and several distinctive styles of goldworking developed throughout the region from the 1st century BC/AD; the Muisca style itself dates from the 8th century AD. The Spaniards learned the story of the golden king from many sources, including Chibcha who had actually witnessed the ceremony before the Spaniards arrived. Every conquistador and chronicler of this area mentions the Golden Man, but the most complete account is that of mid-17th-century chronicler Rodríguez Freyle, who was told the legend by his friend Don Juan, the nephew of the last independent lord of Guatavita.

The ritual that gave rise to the legend was performed at the inauguration of a new king. The heir to the throne spent the days before the ceremony secluded in a cave. During this time, he was required to abstain from women and was forbidden to eat chilli peppers or salt. Then, on the appointed day, he made his first official journey to Lake Guatavita, to give offerings to the gods. At the lakeside, a raft of rushes was prepared and bedecked with precious decorations and treasures. Four lighted braziers were placed on the raft, in which *moque* incense and other resins were burned. Braziers of incense were also lit on the shore, and such a quantity of smoke was produced that the light of the sun was said to be obscured.

The king-to-be was then stripped naked and his body smeared with sticky clay or resin. Over this he was entirely covered with glittering gold dust, shown being blown from a tube in an engraving of 1599. He then boarded the raft, accompanied by four principal subject chiefs, all of whom were richly attired in "plumes, crowns, bracelets, pendants and earrings all of gold", but also otherwise naked. The king remained motionless on the raft while at his feet was placed a great heap of gold ornaments and precious stones (referred to as "emeralds" by Freyle).

The raft was pushed off across the lake, whereupon musicians on shore struck up a fanfare of trumpets, flutes and other instruments, and the assembled crowd began to sing. When the raft reached the centre of the lake, a banner was raised as a signal for silence. The gilded king then made his offering to the gods: one by one, the treasures were thrown into the lake by the king and his attendants. Then the flag was lowered again, and the raft paddled towards shore to the accompaniment of loud music, singing and wild dancing.

Upon reaching the shore, the new king was accepted as lord and master of the realm.

THE SPANISH LEGEND of El Dorado ("the gilded man") (above) originated with tales of the investiture ceremonies for a Chibcha chief. The ruler-to-be was dusted with fine gold dust, then paddled out into the middle of Lake Guatavita on a raft laden with gold objects (top left), to be offered into the lake waters.

THE CEREMONY of El Dorado took place on Lake Guatavita, Colombia (below left). So convinced were the Spanish that a fortune in gold lay beneath the waters of the lake that several attempts, all unsuccessful, were made to drain it. In the 1580s the merchant Antonio de Sepúlveda tried by cutting a huge notch to drain the water out (still visible to the left of the picture).

EL-LAL was the legendary culture hero of the *ONA* and *YAHGAN* tribes of Patagonia, and was regarded as the teacher of mankind.

When he was about to be born, his father, Nosjthej, snatched him from his mother's womb because he wanted to eat him. El-lal was saved by a rat, who carried him off to his nest, fostered him and taught him the sacred lore. Having learned well, El-lal came back to the surface and made himself master of the earth through his invention of the bow and arrow. With this weapon he fought Nosjthej, and the giants who dwelt on the earth long ago, overcoming them all.

Eventually, he tired of the earth and decided to leave it behind. As he departed, he declared that humans would thenceforth have to look after themselves.

ENDOCANNIBALISM
see *CANNIBALISM*.

EXOCANNIBALISM
see *CANNIBALISM*.

37

UNIVERSALITY, CONTINUITY & CYCLICITY

FOR THE PEOPLES OF ANCIENT ANDEAN and coastal civilizations the endless cycle of time began with the daily movement of the sun across the sky and then progressed through seasonal change to repetitious decades to the religious concept of *pachacuti*, or the "revolution of time and space". Andean and western coastal peoples believed in the existence of an overall supreme power, and that the course of history and civilization formed an inevitable succession of repetition and renewal. Collecting and collating their own beliefs and those of the peoples they conquered, the Incas believed in an elaborate succession of worlds or creations, inhabited by different races of beings and/or civilizations. Each "Age" was referred to as being ruled over by a sun, and the general course of development was from the more primitive to the sophisticated. Each world ended in its destruction by some catastrophic event. Naturally, they considered the Inca Empire to be the supreme achievement in this progression, and manipulated the creation myths to convince themselves and their subjects of their divine right to rule. That the Spanish conquest has merely interrupted this course of events is embodied in the concept of *Inkarrí*, the return of the Inca king.

THE ENDLESS *daily cycle of the sun was considered vital in Inca religion. The sun god Inti was special to the Inca and in the later empire began to rival even the creator god Viracocha in importance. The movement of the sun through the year was carefully charted by Inca priests, and two of the most important annual festivals were the summer and winter solstices, known respectively as Capac Raymi (December in the southern hemisphere) and Inti Raymi (June).*

TWO VITAL ELEMENTS in the economies of Andean and coastal civilizations were corn (maize) (silver representation, top) and the llama herds (above). It was important to chart the seasons carefully, relating them to botanical and zoological cycles so that steps could be taken during the agricultural year and herding seasons to ensure the wellbeing of the people.

THE CYCLE of the seasons was carefully plotted from the movements of the sun, and of the Milky Way (Mayu) and other stars and celestial bodies from observation posts carefully placed in relation to marker pillars at strategic points on local horizons. As well as in the capital Cuzco itself, there were observation platforms in several Inca cities. For example, at Kenko near Cuzco there was an intihuatana or "Hitching Post of the Sun" (above), perhaps less well known than its monolithic brother at the Inca mountain retreat at Machu Picchu.

INKARRÍ, the return of the Inca king, is the ultimate extension of Inca pachacuti or "revolution of time and space". This post-Spanish conquest development of Inca mythology or religion believes that the interlude of Spanish rule will ultimately end when the Inca return to power with the arrival of a new Sapa Inca (emperor). The festival of the sun celebrated today (right) is perhaps a wistful rehearsal for that time, as well as a revival of the ancient solstice rituals.

G

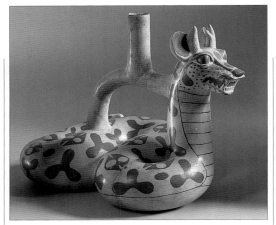

FANGED GOD

FANGED GOD, a general term, is sometimes used for beings depicted by several Andean cultures. Even before the Early Horizon religious prominence of CHAVÍN, many U-shaped ceremonial centres in the coastal valleys of Peru demonstrated an apparently widespread religious coherence, displaying fanged beings and painted figures on sculptured architecture at many sites, for example at Garagay, Sechín Alto and Cerro Sechín.

Faces with grimacing mouths and protruding fangs were especially prominent in Early Horizon Chavín and in later MOCHE art of the Early Intermediate Period. For example, a being with thick, upturned lips and fangs was a common image in the Chavín pantheon. The DECAPITATOR GOD of Moche, identifiable by his distinctive protruding fangs and double ear-ornaments, was depicted in numerous painted scenes on pottery and walls, and on the contents of tombs; and the sky or creator god AI APAEC of the Moche (and later the CHIMÚ) also had a distinctive fanged FELINE mouth.

Farther south, in the Early Intermediate Period NAZCA culture, fanged creatures were also frequently depicted on pottery. Such common imagery no doubt reflects a certain basic animism and naturalism in Andean iconography, which prevails through centuries of religious practice. At the same time, the variations of detail in the fanged beings portrayed belies a wealth of imagination in conjuring up fearful gods/goddesses to strike awe in the intended worshippers.

FELINES

FELINES, like SERPENTS, were pan-Andean. JAGUARS in particular, inspired a ubiquitous imagery used by many Andean cultures from the very earliest times. The most prominent aspect was long, curved canine teeth. (See also CHAVÍN, DECAPITATOR GOD and FANGED GOD)

FEMALE DOMINATION

FEMALE DOMINATION is a widespread mythological theme, recounted with many variations among South American tribes, from the Amazon rain forests to Tierra del Fuego (see JURUPARI, TEMAUKEL, WATAUINEIWA). For various reasons, the situation was reversed among the gods. In general, among the rain forest tribes, women are associated with natural fertility, ignorance of spiritual matters, and chaos; in contrast, men are associated with cultural fertility, sacred knowledge and order.

FEMPELLEC

FEMPELLEC was the 12th ruler in the legendary line of NAYAMLAP in the LAMBAYEQUE VALLEY dynasty of northern coastal Peru. In myth, he is remembered as the king fated to bring disaster on the kingdom.

RECOGNIZABLE FELINES, especially jaguars, were depicted in all media, including metals, as here, in a gold and copper jaguar head from the Lambayeque Valley.

THE FANGED GODS, represented from before the Early Horizon, were especially favoured by Moche craftspeople, as here, in a composite fanged feline/deer/serpent.

He insisted on moving the stone idol of YAMPALLEC, symbol of the dynasty, from the capital at CHOT to another city – an act of which his priests heartily disapproved. Before he could accomplish this sacrilege, however, a demon appeared to Fempellec in the form of a beautiful woman. She seduced him, after which it began to rain heavily, an event all too rare in this arid region of the coastal valleys. It rained for 30 days, and then followed a year of drought and – inevitably – hunger, as the crops failed. By this time, the priests had had enough. They seized Fempellec and tied his hands and feet; then they carried him to the sea, threw him in, and left him to his fate, thus ending the dynasty of Nayamlap.

GATEWAY GOD
see under TIAHUANACO.

GATEWAY OF THE SUN
see under TIAHUANACO.

GENTE BRUTA

GENTE BRUTA ("brutish/ignorant folk") were the "stupid folk" taken in by a ruse to lay the foundations for MANCO CAPAC's claim to rule CUZCO in the INCA state foundation myth.

"GOLDEN ENCLOSURE"
see CORICANCHA.

GRAN CHACO see CHACO.

GREAT IMAGE see CHAVÍN.

GUACA BILCAS

GUACA BILCAS, supernatural devils (see PACHACUTI).

THE GUARI

THE GUARI were one of the legendary lineage AYLLUS of CAJATAMBO. They were conquered by, then confederated with, the LLACUAZ ayllu and shared ritual beliefs with them.

GUASCAR see HUASCAR.

GUAYNA CAPAC see HUAYNA CAPAC.

GUECUFU

GUECUFU was the evil spirit of the AUCA peoples of northern Chile, the ultimate source of misfortune. It was Guecufu who sent the floods that could destroy humankind.

GUINECHEN

GUINECHEN ("master of men") was the supreme god of the AUCA peoples of northern Chile. Guinechen was a deity of all natural

phenomena: animals, plants, humans, crops, flocks and their fertility. Because of this, he was also known as Guinemapun (literally "master of the land").

GUINEMAPUN see *GUINECHEN*.

HANAN AND HURIN CUZCO (*INCA*) literally "upper *CUZCO*" and "lower Cuzco" were the two groups or social divisions of the populace of the city. In Inca legend, the division was believed to have been ordered by the first ruler, *MANCO CAPAC*, and the two groups prevailed up to the time of the arrival of the Spaniards. The two parts of Cuzco were also associated with a similar division of the system of *CEQUE* lines that regulated sacred ritual and astronomical observations. An upper set of *ceques* was associated with Hanan Cuzco, and with the quarters of *CHINCHASUYU* and *ANTISUYU*, while a lower set was associated with Hurin Cuzco, and with the quarters of *COLLASUYU* and *CUNTISUYU*.

Divisions into *hanan* and *hurin* were also generally used among the *MOIETY* groupings of *AYLLUS*. The division was based on locally important topographic features in the area inhabited by the group, and on distribution rights to water.

HATUNRUNA (meaning "the great people") were the *INCA* commoners. They were of lower social rank than the royal *PANACAS* and lesser nobility and made up the majority of the populace, especially in the provinces of the empire. They were organized into tens of thousands of *AYLLUS*, or kinship lineages. Members of higher-ranking lineages of the *hatunruna*, called *CURACAS*, held hereditary lordships and served the Inca state as imperial agents and local authorities to supervise provincial affairs.

The value of the *hatunruna* in the study of Andean mythology lies in the fact that their religious beliefs were recorded in the *IDOLATRÍAS*

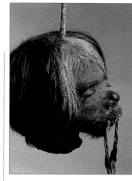

("idolatries"), which comprised a multitude of local traditions, legends and beliefs.

The Inca practice of redistributing large groups of *hatunrunas* as *MITIMAES* throughout the empire not only resulted in a stabilizing economic, ethnic and social mix, but also served to transfer, alter and amalgamate *hatunruna* notions of geographic identity and religious/mythological concepts.

Although there are fewer sources for local religion and mythology than for official Inca state religion, one particular text, the *HUAROCHIRÍ MANUSCRIPT*, provides a detailed record of such provincial beliefs in the western Andes of central Peru, to the east of Lima.

HAYSQUISRRO was the *INCA* ancestors' fourth place of sojourn during their wanderings related in the Inca state foundation myth, and where the plot to get rid of Ayar Cachi was conceived (see *MANCO CAPAC*).

HEAD-HUNTING was a ritual practice among several tribes of the Amazonian rain forest, persisting, for example, among the Ecuadorian-Amazon Jivarro tribe into the 1960s. The taking and keeping of human heads was restricted to a select group of especially fierce male warriors, who became feared killers.

The Jivarro head-hunter was thought to possess two souls in conflict. The first, called *Arutam*, gave the owner permission and power to kill and head-hunt, but not without impunity, for the second soul,

AFTER HEAD-HUNTING, to prevent revenge, the head was shrunk in order to block the power of the Muisak, *or second soul of the victim.*

Muisak, was meant to avenge the death of the hunted. To prevent it from taking revenge, the head was shrunk, thus drawing *Muisak* into it, from which it was believed to be powerless to escape.

"HITCHING POST OF THE SUN" see *INTIHUATANA*.

HUACA (*INCA* and, more generally, central Andean) was a sacred place or object in the landscape (see also *ZEMÍ*). As well as the powerful central deities of the Inca pantheon, each of which was given a special temple in the *CORICANCHA* in *CUZCO*, the Andean peoples recognized a host of lesser nature gods, spirits and oracles throughout the land.

Huacas were hallowed places where significant mythological events had taken place and/or where offerings were made to local deities. They were frequently natural objects such as mountain tops (*APU*), caves, springs, and especially stones or boulders (*APACHETA*, *HUANCA*), but could also be locations along a sacred *CEQUE* line or man-made objects, such as the pillars erected on the western horizon above Cuzco for viewing the sunset from the *CAPAC USNU* for special astronomical observations. Other examples include the stones (the *PURURAUCAS*) around Cuzco that rose up to help *PACHACUTI INCA YUPANQUI* defend Cuzco against the *CHANCAS*, and the sacred shrines and statues of *VIRACOCHA* at *CACHA* and *URCOS*. In some cases, the *huaca* was a combination of the natural and the miraculous. One example was the stone of the ancestor brother *AYAR UCHU* atop *HUANACAURI* mountain, a principal Inca *huaca* believed to be the lithified body of that ancestor; another example was that of *PARIACACA*,

who seems to have been simultaneously a mountain and a mobile deity/culture hero.

Most Andean "nations" and towns had a particular place that they recognized as their own *huaca*, as did most of the *AYLLUS*, or kinship groups. It was their belief that the spirit of the *huaca* exerted a special and beneficial influence over the lives and destinies of the members of the group.

Huacas continue to be recognized by local peoples in the Andes today, in a mixture of pre-Christian and Catholic belief.

HUACA CHOTUNA, an archaeological site in the *LAMBAYEQUE VALLEY*, was almost certainly the *CHOT* of *NAYAMLAP*.

HUACAS, both natural and man-made, were a common aspect of ancient Andean landscapes. As well as using natural features, stone pillars were also frequently erected by the Incas for use in astronomical sightings, such as the ones shown here at Kenko near Cuzco.

HUACA DE LA LUNA
see *DECAPITATOR GOD* and *MOCHE*.

HUACA DEL SOL
see *MOCHE*.

HUACA FORTALEZA
see *MOCHE*.

HUACO see *MAMA HUACO*.

HUALLALLO CARHUINCHO

(pre-*INCA*) was the principal god of the indigenous people of the Huarochirí region described in the *HUAROCHIRÍ MANUSCRIPT*.

He was a fierce, fire-breathing, volcanic god of ancient origin, long predating the Inca conquest of this region in the western Andes east of Lima. The manuscript refers to the people of Huarochirí as *Lurin* (lower) and *Anan* (upper) *Yauyos*, a kinship *AYLLU* dichotomy implying that there were also "outsiders" among the indigenous population. The manuscript is principally concerned with the *Lurin Yauyos*.

According to the Huarochirí creation myth, Huallallo Carhuincho was present at the beginning of time, and exercised unchallenged power and control over the daily lives of the people. At that time, Huarochirí province had a climate that was comparable to the adjacent warm coastal lowlands. The land was filled with snakes, toucans, *JAGUARS* and other animals associated with warmer coastal regions. It was presumably during this early time that agriculturalist *Yauyos* migrated into or invaded the area.

The story itself begins some time after Huallallo Carhuincho had been ruling his people in this autocratic manner. At the beginning of the Huarochirí Manuscript he was challenged by another god, *PARIACACA*, a five-fold being who had been born on a distant mountain. Pariacaca was the principal deity of the *Checa* portion of the *Yauyos*, the pastoralists, and is described as the ancestor(s) of these more recent immigrants to the region. In the end, Huallallo Carhuincho was defeated, despite the help he received from *MAMA ÑAMCA*, and fled to the low country to the north, called Antis (that is, *ANTISUYU*). He left behind him a huge two-headed snake, which Pariacaca transformed into stone.

Huallallo Carhuincho also had a penchant for cannibalism. He

issued the command that the *Lurin Yauyos* be allowed to have only two children per household, one of which was to be handed over to him for his meals.

HUANACAURI, or Huana Cauri,

was the mountain at Quirirmanta described in the *INCA* state foundation myth. It was from this place that the Inca ancestors first viewed the Valley of *CUZCO* after their wanderings. Huanacauri was also the name of *MANCO CAPAC*'s father's principal idol.

HUANAYPATA was the final stop-

ping place of the *INCA* ancestors in their wanderings, where the centre of *CUZCO* was established and where *AYAR AUCA* was turned into a stone pillar (see *MANCO CAPAC*).

HUANCA was the *INCA*/central

Andean term for a particular type of *HUACA*. As opposed to obvious mountains, springs or caves, these were especially prominent or large boulders in the landscape, which were believed to incorporate the essence of an ancestor of one or more local *AYLLU* kinship groups. (See also *APACHETA*, *APU*, *CEQUE*)

HUARI (*INCA* and Spanish colo-

nial) was the principal deity of the *GUARI AYLLU* of *CAJATAMBO*.

HUARI, or Wari, an ancient site

and kingdom in the Andes of south-central Peru, dominated the highlands and coastal regions of Peru and in due course, during the

Middle Horizon, expanded into the regions to the north, almost to the Ecuadorian border. One of its northernmost outposts was the city of Cajamarca in northern Peru; its southernmost was Pikillaqta near Cuzco. Although major constructions in Huari began earlier – not long after those at its chief rival *TIAHUANACO*, to the south near Lake *TITICACA* – its main period of expansion and imperial power lasted from about AD 600 to 800. The two empires confronted each other across the mountain pass of La Raya, south of Cuzco, and appeared to agree to make this region a buffer zone between them. Despite their obvious military and political rivalry, both cultures shared a religious iconography and mythology.

The city of Huari occupied the plateau of an intermontane valley at some 2,800 m (9,180 ft) above sea-level between the Huamanga and Huanta basins. Serving as a civic, residential and religious centre, it grew rapidly to cover more than 100 hectares (247 acres), expanding to 300 hectares (740 acres), with an additional periphery of residential suburbs occupying a further 250 hectares (620 acres). From *c.* AD 600, alongside its military expansion, Huari spread a religious hegemony that was characterized by a distinctive iconography, much of which shows continuity with the ancient traditions of *CHAVÍN*, which survived the political fragmentation of the Early Intermediate Period. Shortly before AD 800, however, there appears to have been a political crisis that caused building within the capital to abate rapidly and then cease. At the same time, *PACHACAMAC*, a political centre and religious shrine on the central Peruvian coast, which had flourished since the later Early Intermediate, and which had been recently occupied by the Huari, began to reassert itself and possibly even to rival Huari power. Huari expansion ended abruptly, and the capital was abandoned by AD 800.

The architecture of the site, although megalithic, has not lasted well. Some of it approximates to the ceremonial architecture at Tiahuanaco, although more crudely, including several rectangular compounds. In contrast to Tiahuanaco, however, the rapid expansion of Huari appears to have occurred at random, without the deliberate and preconceived planning of its competitor. The huge enclosure of Cheqo Huasi (or Wasi) included dressed stone-slab chambers. Two of the most important temple complexes were Vegachayoq Moqo and

THE HUARI military empire of central Peru conquered as far south as Pikillaqta (above), near Cuzco, where its fortress confronted its rival Tiahuanaco, beyond the La Raya Pass to the south.

Moraduchayoq, the latter a semi-subterranean compound similar to that at Tiahuanaco. In keeping with the comparatively frenetic pace of Huari's development, the Moraduchayoq Temple was dismantled in about AD 650.

Much of the religious and mythological iconography of Huari and Tiahuanaco was virtually identical, and originated in Early Horizon and Early Intermediate times. Despite the two capitals' obvious military opposition, scholars think it possible that religious missionaries from one city visited the other. It may have been that the priests were willing to let religious beliefs transcend politics.

Shared religious imagery included, in particular, the STAFF DEITY image, winged beings (sometimes referred to as "angels") in profile – sometimes with falcon and condor heads – and severed trophy heads. Winged beings appear both accompanying the Staff Deity and on their own; and are shown running, floating, flying or kneeling. The frontal Staff Deity – with mask-like face, radiating head rays (sometimes ending in serpent heads) and tunic, belt and kilt – appears on pottery and architecture and might have been the prototype for the creator god VIRACOCHA.

HUARI CULTURE shared many features with other Andean cultures that flourished both before and afterwards, including ancestor worship through mummy bundles (below) of dead forebears.

Yet, despite this apparent religious unity, the focus of the imagery at Huari differed from that at Tiahuanaco. At Huari it was applied primarily to portable objects, particularly ceramics; at Tiahuanaco it was applied to monumental stone architecture, but rarely appeared on pottery. Thus, while Huari ceramics spread the word far and wide, Tiahuanaco imagery was confined to standing monuments at the capital and a few other sites. Religious ceremony at Huari appears to have been quite private, confined to small groups, judging by the architecture, while at Tiahuanaco it seems to have been more public, taking place within large compounds designed for the purpose.

Given such differences within the similarities, the exact nature of the relationship between the two powers remains a keenly debated subject. What is indisputable is that religious imagery and concepts continued through politically divided times as well as more unified imperial times, as states, kingdoms and empires rose and fell during the fragmented Middle Horizon.

THE HUAROCHIRÍ MANUSCRIPT,

a post-Spanish-conquest INCA document, composed in the early 17th century (c. 1608), was one of the most valuable and detailed sources of pre-Spanish conquest religious belief among the HATUN-RUNA commoners of the Inca Empire. Written in QUECHUA, it was almost certainly the work of a native chronicler and, like the IDOL-ATRÍAS, compiled at the instigation of the local "extirpator of idolatries", Francisco de Avila (see also CAJATAMBO).

Huarochirí was an Inca province in the western Andes, east of present-day Lima. The inhabitants were of the AYLLU kinship lineage of Yauyos, and, reflecting Inca imperial practice in the capital, were divided into two groups – Anan (or "upper") Yauyos and Lurin (or "lower") Yauyos (see also HANAN and HURIN Cuzco). The information recounted in the manuscript concerns two subgroups of the Lurin Yauyos, called the Checa and Concha, who were respectively pastoralists and agriculturalists. The label "Yauyos" was a general social classification for "outsiders", implying that at least part of the ayllu, the pastoralists, came into the region only relatively recently, probably from the south, and established themselves in complementary opposition to the indigenous lowland agricultural population. The

HUASCAR was the Inca emperor who seized power after the death of his father Huana Capec. (NUEVA CORÓNICA Y BUEN GOBIERNO, FELIPE GUAMAN POMA DE AYALA, 1583–1613.)

agriculturalists, however, also Yauyos, had probably themselves moved into the region much earlier and become integrated with the people already there.

The principal deities of the Huarochirí Yauyos were HUALLALLO CARHUINCHO, a fierce, powerful, fire-breathing god, and his Checa rival PARIACACA, who was "born" on a distant mountain top.

HUASCAR, or Huascaran, was the 13th Inca emperor (ruled 1526–32), having seized the throne after the sudden death of his father HUAYNA CAPAC and the heir-apparent from smallpox. Although some sources indicate that he had a more legitimate claim to the throne, his rule was contested by his half-brother ATAHUALPA, who captured him and took control in 1532.

HUATHIACURI was a lesser deity/culture hero of the pre-INCA Yauyos of the Huarochirí region in the western Andes of central Peru. He was the son of PARIACACA, god of rain, thunder and lightning. He met a rich man whose wife had committed adultery. Because of her impiety, two SERPENTS were slowly eating away the jilted husband's life; Huathiacuri confronted the wife and forced her to confess, thereby causing the serpents to die and saving the husband's life.

I

HUAYNA CAPAC was the 12th *INCA* emperor, who ruled from 1493 to 1526. He died suddenly of smallpox in 1526 along with his heir apparent. The Spanish sources leave some doubt as to whether he had actually designated his successor, whether he favoured his son *HUASCAR*, or whether he secretly hoped that another son, *ATAHUALPA*, would use his own control of the army to supplant Huascar – or whether he had planned to divide the empire among several sons.

Huayna Capac's place in Inca "myth" lies in the fact that, as smallpox spread rapidly south from Mesoamerica, where it had been introduced to the Americas by the Spaniards, he received reports from traders from the north of bearded strangers who sailed in strange ships. These reports coincided with of a series of ill omens, and his priests prophesied evil and disaster when they witnessed the death of an eagle, which fell out of the sky after being mobbed by buzzards during ceremonies in honour of the sun god *INTI*.

HUAYNA PICCHU see under *MACHU PICCHU*.

HUITACA was the *CHIBCHA* goddess of evil, and the patroness of misbehaviour and drunkenness. She challenged the work of the preacher hero *NEMTEREQUETEBA*. In one version of the myth, he transformed her into the moon, and she is therefore sometimes confused with the moon goddess *CHIE*.

HURIN CUZCO see *HANAN AND HURIN CUZCO*.

IAE was the *KAMAIURA* moon god (see *KUAT*).

IAMURICUMA WOMEN, among the tribes of the Brazilian *XINGU* River region, were a tribe of female warriors who, like the Amazon warriors of Greek myth, cut off their right breasts so that they

EL ONZENO INGA
GUAINACAPAC

Reyno chacha poya qui to Cataconga
ciescho guanca bilca cayan bi canaxi–
guayna

HUAYNA CAPAC, the 12th Inca emperor, was the last to rule a relatively peaceful empire before civil war and the arrival of the Spaniards. (IMAGINARY SKETCH BY FELIPE GUAMAN POMA DE AYALA IN HIS NUEVA CORÓNICA Y BUEN GOBIERNO WRITTEN BETWEEN 1583 AND 1613.)

could draw their bows and shoot arrows more effectively. They could transform themselves into spirits and could capture anyone who looked upon them. When 16th-century Europeans heard these stories, they thought they had discovered the land of the Amazons and thus gave the area its name.

IDOLATRÍAS ("idolatries") are the records of the investigations of Spanish priests into idolatrous practices in the countryside. In the first few decades after the Spanish conquest, the conversion of the peoples of the *INCA* Empire to Catholicism appeared, on the surface, to be successful. In reality, however, for more than a century Spanish priests continued to discover, and struggle with, a wealth of ingrained local belief and ritual practice "behind the altar" and, in fact, many local legends and "beliefs" continue to the present day.

This conflict of religions was particularly fierce during the late 16th and early 17th centuries, and knowledge of the struggle, and thus of provincial Inca religious belief among the *HATUNRUNA* commoners, comes mostly from the local nobility, the *CURACAS*, who were interviewed and enlisted by Spanish priests. Through them, the priests were able to interrogate local curers, "witches", diviners, and communal leaders about the persistent worship of ancestral mummies (*MALLQUIS*) and celestial bodies (see *MAYU*), and reverence for the spirits of local *HUACAS* (sacred places).

Another important source for pre-Spanish Andean provincial religion, and one of the most detailed,

INCA BELIEF in and practice of their ancient religion well into the 17th century prompted the Spanish authorities to attempt to extirpate such practice. This Idolatría records their efforts.

is the work of the Spanish-trained native acolyte Felipe Guaman Poma de Ayala from Huamanga, an Inca town in the central Peruvian Andes. Guaman Poma claimed to be the son of a *curaca* who had served as an emissary of Inca *HUASCAR* to Francisco Pizarro at Cajamarca. His monumental work, *Nueva Corónica y Buen Gobierno*, written over the course of 30 years, was completed in 1613. Perhaps prompted by the descriptions in myth of *VIRACOCHA* as a bearded white god, Guaman Poma was convinced that the Andean peoples knew the God of Christianity before the conquests of the Inca state, and thus were practising Christians until corrupted by Inca religion. He even identified Viracocha as St Bartholomew.

Yet another important and detailed source is the *HUAROCHIRÍ MANUSCRIPT*, which came from a town in the western Andes east of Lima, the nature of which has been used to argue that it was written by a native under the guiding hand of the local "extirpator of idolatries", Francisco de Avila.

As well as the information on religious beliefs and practices, these sources relate detailed information

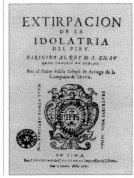

EXTIRPACION
DE LA
IDOLATRIA
DEL PIRV.

DIRIGIDO AL REY N. S. EN SV
REAL CONSEJO DE INDIAS.
Por el Padre Pablo Ioseph de Arriaga de la
Compañia de IESVS.

EN LIMA,
Por GERONYMO DE CONTRERAS impressor de Libros.
Año 1621.

A FANCIFUL reconstruction of an Inca procession, which attempted to convey the near-divine status of the Inca emperor. (PAINTING BY ALBERTO FEBALLOS FRANCHI, 1905.)

on everyday *hatunruna* life. This detail provides valuable contextual background for interpreting the myth and legend of the official Inca state religion and for understanding the intricacies and permutations of local pre-Inca beliefs. The most revealing aspect of the *idolatrías* is their demonstration of the intimate bond between the peoples of local communities and their "personal" sacred *huacas* and local deities. Although few *idolatrías* have been published, those of Huarochirí province and *CAJATAMBO* are particularly informative.

The *idolatrías* show us the mythology of Inca commoners – how they believed their communities were created, how they regarded the relationship between the living and the dead, their sense of how the supernatural regulated and influenced daily life, and their integration, both religious and social, into official Inca state religion. At the same time, they show the relationships between religion and the social structure, the opposition and co-operation between highland and lowland communities, and the relationships among *AYLLU* kinship groupings, and between pastoralists and agriculturalists. Local legends have been, and continue to be, recorded by anthropologists. One of the most enduring, universal themes in the Andes is that of the return of the Inca, the *INKARRÍ* legend.

ILLA see *ILYA.*

ILLAPA was the *INCA* weather god of thunder, lightning and rain. One of the temples in the sacred *CORICANCHA* in *CUZCO* was dedicated to him, and he was offered prayers and gifts to bring fertilizing rain for the crops. The Incas appear to have modelled him on the thunder god *THUNUPA* of *TIAHUANACO.*

Illapa was usually portrayed holding a war club in one hand and a sling in the other (perhaps corresponding to the spear-thrower and spears of Thunupa). He drew water from *MAYU*, the Milky Way, which was regarded as a "celestial river". The water was kept in a clay jar owned by his sister, and when Illapa wanted to send down rain to earth he would shatter the jar with a stone from his sling. Thus the whir and crack of his slinging made the whistle of the winds and the thunder, while his brisk movements caused the shining garments he wore to flash as lightning.

ILLMA was a pre-*INCA* name for *PACHACAMAC.*

ILYA ("light") was one of the many epithets used by the *INCA* to refer to *VIRACOCHA.*

ILYAP'A see *ILLAPA.*

IMAYMANA VIRACOCHA was the elder son or special aide of *CON TICCI VIRACOCHA* in different versions of the central Andean creation myth. After the creation of the world by *VIRACOCHA* at Lake *TITICACA*, Imaymana Viracocha set off northwestwards along a route bordering the forests and mountains. He called forth the clay models of people made by his father, named the trees and plants and established when they would flower or bear fruit, instructing the people on which were edible or medicinal. He

eventually rejoined his father and brother, *TOCAPO VIRACOCHA* at *MANTA* on the Ecuadorian coast, where they disappeared out to sea by walking across the waters.

INCA was the name of one of the peoples of the Valley of Cuzco, who rose to prominence and eventually built a vast empire throughout the Andes, and the adjacent western coastal regions and eastern rain forests. Their empire, traditionally founded by *MANCO CAPAC* and the ancestors, began about 1100 and lasted until the Spanish conquest of the 1530s. They called their lands *TAHUANTINSUYU*, literally "the land of the four quarters".

The two principal gods of the Inca were *VIRACOCHA* and *INTI*, although the latter became increasingly favoured shortly before the arrival of the Spaniards. Other important deities included *QUILLA*, *CHASKA-QOYLOR*, *ILLAPA* and *CUICHU.* The two principal temple complexes in *CUZCO* were the sacred *CORICANCHA* precinct and the imposing *SACSAHUAMAN* edifices. *SAPA INCA* was the honorary title given to the Inca emperor.

INCA ROCA was the legendary sixth *INCA* ruler of *CUZCO*, probably sometime in the 13th century.

INCA ROCA was the sixth legendary Inca emperor, who ruled at some point in the 13th century. (IMAGINARY SKETCH BY FELIPE GUAMAN POMA DE AYALA IN HIS NUEVA CORÓNICA Y BUEN GOBIERNO, WRITTEN BETWEEN 1583 AND 1613.)

Like all Inca rulers, he was considered to be a direct descendant of the ancestors, *MANCO CAPAC* and Mama Ocllo.

INCA URCO, or Urcon, the ninth *INCA* ruler of *CUZCO*, had the shortest reign of any pre-Spanish-conquest Inca king, traditionally less than a year in 1438. He had been chosen by his father, *VIRACOCHA INCA*, to be his successor but had fled from Cuzco with his father at the approach of the army of the rival city-state of *CHANCA*, leaving his brother, *PACHACUTI INCA YUPANQUI*, to defend the city.

INCA YUPANQUI see *YAHUAR HUACAC.*

INKARI was the name of the first man in the *Q'ERO/INCA* central Andean variation of the creation myth (see *ROAL*).

INKARRÍ was/is the central character in a post-Spanish conquest *INCA* millenarian belief in the "dying and reviving Inca". The derivation of the name itself is a combination of *QUECHUA Inca* and Spanish *rey*, meaning both king or ruler. The myth foretells a time when the current sufferings of the original peoples of the Andes will be ended in a cataclysmic transformation of the world, in which Spanish overlords will be destroyed. The true Inca will be resurrected and reinstated in his rightful place as supreme ruler, and prosperity and justice will return to the world.

Many slightly different versions of the Inkarrí myth were collected and recorded by the Peruvian anthropologist Josémaria Arguedas in the 1950s in southern Peru. A typical example recounts how Inkarrí was the son of a savage woman and Father Sun. Inkarrí was powerful; he harnessed his father and the very wind itself. He drove stones with a whip, ordered them around, and founded a city called K'ellk'ata, probably *CUZCO*. Then he threw a golden rod from a mountain top, but found that Cuzco did not fit on the plain where it had landed, so he moved the city to its present location. When the Spaniards came, however, they imprisoned Inkarrí in a secret place, and his head is all that remains. But Inkarrí is growing a new body and will return when he is whole again.

Such belief is clearly in keeping with the Andean concept of *PACHACUTI*, the revolution of time and space, and understandably arose from a sense of oppression and injustice to the native populations by the Spaniards. It probably harks back to events of the first few decades after the Spanish conquest, during which the last Inca emperor *ATAHUALPA* was beheaded by Francisco Pizarro, and to the beheading of *TUPAC AMARU*, a claimant to the Inca throne who led an unsuccessful revolt against Spanish rule in the 1560s and 1570s. In different

accounts, the heads were taken to Lima or to Cuzco, but in both cases the belief is that, once buried in the ground, the head becomes a seed that regrows its body in anticipation of Inkarrí's return.

INTI, the *INCA*/pan-Andean manifestation of the sun, was the life-giving force universally recognized by Andean peoples, undoubtedly from earliest times and by numerous, now lost, names. The sacred *CORICANCHA* precinct in *CUZCO* was the centre of the official state cult dedicated to his worship. By Inca times, Inti rivalled in importance the creator god *VIRACOCHA* himself, owing in particular to his special relationship with the Inca emperor, the *SAPA INCA*, and to the splendour and importance of his temple within the Coricancha. So powerful and important was Inti that an incident witnessed by the priests during ceremonies in his honour appeared to foretell the downfall of the empire. The event – the ill omen of an eagle, mobbed by buzzards, falling from the sky – occurred in the reign of *HUAYNA CAPAC*, the 12th emperor (1493–1526), and coincided with reports of the spread of an unknown and deadly menace from the north – now known to have been smallpox spreading from Mesoamerica.

The universality of the sun notwithstanding, the sun god as Inti was in many respects a uniquely Inca deity; the emperor became regarded as the manifestation of the sun on earth. Although regarded with awe because of his power, Inti was believed to be a benevolent and generous god. Nevertheless, solar eclipses were regarded as signs of Inti's anger.

The image of Inti was most frequently a great mask of sheet gold, moulded as a human-like face, wide-eyed and showing a toothy grin. Surrounding the face were rays of sheet gold, cut in zig-zags and ending in miniature human-like masks or figures.

By the second half of the 15th century, when the Inca Empire was reaching the limits of its expansion and power, Viracocha had become a somewhat remote deity. Inti came to be regarded as his intermediary, with the weather god *ILLAPA* and others. This relationship was carefully emphasized by the Sapa Incas, and it became the basis for their own intimate association with Inti, putting forth themselves as the intermediary between the sun and the people. The Sapa Inca's presence was regarded as essential to assure the light and warmth of the sun to make the world habitable. Ritual ceremonies and offerings to Inti served to reinforce this melding of god and king, and to legitimize Inca power and right to rule. The Incas were painstaking in their

efforts to establish, and to permute as necessary, an elaborate mythology to support this close association of Inti, the emperor and power.

Historical and archaeological evidence shows that expansion of the empire beyond the Valley of Cuzco began in earnest with *PACHACUTI INCA YUPANQUI*, the tenth ruler of Cuzco (1438–71), and his son *TUPAC INCA YUPANQUI* (1471–93). Much of the appearance of the capital described by the Spanish conquistadors was the work of these rulers. It also appears that development of the Inti–Sapa Inca bond and perfection of the state foundation myth took on increasing importance during their reigns. It became necessary for the Incas to demonstrate their right to rule, and to unify the empire, by proving that all peoples were descended from the same ancestors, namely the Inca ancestors. The beliefs and cosmologies of those they conquered needed to be incorporated into a universal state religion, and to do this alongside continuous acquisition of territories and peoples required an equally unremitting campaign of addition to and alteration of the state mythology (for example, see *MINCHANÇAMAN*). It was also important to extend this continuity back to the first ruler of Cuzco, Ayar *MANCO CAPAC*, and even to link the state foundation myth with creation mythology itself. This was the task allocated to the *AMAUTA* and *QUIPUCAMAYOQ* record-keepers.

In the official mythology of the ancestors' wanderings after their emergence from the cave at *TAMBO TOCO*, Manco Capac was given divine sanction when his brother Ayar Uchu flew up and spoke to the sun. The message he brought back was that Ayar Manco should thenceforth be called Manco Capac and rule Cuzco in the name of the sun.

In other versions of the state creation myth, Inti is named as the father of Ayar Manco Capac and Mama Coya (otherwise known as *MAMA OCLLO*) and of the other Ayars and their sister/partners, collectively known as the ancestors. Manco Capac and Mama Ocllo were sent down to earth specifically to bring the gifts of civilization to humankind, namely corn (maize) and potato cultivation, and this myth established the Incas' right to rule on the basis of their benevolent influence. In a somewhat more sinister variation on this theme, however, interpreted by some as an attempt by disgruntled members of the empire to discredit Inca rule, "Son of the Sun (Inti)", was the nickname given to Manco Capac by his (human) father in a ruse to trick the populace of Cuzco into handing over power and the rulership of the city. This and another

rendition describe how Manco Capac bedecked himself in gold plates to lend credibility to his "divine" dawn appearance to the people of Cuzco.

Further elaborate permutations and details are given in other myths, especially those involving Pachacuti Inca Yupanqui. His discovery of the crystal tablet, with its image of Viracocha, at the spring of *SUSUR-PUQUIO*, together with his renewed construction and rearrangement of the sacred Coricancha to give

greater prominence to Inti, can be interpreted as an attempt to bond the creator, the sun and the emperor in one stroke. This appears to be the beginning of the "solarization" of Inca religion and of the empowerment of a state cult meant to accommodate and include all the peoples of the empire. The construction of *SACSAHUAMAN* at the northwest end of the capital (probably begun by Pachacuti Inca Yupanqui), its use as a sacred precinct and place of sacrifice to Inti,

and the probability that it was used for cosmological observations (see *MAYU*) further link Inti, the Sapa Inca and the people in a clear hierarchy. Further still, the mountain fortress and sacred estate of *MACHU PICCHU*, also

THE INCAS built temples to Inti throughout the empire. One of the best preserved is at Ingapirca, Ecuador, one of the most northerly sites of the empire.

begun by Pachacuti Inca Yupanqui, held the *INTIHUATANA* or "Hitching Post of the Sun".

After the death of Pachacuti Inca Yupanqui, his body was embalmed and mummified. Along with the mummified body of his principal consort, he was kept in a special palace tomb, where both were looked after by a dedicated cult of young women called the *ACLLAS* ("chosen women"). In biannual official state celebrations of the

THE INTIHUATANA, literally the "Hitching Post of the Sun", at Machu Picchu, comprised two "shadow clocks" for Inca priests to observe and record the movements of the sun.

summer and winter solstices, *CAPAC RAYMI* and *INTI RAYMI*, the royal *MALLQUIS* were carried in procession on gold-covered seats from the tomb into the Coricancha, to the Temple of Inti, where they were offered food and drink.

Incorporation of "foreign" mythologies as conquests increased is well illustrated by the Inca Empire's encounter with the ancient and powerful kingdom of *PACHACAMAC* on the central Peruvian coast. Here the Incas met an ancient culture and polity with its own long-standing religious entity. It was a coastal religion, and thus more alien than, for example, that of *CHIMÚ* which, as an Andean culture, shared most of the basic tenets of Inca beliefs. To reconcile the traditions and ease potential tension between them – while insuring that Inca belief remained primary and all-inclusive – the *quipucamayoqs* and *amautas* included the ancient oracle site of Pachacamac in the story of *CONI-RAYA VIRACOCHA* (thus probably identifying him with *VIRACOCHA*),

A MODERN MURAL in Lima depicts the honouring of Inti with the offer of a herd of llamas. (CHAVEZ BALLON COLLECTION.)

demonstrating that the creator was already associated with Pachacamac and recognizing a connection in all but name between the two creator-god centres – Pachacamac and the *ISLAND OF THE SUN* in Lake *TITI-CACA*. Significantly, the shrine of Pachacamac was allowed to continue functioning but, to strengthen the link, the Incas established a temple to Inti alongside it.

Provincial peoples were continually reminded of their bond with Inti and the Sapa Inca by *CAPA-COCHA* sacrifices to Inti. Annually, the chosen victims were brought to the capital, then marched back out to their respective provinces again for ritual immolation.

INTI RAYMI, the *INCA* winter solstice festival in honour of the sun god *INTI*, was held in June (see also *CAPAC RAYMI*).

INTIHUATANA (the "Hitching Post of the Sun") was a stone pillar at *MACHU PICCHU*, carved atop a massive stone block. This and other stone pillars were used as "shadow clocks" , from which *INCA* priests observed and recorded the regular movements of the sun in order to understand the cycles of cosmic events and to predict the future. At solstices, they would symbolically tie the sun to the pillar with a cord to prevent it from disappearing.

STAFF DEITY
& FANGED GODS

THE RELIGIOUS BELIEFS OF ancient Andean and western coastal civilizations imagined the gods in many forms, and as possessing different powers and rulership in different spheres. Thus a pan-Andean pantheon included a creator deity, a sun god, a moon god or goddess, a rain and weather deity, a sea god and a less universal collection of other deities of more specific natural phenomena, such as the rainbow or thunder, or of specific cultural commodities, such as crops or metalworking.

Running through the sequence of Andean civilization is the persistence of several iconographic themes and imagery. From earliest times, architecture, ceramics, textiles and even geoglyphs repeatedly used images of composite beings incorporating serpentine, feline and avian features. From at least as early as the Chavín civilization, the Staff Deity – a deity portrayed frontally, with outstretched arms holding staffs – and fanged, clawed, winged and bird-headed beings were depicted in various culturally distinctive styles. The jaguar also features prominently in Amazonian mythology, and many rain forest animals, including the jaguar, strongly influenced Andean art from the earliest times.

ONE OF THE MOST enduring iconoclastic images used from the Chavín culture of the Early Horizon (c. 900–200 BC) to the Late Horizon (15th–16th century AD) Inca was the Staff Deity. Male (left) or female (above), he/she was represented on every medium – stone, ceramics, paint on cloth, wood and metal. Although details of the imagery varied greatly from one culture to another, the essential elements were always included: a frontal stance and outstretched arms holding staffs or corn stalks. The imagery was clearly associated with fertility.

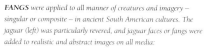

FANGS *were applied to all manner of creatures and imagery – singular or composite – in ancient South American cultures. The jaguar (left) was particularly revered, and jaguar faces or fangs were added to realistic and abstract images on all media:*

A FANGED STONE *mask with jaguar snout and mouth, human head and ears (centre left) comes from the La Tolita culture of Ecuador (c. 500 BC–AD 500).*

FROM THE CHAVÍN *culture of the Early Horizon (c. 900–200 BC) is a pugnacious-looking stone bowl or mortar (below left) in the form of some type of feline.*

A 15TH-CENTURY *Inca ceramic painted kero, or drinking cup, (above) is in the form of a jaguar.*

J

IPACURA see *MAMA IPACURA*.

IRIN-MAJE see *MONAN*.

IRMA, a pre-*INCA* name for *PACHACAMAC*.

THE ISLAND OF THE MOON is an island in Lake *TITICACA* in the highland Andean Titicaca Basin. In many versions of pan-Andean mythology describing the creation of the contemporary world, it was the place from which the moon first rose into the sky and was set into motion at the command of *VIRACOCHA*. (In other versions, the moon arose, along with the sun and the stars, from the *ISLAND OF THE SUN*.)

THE ISLAND OF THE SUN is an island in Lake *TITICACA* in the highland Andean Titicaca Basin. In pan-Andean mythology it was the

and the *CORICANCHA* in *CUZCO*, was one of the most sacred in the Inca realm until it was sacked by the Spaniards.

In one version of the origins of the Inca state, *MANCO CAPAC* and his sister/wife *MAMA OCLLO* were associated with the Island of the Sun in a deception meant to justify Inca conquest of the local peoples. In another rendering, Manco Capac was said to have led the "ancestors" underground from Lake Titicaca to the cave of *PACARITAMBO*.

THE ISLAND OF THE SUN (right) and the island of the Moon (above) in the middle of Lake Titicaca were two of the most sacred sites of Andean religion. It was believed that the sun, moon and stars rose from the islands over the lake waters and were set in motion by the creator god Viracocha.

place from which the sun – and, in some versions, the moon and the stars as well (see also *ISLAND OF THE MOON*) – first rose into the sky and was set into motion at the command of *VIRACOCHA*. The *INCAS* identified and named the island, and built a shrine to Viracocha there, which was the focus of an annual pilgrimage by the Inca emperor and nobility. This shrine, along with that of *PACHACAMAC*

FANGED GOD imagery from the earliest times to the *INCA* Empire. The beast itself was depicted frequently in wall paintings and stone carvings, on ceramics and textiles, and in metalwork and other portable artefacts. The beast-like monster gods of *CHAVÍN*, the *MOCHE*, the *CHIMÚ* and other cultures incorporate features and characteristics of the jaguar or felines in general, such as fangs and claws.

Such general recognition of the ferocity and power of the jaguar was, and still is, also prominent among Amazonian, Orinoco and *XINGU RIVER* peoples. There they regard the jaguar as the spirit of the rain forest, and their mythology refers to jaguars as the first beings to inhabit the world, in much the same role as later occupied by humans (see *BOTOQUE*). The jaguar represents power, fertility and an

JAGUARS AND JAGUAR-HUMANS were universal sources of imagery and mythology among the peoples of South America, as they were in ancient Mesoamerica. Among the cultures of the Andes and the west coast, the jaguar face has clearly inspired much of the

ambivalent force that needs to be mastered, or controlled and kept in check, by *SHAMANS*. Among the rain forest peoples of eastern Bolivia, men, in order to win their warrior status, must go into the forest alone and armed only with a wooden spear to kill a jaguar.

INTI RAYMI, the winter solstice festival in honour of Inti the sun god, has been rejuvenated and is held in Cuzco at the temple of Sacsahuaman.

Shamans and spiritual healers of the rain forest tribes don jaguar skins, wear necklaces of jaguar canine teeth (see also *KUAMUCUCA*) and, in their ritual trances, even growl like jaguars. The jaguar is regarded as their alter ego so that,

THE POWERFUL IMAGE of the jaguar was used from the earliest times by Andean cultures on everyday objects, such as this Chimú wooden vessel, as well as for architectural embellishment.

when a shaman dies, it is believed that his soul becomes a jaguar – a prowling jaguar seen at night near a village or burial ground is greatly feared because it is believed to be the metamorphosed body and soul of a dead shaman.

THE JIVARRO are an Ecuadorian rain forest tribe (see *HEAD-HUNTING*).

THE JURUNA are a rain forest tribe of the *XINGU RIVER* region of Brazil; see *SINAA* and *UAICA*.

JURUPARI is the central character in the Brazilian *TUPI* tribal myth, accounting for the present dominance of men in their society. The

K

myth typifies the widespread belief among many South American tribes of original female dominance.

The Tupi believe that the sun became angered at the domination of the earth by women, and decided to reverse the situation. First, he caused Ceucy, a young female virgin, to become pregnant from the sap of the *cucura* tree. When she gave birth to a boy named Jurupari, the precocious child took power away from women by teaching men to hold ritual feasts in order to gain and keep knowledge and power. Women were forbidden to attend the feasts on pain of death. A precedent was set when Jurupari caused the death of his own mother as punishment.

Jurupari's other task was to find a perfect woman to be the wife of his father the sun but, so far, he has not succeeded in finding one.

KALASASAYA see *TIAHUANACO*.

THE KAMAIURA are a *XINGU RIVER* tribe of central Brazil (see *KUAT* and *MAVUTSINIM*).

KANASSA is a creator god of sorts to the Kuikuru of the *XINGU RIVER* region of central Brazil.

At the beginning of time, in the darkness, Kanassa could not see what he was doing. He traced the outline of a ray in the mud of the river bank but, in the darkness, stepped on it and was stung by it. The ray then plunged into the water and swam away. Thus was the alligator given its flat tail.

Kanassa blamed all on the firefly, because it refused to give light for him to see by. Then he recalled that the vulture king, Ugwvucuengo, was also the master of fire. Kanassa went to him and seized him by the leg, refusing to let go until the vulture brought down an ember from the sky. When Kanassa used the ember to create fire, the frogs tried to squirt water on it to put it out, but Kanassa, with the help of the serpent, moved the fire

THE KAYAPO of the central Brazilian rain forest believe themselves to have been the original "beasts" of the forest until they stole the jaguar's knowledge of fire and the bow and arrow for hunting.

safely away from the water's edge. Thus was fire brought from the sky to humankind (see also *KUAT*).

Kanassa also taught ducks how to swim and gave the curassow bird its brilliant feathered headdress.

KASOGONAGA was a sky goddess (see *CHACO*).

KASPI are the souls of the Tierra del Fuegan *ONA*, who join their creator *TEMAUKEL* after death.

THE KAYAPO are a rain forest tribe of central Brazil (see *BOTOQUE*).

K'ELLK'ATA was the legendary city founded by *INKARRÍ*.

KHUNO, the storm god of the high Andes, brought rain and snow to the high mountain valleys when humans began to clear the forests for agriculture.

KHUNO was a storm god of the peoples of the high Andean valleys, where snow was frequent. According to myth, when people began to clear the highest valleys for farming by burning the trees, Khuno became angry because of the smoke and smut that blackened his snow. In retaliation, he sent a flood to wipe out the people, but some survived by hiding in caves. When the waters subsided and they came out there was nothing to eat. It was then that humans discovered the

coca plant (*Erythroxylon coca*) and found that, when they chewed its leaves, they lost all sense of hunger, cold and unhappiness.

KILLA see *QUILLA*.

KILYA see *QUILLA*.

KONONATOO ("our maker") is the creator god of the Warao tribe of the lower Orinoco River. The Warao believe that they originally lived in heaven with their maker, who

desired that they stay there with him. One day, however, the Warao descended to earth, when a young hunter discovered a hole in the sky and led the people through it. Later they were unable to return because a fat woman got lodged in the hole and blocked it up. As well as this, Kononatoo was disappointed in the Warao's disobedience, and so

he refused to create another entrance for them to return to the sky (see also *TOBA*).

The Warao are reluctant to bathe in lakes and rivers because, on earth, two girls once swam in a lake forbidden by Kononatoo and became pregnant by a water god, thus creating snakes.

KOYLLUR see *QOYLOR*.

KUAMUCUCA is a culture hero of the tribes of the Brazilian *XINGU RIVER* region. With the help of the sun and the moon, he invaded the village of the *JAGUARS* and killed them all, after which Kuamucuca and his fellow warriors collected the jaguars' claws as trophies with which to make necklaces. They were warned by the sun, however, not to eat the meat, and so the people of the Xingu tribes never eat jaguars when they kill them.

KUARUP is the name given to the rituals performed among the *XINGU RIVER* tribes when a person of importance has died (see *MAVUTSINIM*).

KONONATOO, the creator god of the Orinoco River Warao tribe, refused to allow them to rejoin him in the sky after a young warrior led them through a hole down to the earth.

L

KUAT is the sun god and culture hero of the *XINGU RIVER KAMAIURA* tribe. His brother Iae is moon god.

At the beginning of time, humankind lived in a world of total darkness, for it was always nighttime. Humans lived near termite hills, and their lives were wretched. The birds, however, lived in a kingdom of shining light ruled by the vulture king, Urubutsin. Kuat and Iae wanted to make life better for their fellow humans but could not think what to do, for they could not make light. So they plotted, and decided on a ruse to steal the birds' daylight and bring light into the world of humans.

They made an effigy in the form of a rotting corpse, buzzing with flies and crawling with maggots, and sent it to Urubutsin. But Urubutsin could not understand the flies' humming until one of his subjects interpreted the effigy as an offering and the maggots as a gift for the vulture king to eat. Then Urubutsin understood that the flies were inviting him to visit Kuat and Iae, who would give him more maggots to eat.

Meanwhile, Kuat and Iae had made another effigy corpse, and concealed themselves inside it. The vultures shaved their heads and made their way to Kuat's and Iae's village. The very moment that Urubutsin alighted on the corpse

THE LAMBAYEQUE VALLEY was ruled by a succession of powerful kingdoms – Moche, Sicán and Chimú. Each left monuments of their power, such as the Sicán pyramids at Túcume.

to feast, however, Kuat leaped out and caught hold of his leg. The other birds flew off in fright. Kuat refused to release Urubutsin until he promised to share the light of day with humans, so the secret of daylight was bought as a ransom. Urubutsin explained that day and night must alternate, promising that day would always return. So it was that humans began to live in the endless cycle of day and night (see also *KANASSA*).

THE KUIKURU are a *XINGU RIVER* tribe of central Brazil (see *KANASSA*).

KULIMINA was the *ARAWAK* creator of women (see *KURURUMANY*).

KURURUMANY is one of two Orinoco River *ARAWAK* tribal creator deities (see also *ALUBERI*). Kururumany created men, while the goddess Kulimina created women. He was also responsible for introducing death to humankind when he saw that his creations were not

KUAT and his brother Iae, the culture heroes of the Kamaiura Xingu River tribe, wanted to better the life of their fellow humans, so they stole the sunlight of the forest birds from the vulture king Urubutsin. Kuat became the sun god and Iae the moon god, thus initiating the endless cycle of night and day.

perfect. To plague humans, he also created serpents, lizards, mosquitoes, fleas and other biting creatures.

LAKE TITICACA see *TITICACA*.

LAMBAYEQUE VALLEY, in northern coastal Peru, was one of several valleys in this region where the *MOCHE*, *SICÁN* and *CHIMÚ* kingdoms developed from the Early Intermediate Period to the Late Horizon. In myth and legend, the Lambayeque Valley was invaded and settled by *NAYAMLAP*, with his idol *YAMPALLEC*, and his descendants, and later invaded by *CHIMO CAPAC* from the Moche Valley. It came under *INCA* rule after the conquest of Chimú in the 1470s.

LANZÓN IDOL see *CHAVÍN*.

THE LLACUAZ were one of the legendary lineage *AYLLUS* of *CAJATAMBO*. They conquered the *GUARI ayllu*, and shared ritual beliefs.

LLASCA CHURAPA was one of the five selves that made up the pre-*INCA* god *PARIACACA* in the *HUAROCHIRÍ MANUSCRIPT*.

LLAUTO was a common *INCA* headdress; one was worn by the image of *VIRACOCHA* seen by *PACHACUTI INCA YUPANQUI*.

LLIBIAC see under *CAJATAMBO*.

LLOQUE YUPANQUI was the legendary third *INCA* ruler of *CUZCO*, probably sometime in the 12th century AD. Like all Inca rulers, he was considered to be a direct descendant of the ancestors, *MANCO CAPAC* and *MAMA OCLLO*.

LLOQUE YUPANQUI was the third legendary Inca emperor. (IMAGINARY SKETCH BY FELIPE GUAMAN POMA DE AYALA IN HIS NUEVA CORÓNICA Y BUEN GOBIERNO, WRITTEN BETWEEN 1583 AND 1613.)

LLULLAILLACO, a mountain peak in the northern Argentinian Andes, was the site of the *INCA* ritual sacrifice of two young girls and a boy between the ages of 8 and 14. Two of the bodies were buried about 2 m (6 ft) deep in the ground, possibly alive, in a child sacrifice (see *CAPACOCHA*) to the sun god *INTI*, or perhaps to the creator *VIRACOCHA*. Conditions at the site, discovered in 1999 at 6,700 m (22,000 ft) froze the bodies in near-perfect condition, and this has enabled scientists to study their diet and any genetic relationships (see also *AMPATO*).

M

MACHU PICCHU, *a remote mountain retreat north of Cuzco, was one of the Incas' most sacred sites. The even more remote retreat of Huayna Picchu was perched on a rocky outcrop above the main site.*

MASSIVE *polygonal stone structures such as the Intihuatana ("Hitching Post of the Sun") and numerous other temples and ritual locations were incorporated at Machu Picchu, as well as natural Huacas.*

LURIN YAUYOS see *HUAROCHIRÍ MANUSCRIPT*.

MACAW see *YURUPARY*.

MACHAY (caves) see under *CAJATAMBO*.

MACHU PICCHU was a remote *INCA* mountain retreat above the Urubamba Valley, north of *CUZCO* – possibly of military significance to commemorate the conquest of the eastern provinces, but certainly much more important as a sacred site and Inca royal estate. Its construction was begun by *PACHACUTI INCA YUPANQUI*, and it served as an estate for his descendants until it was abandoned shortly before the Spaniards arrived. Its vast natural and polygonal stone construction incorporates several ritual locations, including the *INTIHUATANA* or "Hitching Post of the Sun", the Torreón Sun Temple and the Temple of Three Windows, all significant for ritual and astronomical observation. An even more isolated retreat, Huayna Picchu, is reached by a flight of stone steps from Machu Picchu to a rocky outcrop above it. In addition, a chain of 16 spring-fed water catchments supplied water and may have been used in the ritual control and manipulation of water (see also *CHAVÍN*, *SACSAHUAMAN* and *TIAHUANACO*).

MAIRE MONAN see *MONAN*.

MALLQUIS (*INCA* and pre-Inca) were the mummified remains of the ancestors of a kinship or lineage *AYLLU*, including the mummies of Inca emperors and their queens. The care and veneration of *mallquis* were a central and essential part of Andean religious practice. They were usually stored in caves seen as sacred places, and at festivals for the gathering of *ayllu* members they were dressed in rich clothing, put on display, and offered food and

MALLQUIS, *the carefully preserved mummified remains of ancestors, formed an important element in the religious structure and played a vital role in the rituals of Inca and earlier cultures.*

drink. The *mallquis* were the focus of veneration and provided a setting for the recounting of the clan's origin myths, thus passing the knowledge down the generations. Such ceremonies were regarded as crucial in order to ensure the fertility of crops and herds, and to maintain cosmic order.

Judging from archaeological finds of well prepared and cared for mummies in the Andes and among the southern coastal cultures of Peru, the practice appears to have begun as early as the Early Horizon. Mummies also played an early and important role in the myth of the creation of the Inca state. The name *Ayar* itself, given to each of the male brothers/husbands of the Inca founders/ancestors, means "corpse", linking the ancestors and the mummified bodies of the deceased Inca rulers. According to the late 16th-century chronicler Cristobal de Molina, *MAMA HUACO*, the sister/wife of the founder/ancestor *AYAR AUCA*, was embalmed and mummified, and *chicha* (corn/maize beer), fermented from the corn of a special field believed to have been planted by her, was drunk by the keepers of her cult. Emperor *PACHACUTI INCA YUPANQUI* and his main consort were similarly honoured.

Although the *mallquis* of the Inca emperors were destroyed by the Spaniards in Cuzco, reverence for *mallquis* lasted into the 17th century in the provinces, much to the consternation of Spanish priests. Special "extirpators of idolatries" appointed to search out and destroy them discovered hundreds hidden in caves near provincial towns (see *IDOLATRÍAS*, *CAJATAMBO*).

MAMA COCA was the *INCA* goddess of the sea. She was a lesser deity in the Inca pantheon. As a highland people, the Incas had less to do with the sea than did the coastal cultures, except to trade with the latter for their products.

MAMA COYA see *MAMA OCLLO*.

MAMA CUNAS see under *ACLLAS*.

MAMA CURA see *MAMA IPACURA*.

MAMA HUACO was the sister/wife of *AYAR AUCA* (although one chronicler names *AYAR CACHI* as her husband) and one of the original *INCA* ancestors (see *MANCO CAPAC*).

MAMA IPACURA was the sister/wife of *AYAR CACHI* and one of the original eight *INCA* ancestors (see *MANCO CAPAC*).

MAMA KILYA see *QUILLA*.

MAMA ÑAMCA (pre-*INCA*) was the female ally of *HUALLALLO CARHUINCHO*. Both fought *PARIACACA* (see *HUAROCHIRÍ MANUSCRIPT*).

MAMA OCLLO, also Cori Ocllo, Mama Coya, or Ocllo Huaco, was the sister/wife of *MANCO CAPAC* and mother of *SINCHI ROCA*. She was one of the eight *INCA* ancestors.

MAMA RAUA was the sister/wife of *AYAR UCHU* and one of the original eight *INCA* ancestors (see *MANCO CAPAC*).

MAMACUNA was the *INCA* Temple of the Sun at *PACHACAMAC*.

MAMA OCLLO, *wife of the first Inca ruler, holds a symbol of Quilla (the moon), which she represents.* (ILLUSTRATION FROM THE GENEALOGY OF THE 18TH-CENTURY "CUZCO SCHOOL.")

53

MANCO CAPAC, or Ayar Manco, was the legendary first *INCA* ruler and founder of the Inca dynasty, known as Hurin Cuzco (see *HANAN AND HURIN CUZCO*). His alternative name was in keeping with his brothers' names, all of which had Ayar as the first element. Manco Capac was the principal character in Inca mythology surrounding the origins of the state and in Inca hegemony. Manco Capac was also the name of one of the four kings who figure in the myth of the *UNNAMED MAN*, concerning the origin of the four-fold division of the Inca Empire.

The Incas vigorously promoted their own political agenda. They were particularly keen to establish their origins as special, and to convince others that their own place of origin was the same as that of the Incas. In the words of the 17th-century Jesuit priest, Bernabé Cobo, this official line was "caused by the ambition of the Incas. They were the first to worship [at] the cave of *PACARITAMBO* as the [place of the] beginning of their lineage. They claimed that all people came from there, and that for this reason all people were their vassals and obliged to serve them."

Permutations of the state creation myth seem to have prevailed simultaneously. The most prominent version, in outline, described how four brothers and four sisters came forth from the central one of three "windows" or caves in the mountain of *TAMBO TOCO* ("window mountain"). These were "the ancestors", and their leader (the eldest brother) was Manco Capac or Ayar Manco. The ancestors led the people who lived around Tambo Toco in search of a new land to settle. After much wandering, they came to a hill overlooking the Valley of Cuzco. Certain miraculous signs informed them that here was where they should settle, so they came down from the mountain, overcame any local resistance, and took possession of the land.

This standard version comes from the 16th-century chronicler Sarmiento de Gamboa's *Historia de los Incas* (1572), an early source and one that relied heavily on interviews with keepers of the Inca state records, the *QUIPUCAMAYOQS*.

Pacaritambo was the "inn, or house, of dawn", the "place of origin". According to the chroniclers it was six leagues (about 33 km/20 miles) south of Cuzco; in fact, it is closer to 26 km (16 miles). The mountain there, Tambo Toco, had three windows, the central one of which was called Capac Toco ("rich window"). From this window stepped the four ancestral couples, the brother/sister–husband/wife pairs: Ayar Manco Capac with Mama Ocllo, Ayar Auca with Mama Huaco, Ayar Cachi with Mama Ipacura or Mama Cura, and Ayar Uchu with Mama Raua. From the flanking windows, Maras Toco and Sutic Toco, came the Maras and Tambos, both allies of the Incas. A divine link was immediately established in the promotion of the myth by the claim that the ancestors and their allies came out of the caves at the urging of *TICCI VIRACOCHA*.

Ayar Manco declared that he would lead his brothers and sisters, and the allies, in search of a fertile land, where the local inhabitants would be conquered and their land seized. He promised that he would make the allies rich. Before setting out, the ancestors and allies were formed into ten lineage groups called *AYLLUS*. (This was the origin of the ten *ayllus* of commoners at Cuzco, as opposed to the *PANACA*, the ten royal *ayllus*, who were the descendants of the Inca emperors.)

Ayar Manco led his followers north, towards the Valley of Cuzco. He had a golden bar, brought from Tambo Toco, with which he tested the ground for fertility by thrusting it periodically into the soil.

Progress was slow, and there were several stops. At the first stop Ayar Manco and Mama Ocllo conceived a child. At the second stop a boy was born, whom they named *SINCHI ROCA*. A third stop was made at Palluta, where they lived for several years, but eventually became dissatisfied with the fertility of the land, and so moved on to a place called Haysquisrro. It was here that the first breaking up of the company occurred.

Ayar Cachi was known to be unruly and sometimes cruel. Wherever the ancestors passed through or stopped he caused trouble with the local inhabitants. He was also a powerful slinger and could hurl stones hard enough to split mountains open, causing dust and rocks to fly up and obscure the sun. The other ancestors began to consider him a liability and a hindrance to their prospects, so the brothers and sisters formed a plan to dispense with him. Ayar Manco told him that several important objects that should have accompanied the golden rod had been left in Pacaritambo: a golden cup (*topacusi*), a miniature llama figurine (called a *napa*) and some seeds. Ayar Cachi at first refused to return to Capac

Toco, but agreed to do so when his sister, Mama Huaco, herself a forceful character, chided and accused him of laziness and cowardice.

Ayar Cachi journeyed back to Capac Toco with a Tambo companion called Tambochacay (literally, "the window entrance-bearer"). He was unaware, however, that Ayar Manco and the others had convinced Tambochacay to dispose of him. So, when Ayar Cachi went into the cave to retrieve the forgotten items, Tambochacay sealed the entrance, trapping Ayar Cachi inside forever. The site, later known as *MAU-QALLAQTA*, became an important Inca *HUACA* and place of pilgrimage.

The ancestors' next stop was at Quirirmanta, at the foot of a mountain called Huanacauri. They climbed the mountain and, from the top, saw the Valley of Cuzco for the first time. From the summit, Ayar Manco threw the golden rod into the valley to test the soil. To their amazement the entire rod vanished into the earth, and a rainbow appeared. Taking these as propitious signs, they decided this was the place that should become their homeland.

Before they could descend the mountain, however, Ayar Uchu became the second to depart from the company. He sprouted huge wings and flew up into the sky, where he met the sun. The sun told Ayar Uchu that thenceforth, Ayar Manco, the eldest brother, should be called Manco Capac ("supreme rich one"), and that they should go into the valley to the place of Cuzco, where the ruler of that place, *ALCAVICÇA*, would welcome them. Ayar Uchu returned to his brothers and sisters, told them this news, and was transformed into stone. A stone, identified by the Incas as Ayar Uchu, became another of their principal *huacas*.

The remaining ancestors did not, however, proceed straight to Cuzco and Alcavicça. They stopped first at a place called Matao, near Cuzco, where they remained for two years. During this period another strange event occurred. Mama Huaco, like Ayar Cachi, was also an expert slinger. She hurled a stone at a man in Matao and killed him. Splitting open his chest, she removed his heart and lungs, and blew into the lungs to make them inflate. When she displayed these to the people of the town, they fled in terror.

Finally, Manco Capac led the ancestors to Cuzco. They met Alcavicça and declared that they had been sent by their father, the sun. This news convinced Alcavicça, who allowed them to take over the town. In return, the ancestors "domesticated" the inhabitants by teaching them to plant corn (maize). (In one version it was Manco Capac who planted the first field; in another it was Mama Huaco.) At the place that would become the centre of the Inca city of *CUZCO* – the plaza called Huanaypata – the last remaining brother ancestor, Ayar Auca, was turned

MANCO CAPAC *was founder ancestor and first ruler of the Incas. (CONCEIVED AND SKETCHED BY FELIPE GUAMAN POMA DE AYALA IN HIS* NUEVA CORÓNICA Y BUEN GOBIERNO, *WRITTEN BETWEEN 1583 AND 1613.)*

into a stone pillar, which, like the stone of Ayar Uchu on Huanacauri, became a revered *huaca*.

This left Manco Capac, his four sisters and his son Sinchi Roca to organize the building of Cuzco: a convenient outcome, and in keeping with later Inca imperial practice of sister/wives, and leaving only one descendant to the leadership.

This was the "standard" version. It contains all the necessary elements of Inca legend, including the wandering, conquering, alliances and divine intervention needed to telescope the folk memory of a long and complex history of a people.

So ambitious were the Incas, however, that they felt the need to link this lineage creation myth to the world creation myth, and thus gain the ultimate divine sanction. And in variations, the Incas appear openly devious in their determination to rewrite and shape history to fit their self-image as the supreme and only people fit to rule.

In one version, the ancestors deliberately tricked the inhabitants of the Valley of Cuzco into believing them to be the descendants of the sun itself. Manco Capac made two golden discs, one for his front and one for his back. He then climbed the hill of Huanacauri before dawn so that at sunrise he appeared to be a golden, god-like being. The populace of Cuzco was so awed that he had no trouble in descending the hill and taking over their rule.

In yet another version, Manco Capac achieved rulership, but the account, given by four elderly

QUIPUCAMAYOQS, contains an undercurrent of the resentment that local valley inhabitants might have harboured, even years after ancestors of the Inca had invaded and conquered them. The story can be interpreted as a suggestion that the whole fabric of Inca rule was illegitimate.

In this variation, Manco Capac was the son of a local valley *CURACA* or official in Pacaritambo. His mother had died giving birth to him, so he grew up with his father, who gave him the nickname, "Son of the Sun [*INTI*]". The father died when Manco Capac was about 10 or 12, never having explained to his son that the nickname was just that, and not the truth. What is more, the commoners of the town – referred to as *gente bruta* ("stupid folk") in the chronicle – appear also to have been convinced that Manco Capac was actually the son of the sun. Two old men, the priests of Manco Capac's father's household gods, continued to encourage this belief. As Manco Capac reached early manhood, the priests further promoted Manco Capac's own conviction that he was the son of a god and that he had a natural right to rule on earth. With these ideas in his head, he set off for Cuzco with several relatives and the two old priests; also with his father's principal idol, named Huanacauri. In this version also, Manco Capac wins the rule of the people of Cuzco by appearing at dawn on the mountain of Huanacauri, bedecked in gold as a divine being and dazzling them.

THE TRADITION of the Sapa Inca and the founding of the Incas nation by Manco Capac has recently been revived, and is celebrated annually in Cuzco with a representative, symbolism and ritual attire.

In a final variation, Manco Capac and his sister/wife Mama Ocllo were associated with the *ISLAND OF THE SUN* in Lake *TITICACA*, a deception meant to justify Inca conquest of local peoples. This version provides another example of Inca efforts to reconcile the beliefs of the local peoples with creation in general and with the origins of the Inca state – efforts whose ulterior motive was to justify and secure divine sanction for Inca rule. As in the other renditions, Manco Capac, as the legendary first Inca "emperor" and founder of the state to be, identified himself as the son of the sun. Titicaca Basin myth described a great deluge that had destroyed the previous world, and told that the sun of the present world first shone on the Island of the Sun. In this version, therefore, a fable was concocted that, after his creation, the sun placed his two children, a male and a female, on the island with the task of teaching the "barbarous" people of the region how to live in a civilized manner. Undoubtedly these two must have been Manco Capac and Mama Ocllo.

A further connection with the Titicaca Basin was given in an account in which it was claimed that Manco Capac led the "ancestors" underground from Lake Titicaca to the cave of Pacaritambo. In this case, it was even claimed that the creator *VIRACOCHA* bestowed a special headdress and stone battleaxe upon Manco Capac, and prophesied that the Incas would become great lords and conquer many other nations. Both of these renditions have the great advantage of linking Manco Capac and the Inca state with Titicaca and *TIAHUANACO*, which the Incas knew to be revered throughout the Andes as the place where the world began.

MANIOC STICK ANACONDA see *YURUPARY.*

MANTA was the site on the northernmost coast of the *INCA* Empire where, in pre-Inca creation myth, *CON TICCI VIRACOCHA, IMAYMANA VIRACOCHA* and *TOCAPO VIRACOCHA* rejoined each other after their journeys and disappeared by walking northwest out across the ocean.

THE MARAS were allies of the *INCA* ancestors (see *MANCO CAPAC.*)

MARAS TOCO was one of the caves of *TAMBO TOCO* in the *INCA* state foundation myth (see *MANCO CAPAC*).

MATAO was the sixth place of sojourn of the ancestors on their wanderings in the *INCA* state foundation myth (see *MANCO CAPAC*).

MAUQALLQTA ("old town") is the modern name for the ruins of an *INCA* site 26 km (16 miles) south of *CUZCO*. It has been identified as *PACARITAMBO/TAMBO TOCO*, the place of origins of the Inca ancestors (see *MANCO CAPAC*).

MAVUTSINIM was the "first man" of the peoples of the *XINGU RIVER* region. He wanted to bring the dead back to life, so he collected logs (*kuarup*) and brought them to the village, where he dressed them up as people. His plan failed, however, because one member of the village did not complete Mavutsinim's exact instructions, so the logs remained wooden.

According to *KAMAIURA* tribal myth, in the beginning only Mavutsinim existed, and was thus the creator. He transformed a shell into a woman, and with her produced the first boy child. He took the child for himself, away from its mother, who returned tearfully to a lagoon, where she became a shell again. Thus the Kamaiura declare themselves to be the "grandchildren of the son of Mavutsinim".

A variant myth describes how, one day, Mavutsinim was caught in the forest by *JAGUARS*. In exchange for his life, he promised the jaguars his daughters in marriage, but sent wooden figures instead. Two of Mavutsinim's daughters did actually marry jaguars, and one of them became pregnant. Her jealous jaguar mother-in-law, however, killed her, but let her twin boys live. When they grew up, the twins hunted jaguars in revenge and became the sun and the moon.

MAYTA CAPAC was the legendary fourth *INCA* ruler of *CUZCO*, probably sometime in the later 12th century. Like all Inca rulers, he was considered to be a direct descendant of the ancestors, *MANCO CAPAC* and *MAMA OCLLO*.

MAYU (*QUECHUA*, "celestial river") was the Milky Way, the movements of which across the night sky were keenly observed by the *INCA* from points within the sacred *CORICANCHA* precinct in *CUZCO*.

In Inca religion, the observation of this celestial river was the starting point for calendrical correlations with natural changes in terrestrial conditions and seasons. (This is in notable contrast to the calendrical calculations of most other cultures, which proceed from observations of the movements of the closest single celestial bodies, namely the sun and the moon. By contrast, the observation of the Milky Way is of galactic proportions.) This starting point provided a scheme with which to chart the correlations of heavenly positions and terrestrial change, and to organize daily, seasonal and annual labour and ritual.

Observation of the Milky Way is of vast galactic rotation: the plane of rotation inclines noticeably from the plane of the earth's rotation by between 26° and 30°. When the movements are plotted from the southern hemisphere, the broad band of the "river" divides the sky into three sections (above, below, and Mayu itself), and follows a sequence that rocks it slowly through the course of the year, such that during half the year it tilts from right to left, and during the other half from left to right. In the course of 24 hours, Mayu crosses its zenith in the sky, and, in doing so, forms two intersecting or intercardinal axes oriented northeast/southwest and southeast/northwest.

Thus the divisions of the sky provided a celestial grid against which all other astronomical observations could be plotted, including not only the obvious luminated planets and stars, but also immense stellar voids or "dark clouds". To the Incas, these voids were constellations, which they named after animals: adult llama, baby llama, fox, *tinamou* (a partridge-like bird), toad and *SERPENT*. Luminary bodies included *COLLCA* ("granary" – the Pleiades), *ORQO-CILAY* ("multi-coloured llama" – another star group) and *CHASKA-QOYLOR* ("shaggy star" – Venus as the morning "star").

The movements of these celestial bodies were used by the Inca to predict zoological and botanical cycles, wild and domestic, and to regulate the care of their crops and llama flocks. Practical observations and applications were interwoven with myth. For example, the solstices of Mayu coincide with the Andean wet and dry seasons, and thus the celestial river was used to predict seasonal water cycles. The "dark cloud" llama (*YACANA*) disappears at midnight, when it was believed to have descended to earth to drink water and thus prevent flooding. (In contrast, black llamas were starved during October, in the dry season, in order to make them weep, regarded as a supplication to the gods to water the crops with rain.)

The sun's movements were used to calculate the two most important ritual dates in the year – the summer and winter solstices, *CAPAC RAYMI* and *INTI RAYMI*. Similarly, the first appearance of the Pleiades before sunrise was correlated with the regular sidereal lunar months (the 27.3-day period of the rotation of the moon around the earth–moon centre of mass), beginning on 8–9 June and ending on 3–4 May. In *Ayrihua* (the month of April), as this lunar-plotted year ended, ceremonies in Cuzco honoured the royal insignia, and a white llama was dressed in a red tunic and fed *coca* and *CHICHA* (corn/maize beer) to symbolize the first llama to appear on earth after the great flood.

As well as regulating daily and seasonal life, Mayu's movements were reflected in the Inca organization of their empire into four quarters (*TAHUANTINSUYU*), and oriented the routes of the four principal highways out of Cuzco to the quarters: the routes approximated the intercardinal axes of the Milky Way. Mayu's axes were also associated with sacred *CEQUE* ritual alignments, at least one of which correlated to the southernmost point in the Milky Way's movements. (see also *MISMINAY*).

THE MINATA-KARAIA were

a mythical race of beings whom the tribes along the *XINGU RIVER* of Brazil believe existed in the remote past. Minata-Karaia men had a hole in the top of their head, through which they could whistle, and bunches of coconuts grew beneath their armpits. This latter convenience meant that whenever they were hungry, they could simply take a coconut, crack it open against their head and eat it (see also the *OI*).

MINCHANÇAMAN, or Minch-

ancamon, was the pre-*INCA*, partially legendary, king of the *CHIMÚ* dynasty of *TAYCANAMU* in the *MOCHE* valley, the sixth or seventh ruler in that line. During the course of his reign, the valley was conquered by *TOPA YUPANQUI* (or *TUPAC INCA YUPANQUI*) in the 1470s. The Inca account of this (in Garcilaso de la Vega's *Comentarios Reales de los Incas*, 1609–17) demonstrates their method of incorporating new kingdoms into the fabric of their empire, firmly establishing their overlordship while at the same time recognizing the integrity and power of the ruling dynasty: "The brave Chimú [Minchançaman], his arrogance and pride now tamed, appeared

before the prince [Tupac Inca Yupanqui] with as much submission and humility, and grovelled on the ground before him, worshipping him and repeating the same request [for pardon] as he had made through his ambassadors. The prince received him affectionately in order to relieve [his] grief . . . [and] bade two of the captains raise him from the ground. After hearing him, [Tupac Inca Yupanqui] told him that all that was past was forgiven . . . The Inca had not come to deprive him of his estates and authority, but to improve his idolatrous religion, his laws and his customs."

MISMINAY is a town in Peru

situated 25 km (16 miles) south of *CUZCO*. Anthropological research has revealed that the people of the town and region continue to observe the night sky and *MAYU*, the Milky Way, in the manner of the ancient *INCA*, and to apply mythological and cosmological meaning to what they see. The nearby Vilcanota River is regarded as the reflection of Mayu, the "celestial river", and the two are regarded as conduits for recycling water from earth to sky and back again as rain.

MAYU, the Milky Way, was regarded as the "celestial river". Star clusters within it were considered to be celestial signs, one of the most important of which was the Pleiades, called Collea ("the granary").

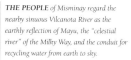

THE PEOPLE of Misminay regard the nearby sinuous Vilcanota River as the earthly reflection of Mayu, the "celestial river" of the Milky Way, and the conduit for recycling water from earth to sky.

As the Milky Way rotates through the sky over a 24-hour period, its zenith traverses two axes that the people of Misminay use to divide the heavens into four quadrants. This grid provides a template for the town itself, which is similarly divided by intersecting footpaths along the two principal irrigation canals, all of which meet at the chapel of Crucero, the name also used for the celestial intersection of Mayu's axes.

The beliefs of the people of Misminay perpetuate ancient Inca perception that all earthly animals and birds have a celestial equivalent, and that the sky beasts govern procreation and sustenance on earth. "Dark Cloud" constellations – stellar voids collectively called *Pachatira* – include llamas, a fox, a toad, a *tinamou* bird and a *SERPENT*, and their influence over their earthly equivalents reflects the concept of the earth mother *PACHAMAMA* and fertility in general. For example, when the "eyes of the llama" – the stars Alpha and Beta Centauri – rise before dawn in November and December, llamas give birth; and the serpent constellation, seen in the sky during the rainy season, brings rain, but is below ground (that is, below the horizon) during the dry season. Rainbows (see *CUICHU*), perceived as multicoloured serpents, rise from the ground after rain showers.

MIT'A ("turns of service") was an

INCA state institutional organization of labour for service to the royal household and for the redistribution of goods; see also *AYLLU*. It could take the form, for example, of tending royal lands and llama flocks, and performing a quota of work at state installations, such as redistribution warehouses.

CULTURE HEROES

THE IDEA OF A LEGENDARY figure as culture hero was an important part of Andean mythology, and continues to be so among rain forest peoples in South America. Among the Andean civilizations, such figures include both divine heroes and teachers, such as Viracocha and his sons, or Bochica in Colombia, and the founders of dynasties, kingdoms and empires, such as Manco Capac and the Ayars, Chimo Capac or Nayamlap. Each of these heroes brought the gifts of civilization, such as agriculture and monumental architecture, to humans and taught them the arts and moral codes by which to live.

A common feature in all of these stories is the eventual departure of the divine or human hero from the world, across the seas or into the sky, leaving humankind to fend for itself. In some cases, the hero existed on the fringes of history and appears to be an inflated version of a real person – for example, Pachacuti Inca Yupanqui. In other cases, the divine nature of the teacher and his description tempted Spanish chroniclers into equating him with a Christian saint.

Among the rain forest tribes, a common belief throughout the vast Amazonian and *pampas* regions is of a hero who learns how to use fire, weapons and tools after having been adopted by jaguar beings, the first masters of the earth who behaved like humans.

Shamans are the tribal spiritual leaders. With the use of hallucinogenic drugs, they gain access to the spiritual "other" world in order to intermediate on behalf of the tribe. Such practice appears to have been a long-standing tradition among ancient Andean cultures as well.

THE ANCIENT USE of hallucinogens to induce trance and gain access to the spiritual world for religious purposes is attested by numerous images on ancient pottery, such as this Moche stirrup vase (left) in the shape of a noble (with large ear discs) and cocaine-induced expression. Similarly, a much later Chimú painted textile (above) depicts a priest or shaman wearing an axe headdress who is apparently in a spirit world. The two anthropomorphized plants in the lower corners are cacti whose hallucinogenic juices induce visions.

A KAYAPO warrior/hunter (above) of the Xingu River region of central Brazil with a jaguar he has killed – ancient Andean cultures and rain forest tribes alike universally revered the jaguar for its power and cunning. Among rain forest tribes, fire and hunting weapons were stolen from the jaguar, thus reversing the roles of the jaguar and man. Shamans imitate jaguars as part of their ritual communication with "other" worlds.

THE CREATOR GOD Viracocha (in some versions accompanied by his sons) travelled throughout the land teaching humankind the arts of civilization. Later inhabitants of alleged stopping places on his legendary journeys honoured him with temples, as at Rachi (or Raqchi), Peru (above).

COCA continues to be used among Andean peoples for divination (above), for example, among the Chipaya people of Bolivia.

PRIESTS AND SHAMANS were/are healers as well as religious leaders – this Moche ceramic model (above) shows a priest with ear discs and a feline headband praying over a sick or deceased person.

MITIMAES was the *INCA* term for groups of people of one province whom they had moved to and settled in another part of their empire.

The practice was used in order to exercise demographic and social control and for economic reorganization. By shifting large groups of people around within the empire, the Incas could redistribute labour and the commodities grown and produced by different groups, as well as mixing peoples' notions of geographic identity and religious/mythological concepts.

The practice undoubtedly had a significant impact in rearranging and conflating the details of creation myth, especially, such that a more generalized pan-Andean/pan-Inca version was propagated. The result provided the Incas with a means of legitimizing their right to rule as a "chosen" people, whose semi-divine ruler had sanction by descent from the creator god *VIRACOCHA* (see also *VIRACOCHA INCA*). The term itself was even established in myth, for it was used in some versions of the creation myth: *CON TICCI VIRACOCHA* ordered the two survivors of the great flood, thrown up on land at *TIAHUANACO*, to remain there as *mitimaes*.

THE MOCHE, or Mochica, were a culture and people who dominated the northern coastal valleys of Peru through the Early Intermediate Period, succeeding *CHAVÍN* cultural influence in that region and roughly contemporary with the *NAZCA* culture in the southern coastal valleys. A powerful kingdom was developed over several hundred years through conquest and domination of the local valleys to the north and south of the "capital" city at Moche in the valley of the same name (see also *FEMPELLEC* and *NAYAMLAP*).

By AD 450, two huge pyramidal structures, each made of millions of *adobe* bricks, had become the focus of political and religious power. The Huaca del Sol, 40 m

(130 ft) high, comprised a four-tiered, cross-shaped platform whose summit was reached by a north-side ramp; 500 m (1,650 ft) away, across an area occupied by dwellings and workshops, the Huaca de la Luna, at the foot of Cerro Blanco, was a three-tiered structure whose walls were richly decorated with friezes depicting mythological scenes and deities. The two ceremonial platforms sat within a sprawling urban setting that, at its maximum size, occupied as much as 300 hectares (740 acres).

About 100 years later, evidence indicates that the impingement of a huge sand sheet around Moche choked the canal system and stifled agriculture, and caused the inhabitants to move away. Some of Moche's inhabitants were probably responsible for the settlement of Galindo, farther up the valley, but from this time onwards the focus of Moche politics and religion shifted northwards, to the *LAMBAYEQUE VALLEY* and the sites of Pampa Grande and *SIPÁN*. As well as the element of natural disaster, these movements appear also to have been influenced by the early expansion of *HUARI* power from the southeast, out of the Andes.

Pampa Grande covered an area of some 600 ha (1,485 acres) and lasted about 150 years. Its most imposing structure, the Huaca Fortaleza, appears to have served a similar function to the Huaca del Sol at Moche as a ritual platform. It rose 38 m (125 ft), and its summit was reached by a 290-m (950-ft) ramp. At the very top,

columns supported the roofs of a complex of rooms, one containing a mural depicting *FELINE* beings. The Huaca Fortaleza appears to have been the élite sector of the city, while the residences of the lower classes of Moche society were spread around it.

Like Moche, Pampa Grande was abandoned abruptly, owing to a combination of agricultural disaster caused by an El Niño weather event and the continued expansion of the Huari state. Fierce internal unrest may also have been a factor, for the archaeological evidence shows intense conflagration in the centre of the city – so hot that *adobes* of the Huaca Fortaleza were fired into brick.

Like the Chavín cult before it, Moche imagery reflected a potent religion, with its own distinctive iconography and pantheon, albeit much derived from Chavín. Like Chavín de Huántar, at least one Moche pilgrimage centre has been recognized in the cliff-top site of *PACATNAMÚ*. Moche iconography was characterized by humans and anthropomorphized animal figures, *SERPENTS* and frogs, birds (owls in particular) and sea animals (crabs and fishes), and by standardized groups and ceremonial scenes, including a *coca* ritual recognizable by distinctive clothing and ritual combat. Murals, friezes and vignettes on pottery depict the capture and sacrifice of "enemies", drink offerings by subordinates to lords and gods, and persons passing through the night sky in moon-shaped boats. Rich tombs at

RICH SIPÁN TOMBS of Moche lords reflect the mythological themes enshrined in the Warrior Priest and Decapitator God, including a crescent-shaped back-flap and rattles suspended from his belt.

Sipán (some of the few unlooted tombs of the Andes) contain burials and artefacts, and mural scenes that confirm the images on the walls, ceramics, textiles and metalwork that have been excavated from other Moche sites.

Although we do not know the names of all the Moche deities directly, *AI APAEC* and *SI*, a sky/creator god and a moon goddess respectively, appear to have been prominent, if extended back in time from the later *CHIMÚ* pantheon. In a similar manner, a *MOCHE MOUNTAIN GOD* has been named by some from the many feline-featured beings depicted on Moche ceramics and textiles. Especially prominent, however, were the *FANGED GODS* and the complex ceremony and ritual of the *DECAPITATOR GOD*. In later Moche imagery, there was a mingling with Huari style, presumably imposed, and subtle changes in the depiction of eyes and headdress ornaments suggest the beginnings of the influence of Chimú.

THIS MOCHE CERAMIC *bottle reflects the rich tradition of anthropomorphized animal figures and fierceness, with a fanged feline head, human hands, serpents and warrior insignia.*

MOCHE MOUNTAIN GOD

was a remote and nameless deity with *FELINE* features depicted on *MOCHE* pottery and textiles. He seems to have been a creator god and sky god, but played little part in the affairs of humankind. He was closely associated with *AI APAEC*, who might have been his son.

MOCHICA see *MOCHE*.

MOIETY,

an anthropological term borrowed from the French word for "half" (*moitié*), describes two-part divisions for groups of *AYLLUS*. The organizational device was used throughout the Inca Empire and in precursor cultures. In Inca times, the two moieties were called *hanan* ("upper") and *hurin* ("lower"). The parts were frequently used in recognition of locally important land and water distribution rights, and/or in memory and respect for more ancient complementary oppositions within local or regional social and economic structures – for example pastoralists and agriculturalists, indigenous peoples and invaders, or highlanders and lowlanders.

MONAN

is the creator god of the Tupinambá tribe in Brazil, who live around the mouth of the Tocantins River, southeast of the mouth of the Amazon. He made the sky, the earth and the animals. Then he made humans, but they behaved so badly that Monan destroyed them in a huge fire. Only one man, named Irin-Maje, survived the flames when Monan sent water, which became the ocean, to put out the fire.

After Monan came Maire Monan, who gave names to all the animals and taught the Tupinambá agriculture and the art of civilization.

MORADUCHAYOQ TEMPLE

see *HUARI*.

MUISAK see *HEADHUNTING*.

MUISCA see *CHIBCHA*.

ÑAMCA see *MAMA ÑAMCA*.

NAPA

was a miniature llama figurine alleged by *MANCO CAPAC* to have been left behind unintentionally in the cave of *TAMBO TOCO*.

NASCA see *NAZCA*.

NAYAMLAP

was the principal character in a myth concerning the *LAMBAYEQUE VALLEY* on the north coast of Peru, one of the few accounts of legendary heroes known from outside the Andean highlands. He was the leader of the primordial sea peoples who invaded the valley in a time that seems to have stretched far back in the folk memories of the region.

Nayamlap led a "brave and noble company" of men and women on a fleet of balsawood rafts from somewhere south of the Lambayeque Valley. He was accompanied by his wife, Ceterni, his

NAPA was the miniature llama figurine forgotten by Manco Capac in the cave of Tambo Toco. (BRITISH MUSEUM; GOLD)

harem and 40 followers, among whom the legend lists a trumpeter, a guardian of the royal litter, a craftsman whose task it was to grind conch shells into powder for ritual purposes, a cook and other special attendants and servants. Nayamlap also brought with him a special green stone figurine, the idol known as Yampallec (which is regarded as the origin of the name of the valley). The visage, stature and figure of the idol was a double of the king.

Nayamlap and his men invaded the valley and built a palace at the place called Chot, which archaeologists have identified as the site of Huaca Chotuna in the Lambayeque Valley. The conquest of the local peoples was successful, and the invaders and invaded settled down together in peace. After a long life, Nayamlap died and was buried in the palace; he had arranged in secret with his priests, however, that they should tell his people that upon his death he had sprouted wings and flown away into the sky.

Nayamlap was succeeded by his eldest son, *CIUM*, and by ten other kings in his dynasty, which lasted until the last ruler, *FEMPELLEC*, brought dishonour and disaster to the kingdom.

NAYAMLAP led his band of followers to invade the Lambayeque Valley, bringing with him the green stone idol Yampallec, a deity perhaps represented by this Chimú tumi ceremonial knife handle, made of gold and inlaid with turquoise.

THE NAZCA *culture was associated in particular with geoglyphs and textiles. Geoglyphs could be figures, lines or cleared areas. The famous hummingbird is formed by a single, continuous ritual line.*

THE NAZCA were a people and culture that flourished in the south coastal region of Peru, in the Nazca and adjacent valleys, from about 200 BC to AD 500 through the Early Intermediate Period; the Nazca were roughly contemporary with the *MOCHE* culture in the northern coastal valleys. Two of the most important Nazca settlements were *CAHUACHI* and Ventilla, the first a ritual "city", the second an urban "capital". Ventilla, by far the largest Nazca site recorded, covered an area of at least 200 hectares (495 acres) with terraced housing, walled courts, and small mounds. It was linked to its ceremonial and ritual counterpart by a "Nazca line" across the intervening desert.

Over the centuries, increasing drought in the highlands to the east caused an ever-growing aridity in the coastal plains. Such was the pressure to obtain water that the Nazca people invented an ingenious system of subterranean aqueducts and galleries to collect and channel the underground waters around Cahuachi, to minimize evaporation and to provide at least a small amount of water in the dry season. Access to the galleries is down spiral paths, whose sides were immaculately terraced using smooth river cobbles.

The characteristic artefacts of Nazca culture were textiles and ceramics, the styles of both of which carried on in similar traditions from those of the preceding *PARACAS* culture in the same general area. Both of these media were decorated with mythical beings and deities in a society that was apparently highly preoccupied with and motivated by religious iconography and ceremonial ritual. Effigy vessels were decorated with *SERPENT* beings, monkeys and other animals, and some were made in the shapes of trophy heads. These last were a feature of a trophy-head cult that collected caches of the trepanned, severed skulls of sacrificial victims in Nazca cemeteries.

The dominance of daily life by ritual was further emphasized across the desert *pampa* floor in the form of geoglyphs. These Nazca "lines" began to be made as early as the settlements at Cahuachi, Ventilla and other sites, but increased in number and complexity as Cahuachi was abandoned. They were made by scraping aside the darker surface gravel to expose the underlying lighter rock, and the region's aridity itself has been instrumental in preserving them. (Experimental archaeology has shown that it would have taken little effort and time to create the geoglyphs. In one experiment, nearly 1.6 hectares/4 acres of desert was cleared in about a week.)

There are two principal types of geoglyph: figures on hillsides, placed in such a way that they are obvious to travellers on the plains below; and lines, both straight and curving. Various lines and sets of lines form numerous geometric patterns, clusters of straight lines, and also sometimes recognizable figures, such as animals or birds. Individual straight lines of different widths stretch for long distances across the *pampa* desert, some for more than 20 km (12½ miles). Altogether there are some 1,300 km (808 miles) of such lines. One famous set forms a huge arrow, approximately 490 m (1,600 ft)

THE WEALTH *of Nazca geoglyphs, especially ritual lines and cleared spaces crossing and overlapping each other, shows that they were used over a long period of time and often abandoned.*

long, pointing towards the Pacific Ocean, and is thought to be a symbol to invoke rains.

Figures include a hummingbird, a duckling, a spider, a killer whale, a monkey, a llama, several plants and anthropomorphic figures, as well as trapezoids and triangles of cleared areas, zig-zags and spirals. The patterns and figures often resemble those used to decorate Nazca textiles and ceramic vessels. Although the lines frequently cross, individual patterns or figures are each made of a single, continuous line. Altogether there are some 300 such figures, and, combined with the lines, about 360 hectares (890 acres) of *pampa* floor have been scraped away to create them.

Argument has raged for more than 60 years over the meaning

and purpose of the geoglyphs. Among the theories that have been put forward are proposals ranging from their having been made by beings from outer space – for which there is categorically no evidence – to their use in the making of astronomical observations – which seems quite plausible but which has not been conclusively demonstrated as yet.

The most convincing, and indeed obvious, explanation of their meaning is linked to the very nature of the landscape, climate and accompanying features of Nazca settlement and material culture. The lines were associated with the Nazcas' necessary preoccupation with water and the fertility of their crops, together with the worship of mountains – the ultimate source of irrigation waters – and a pantheon of deities or supernatural beings, who were believed to be responsible for bringing or withholding the rains. Sets of lines frequently radiate from "ray centres"

"OREJONES" was a name given by the Spaniards to Inca nobility after the fashion of enlarging the earlobes by the insertion of golden spools. The practice predated the Inca, as shown by this Moche gold mask.

on hills – 62 such nodes have been identified so far – and some of the lines lead to irrigated oases. The animal and other figures each comprise a single line with different beginning and ending points.

The sheer number of lines and the fact that they were made over a period of some seven to eight hundred years, over-marking each other in great profusion, shows that they were not conceived in any grand overall plan. As with the profusion of ceremonial kin-group mounds at their sacred "city" at Cahuachi, the Nazca lines and figures appear to have been made by and for small groups – or perhaps even individuals – each for a separate but confederately agreed purpose. "Solid" cleared areas might have been for congregations of participants, while "outlines" of figures probably formed the routes of ritual pathways to be walked with specific resolutions and outcomes in mind, by a people and culture attempting to farm their landscape, practise their specialized crafts and make sense of the deeper meanings of their lives through ritual communion with their gods.

Although we do not know the names of Nazca deities, their images appear on pottery and textiles as well as in the geoglyphs. Anthropomorphic and composite beings abound, and, in particular, the Oculate Being (see *PARACAS*) was inherited from the preceding Paracas culture.

NEMTEREQUETEBA, a legendary culture hero of the *CHIBCHA*, was believed to have come from a distant land. He was an old man with a long beard and hair, who travelled around the land teaching the Chibcha and others the art of weaving and civilized behaviour.

His rival was the goddess *HUITACA* (see also *BOCHICA*, *CONIRAYA VIRACOCHA*, *ROAL*, *THUNUPA VIRA-COCHA* and *VIRACOCHA*).

NEW TEMPLE see *CHAVÍN*.

NI was the *CHIMÚ* deity of the western sea (that is, the Pacific Ocean) over which the supreme deity, *SI*, travelled.

NIGHT-TIME SUN (that is, the sun after sunset, when it was thought to pass through a hidden, watery passage into the underworld until the next sunrise) was a deity of the *GUARI* lineage *AYLLU* of *CAJATAMBO*.

NOSJTHEJ see *EL-LAL*.

NYAMI ABE (*TUKANO*), literally the "Night Sun", that is, the moon (see *PAGE ABE*).

OCLLO see *MAMA OCLLO*.

OCLLO HUACO see *MAMA OCLLO*.

OCULATE BEING see under *PARACAS*.

THE OI were a legendary or mythical race of beings from the remote past whom the tribes along the *XINGU RIVER* of Brazil believe existed until quite recently. The Oi were tall people who sang in chorus as they travelled through the forest. Because they were frequently heard by the tribes, and only died out lately, their chants

became known and are still sung by the Xingu tribes (see also the *MINATA-KARAIA*).

OLD TEMPLE see *CHAVÍN*.

OMAM is the *YANOMAMI* creator god, a beneficent deity who made the earth, the sky, sun and moon, humans, all the animals and plants on the earth and everything else that exists.

In the beginning the earth had two layers, but now there are three layers because the upper layer of the original two became worn and a large section fell away. There were two men on the part that became detached, one of whom was Omam. One day while he was fishing, Omam hooked and pulled a woman from the river, but she had no genitalia – only a hole the size of a hummingbird's anus. So Omam took piranha teeth and made sexual organs for the woman. With her, he then proceeded to father many children, the ancestors of the Yanomami. The other races of humans are believed by the Yanomami to have been made of river mist and foam, fashioned into humans of different colours by a huge bird.

ONA are a tribe of Tierra del Fuego (see *EL-LAL*, *KASPI* and *TEMAUKEL*).

OREJONES ("big ears" in Spanish) was an epithet applied to the *INCA* nobility, owing to their practice of piercing their ears and enlarging them by inserting golden

spools. When *VIRACOCHA* summoned *ALCAVICÇA* from the earth at *CUZCO*, he also commanded the *orejones* to rise from the ground, and gave them his divine sanction for rulership.

ORQO-CILAY ("multicoloured llama") was one of the luminary star groups that the *INCA* recognized within *MAYU*, the Milky Way. It was believed to protect the royal llama herd.

PACARITAMBO, also Pacari Tambo, Pacaritampum or Pacariqtambo, was the land in which lay the *TAMBO TOCO* caves, the legendary place of origin of the *INCA* ancestors (see *MANCO CAPAC*, *MAUQALLQTA*).

PACATNAMÚ, a spectacularly cited ceremonial centre on the cliffs above the Jequetepeque River in northern Peru, was a *MOCHE* religious pilgrimage centre in the Early Intermediate Period and later. It has been compared in importance to the coastal pilgrimage centre at *PACHACAMAC*, and, like that site, it retained its ceremonial importance into much later periods, and even after its abandonment as a place of residence around 1370.

PACARITAMBO was where the Inca ancestors emerged from the caves of Tambo Toco. (SKETCH BY FELIPE GUAMAN POMA DE AYALA FROM THE NUEVA CORÓNICA Y BUEN GOBIERNO, 1583–1613.)

P

63

DIVINE KINGSHIP &
ANCESTOR REVERENCE

INTI THE SUN GOD, *the official deity of Inca rulership and the Sapa Inca – the emperor was regarded as the sun's representative on earth. Niches in the walls of the Coricancha Temple to Inti held sheet gold masks, such as this example, which would have formed part of the emperor's accoutrement on ceremonial occasions.*

THE INCAS regarded their emperor, Sapa Inca, as the divine sun's representative on earth, and his principal wife, the Qoya, as the moon's. Persistent iconography and religious imagery makes it logical to interpret these beliefs as the culmination of attitudes in earlier Andean civilizations. One pre-Inca example is the ruler Nayamlap in the Lambayeque Valley, who contrived with his priests to convince his subjects of his divine nature after death. Rich Moche, Sicán and Chimú burials similarly indicate the development of the idea of divine kingship.

Despite the official state view, however, rulership of the Inca Empire began and ended in rivalry – in the conflict between Urco and Pachacuti Inca Yupanqui over the succession to Viracocha Inca, and, when the Inca ideal of rulership by divine right of descent went awry, in a bloody civil war, less than a decade before the Spanish conquest.

Ancestor worship was widespread among Andean civilization. Physical manifestations of such reverence are well documented among the Inca in the mummified remains – *mallquis* – of Inca rulers and queens. Dedicated cults cared for *mallquis*, housed in the Coricancha Temple in Cuzco and accorded them special honours at ceremonies. Similarly, the *mallquis* of rulers and ancestors of provincial towns were kept in special buildings or in caves and honoured at ceremonies. The care for and elaborate nature of Nazca burials at Cahuachi and the rich burials of Moche lords, in the Moche and Lambayeque valleys, to cite just two examples, show that reverence for ancestors was a theme that began in the earliest Andean civilizations. In the 15th century, at Chan Chan, the Chimú made a substantial industry of ruler worship.

EARLY EVIDENCE of Andean ancestor reverence comes from the hundreds of burials (left) now decaying on the desert floor at Nazca. Nazca burials were accompanied by rich ceramics and textiles wrapped around the mummy.

THE CHIMÚ, the Incas and other Late Horizon peoples wrapped honoured ancestors in mummy bundles (above) and stored them for regular ceremonial display rather than burying them. Numerous whole mummies have been found, as well as parts from mummy bundles. A typical, probably 15th-century, example is this Chimú mummy bundle wrapped in woven textiles and given a "head".

TO COMPLETE a mummy bundle, a mask or head was often added. A Late Horizon Chimú beaten copper mummy mask (left) is painted red and decorated with two feather headbands and two flutes; a carved and painted wooden Inca mummy head (right) has inlaid shell eyes and is wearing a tapestry headband.

NUMEROUS chullpa burial towers (right) were used as the mausoleums of ruling families in the "Aymara kingdoms" of the Titicaca Basin in the Late Intermediate Period (c. AD 1000–1400) and later, after the Inca conquest of the region. Chullpas were single structures near settlements or separated groups. One of the largest groups is at Sillustani, west of Lake Titicaca. It includes square and round towers, containing as many as 20 or more adult and child bodies.

PACHA KAMAQ

see PACHACAMAC.

PACHACAMAC, or Pacha Kamaq, ("Earth-maker", "Maker of Earth/ time" or "He who embraces the entire Earth") was the ancient creator deity of the peoples of central coastal Peru and adjacent Andes, and a coastal site – a shrine and place of pilgrimage – and city-state. Archaeological evidence shows ceramic and architectural links with the central-southern Andes, and linguistic studies indicate association through the spread of QUECHUA from the region into the highlands.

The site became important in the latter half of the Early Intermediate Period, when the first phases of the pyramid-platform to the sun and adjoining Temple to Pachacamac were built. It was the centre of an important political power during the Middle Horizon, and later became an outpost of HUARI power from the central-southern Andes. The site's continued religious importance is implied by a wooden post carved with figures of Huari divinities, as well as stone figurines. The upper part of the post depicts a man holding a *bola* and wearing a chest ornament; the lower part has double-headed SERPENTS, JAGUARS, and a figure with attributes like those of the "angels" on the Gateway of the Sun at TIAHUANACO.

Pachacamac was the only serious rival to VIRACOCHA for the title of creator god. His following was very ancient and widespread in the central coastal region. The site remained a shrine and potent oracle into INCA times. Like Tiahuanaco, the shrine drew visitors from throughout the central lowland plains and valleys, and from the adjacent Andes. After their con-

THE SITE of Pachacamac became perhaps the most famous pilgrimage site in South America, drawing pilgrims from Andean and coastal peoples alike to the temple built atop a huge artificial mound of adobe bricks.

quest of this region, the Incas went out of their way to reconcile this potential conflict, since the power of feeling for, and longevity of worship of, Pachacamac presented a potential threat to the official state cult of the sun god INTI.

The cult of Pachacamac lasted for more than a millennium and, alongside the sacred CORICANCHA in CUZCO and the ISLAND OF THE SUN in Lake TITICACA, the site was one of the most revered places in the Inca Empire. The Pachacamac–Viracocha–Inti rivalry constituted a mythical manifestation of the distinctions and liaisons between the worlds of the highlands, represented by Viracocha, the coastal lowlands, represented by Pachacamac, and the newcomer official

PACHACAMAC was the "Earth-maker" to whom humankind owed all existence, and to whom continual sacrifices were offered.
(FELIPE GUAMAN POMA DE AYALA, FROM THE *NUEVA CORÓNICA Y BUEN GOBIERNO*, 1583–1613.)

state cult, represented by Inti.

The potency of Pachacamac, and Inca deference to him and to his temple and idol, was described by the 16th-century chronicler Pedro de Cieza de León in his *Crónica del Peru* (Seville, 1550–3): "They say . . . that . . . aside from those at Cuzco . . . there was [no temple] to compare with this at Pachacamac, which was built upon a small, man-made hill of *adobes* and earth, and on its summit stood the temple, [with] many gates, that, like the walls, were adorned with figures of wild animals. Inside, where the idol stood, were the priests who feigned great sanctimoniousness. And when they performed their sacrifices before the people, they kept their faces toward the door of the temple and their backs to the figure of the idol, with their eyes to the ground, and [were] all trembling and overcome. . . Before this figure of the devil they sacrificed many animals, and [offered the] human blood of

persons they killed; and that on the occasion of their most solemn feasts they made utterances which were believed and held to be true. . . The priests were greatly venerated. . . and beside the temple there were many spacious lodgings for those who came in pilgrimage. . . And the Incas, powerful lords that they were, made themselves the masters of the kingdom of Pachacamac, and, as was their custom in all the lands they conquered, they ordered temples and shrines to be built to the sun. And when they saw the splendour of this temple [to Pachacamac], and how old it was, and the sway it held over the people of the surrounding lands, and the devotion [that] they paid [to] it, holding that it would be very difficult to do away with this, they agreed with the native lords and the ministers of their god or devil that this temple of Pachacamac should remain with the authority and cult it possessed, provided [that] they built another temple to the sun, which should take precedence."

The voice of Pachacamac's oracle was sought from near and far, to the extent that devotees petitioned the priesthood there to establish

sibling shrines in their homelands, where Pachacamac was added to their own pantheons. Reciprocally, and in addition to the main temple and oracle, secondary shrines were established at Pachacamac as "wives", "sons" and "daughters" to the "father", some of which were dedicated to the foreign deities of pilgrims. Prophesy from the oracle was sought for everything from health, fortune and the wellbeing of crops and flocks, to the weather, and the prognosis of Inca battle plans.

Clearly, the Incas recognized Pachacamac's influence in the coastal region, and knew that they needed his oracle to achieve their imperial aims. Several Inca emperors adopted Pachacamac's name and included it in their titles, just as others included Viracocha's name. The Temple of the Sun, or *Mamacuna*, at Pachacamac was an Inca construction, acknowledging the site's potency, but also establishing ultimate authority of the state cult in the region.

There are many threads to the mythology of Pachacamac. His cult developed much earlier than and independent of the Inca cult of Inti, but the predominance of ancient contact between coastal lowlands and Andean highlands inevitably brought the two creator gods, Viracocha and Pachacamac, into "contact" long before the Inca compulsion to incorporate all myths and pantheons into their official state religion. At times, the two gods seem to have had distinct identities, at other times they appear to have been identical. The mythology recorded in the *HUAROCHIRÍ MANUSCRIPT*, from a people living midway between highlands and coast, complicates the matter further by substituting the sun for Viracocha in opposition to Pachacamac, as if in recognition of the Inti cult of their new overlords.

To scholars, these conflicts seem confusing yet important. To the Inca, the imposition of all-inclusiveness was paramount, yet they

imposed it by mixing, combining, recognizing the similarities, and acknowledging the variety and nuances of the gods of all the peoples of their empire. In essence, lowland Pachacamac and highland Viracocha have retained a core of similarities. They created the world; they held control over the creation and destruction of the first people; they travelled throughout the land and taught, often in the guise of a beggar; and they met, named and gave their characters to the animals and plants.

In the principal myth of Pachacamac, he was the son of the sun and the moon. An earlier deity known as Con had created the first people, but Pachacamac challenged and overcame him, and transformed the first people into the monkeys.

Pachacamac then created a man and a woman, but because he did not provide them with food, the man died. The woman solicited the sun's help (or in another version accused the sun of neglecting his duty) and in return was impregnated by the sun's rays. When she bore a son, the woman taught the child how to survive by eating wild plants. Pachacamac, jealous of his father the sun's powers, and angered by the woman's independence and apparent defiance, killed the boy and cut his corpse into pieces. Pachacamac then sowed the boy's teeth, which grew into corn (maize); planted the ribs and other bones, which grew into yucca, or manioc, tubers; and planted the flesh, which grew into vegetables

and fruits – an apparent mythical précis of the discovery of cultivation among coastal peoples.

Not to be outdone, the sun took the penis and navel of the boy, and with these created another son for himself, whom he named Vichama (Wichama) or Villama. Pachacamac wanted to kill this child too, but could not catch him, for Vichama had set off on his travels, so he slew the woman/his mother instead, and fed her body to the vultures and condors.

Next, Pachacamac created another man and woman, and these two proceeded to repopulate the world. Pachacamac appointed certain of these people as *CURACAS* (leaders) to rule the rest. In the meantime, Vichama had returned. Miraculously, he found the bits and pieces of his mother, and reassembled her. Pachacamac was in fear of Vichama's reprisal, and rightly so, for the formerly pursued became the pursuer, and Pachacamac was driven, or fled, into the sea, where he sank in front of the place of the temple of Pachacamac/Vichama. In a further act of revenge, Vichama transformed the people of Pachacamac's second creation into stone, but later partly repented and changed the ordinary stone of the *curacas* into sacred *HUACAS*.

Finally, Vichama turned again to his father the sun and asked him to create another race of people. The sun sent three eggs, one of gold, one of silver and one of copper. The gold egg developed into the *curacas* and nobles, the silver became women,

A PILGRIMAGE SITE from about the second or third century AD, Pachacamac endured as a sacred site despite the waxing and waning of kingdoms and empires, exemplified here by two 20th-century pilgrims making an offering.

and the copper egg became commoners. (A variation of the story of the final peopling of the earth, from another coastal group, states that it was Pachacamac who did the deed by sending four stars to earth. Two of these were male, and generated kings and nobles; and the other two were female and generated the commoners.) Thus this second part of the tale seems to be a mythical précis of the creation of the social order of humankind.

These variations in the Pachacamac–Vichama myth demonstrate the mutability and interchangeability of the creator Pachacamac and the creator sun.

In recognition of the power of Pachacamac exhibited in these myths, defiance of his will was believed to provoke earthquakes. Offerings to him in solicitation of his oracular predictions – and no doubt of much use to the cult priests – included cotton, corn (maize), coca (*Erythroxylon coca*) leaves, dried fish, llamas, guinea pigs, fine textiles, ceramic drinking vessels, and gold and silver.

The Incas' need to alleviate the potential conflict between Pachacamac and Viracocha was accomplished in two ways. First, they believed that the primitive peoples of the First "Age" or Sun named their creator variously *TICCI VIRACOCHA*, *CAYLLA VIRACOCHA* or Pachacamac (see *PACHACUTI*) – there was no conflict of interest. Secondly, they incorporated the shrine of Pachacamac and his wife and daughters into their own mythology in the story of the central Andean deity *CONIRAYA VIRACOCHA*. Both amalgamations were presumably attempts to show that the two deities had in fact always been inseparable.

PACHACUTI (*QUECHUA*), a "revolution" or "turning over or around" (*cuti*) of "time and space" (*pacha*), was a millenarian *INCA*/Quechua/*AYMARÁ* concept of succession and renewal that formed a core belief in Andean and Peruvian coastal cosmology and mythology. The Incas thought of themselves as the final stage in a succession of creations and destructions, a notion of cyclicity that has interesting parallels with Aztec and Maya mythology in Mesoamerica. The term was used frequently by the 16th- and 17th-century Spanish and Spanish-taught native chroniclers and, because of its nature, fuelled the fires of Spanish priestly enthusiasm to read Christian sparks of inspiration within ancient native beliefs.

The Incas and many other Andean peoples regarded themselves as living in the world of the Fifth "Age" or Fifth Sun. Each previous Age was thought to have lasted 1,000 years.

The First Age was embryonic, a time of primordial, metaphorical darkness. The people living at that time were called the *Wari Wiracocharuna*, a name whose Quechua

PACHACUTI, the revolution of time, included a cycle of "ages", the first of which was the primordial time when the primitive Wari Wiracocharuna lived. (ILLUSTRATION FROM THE NUEVA CORÓNICA Y BUEN GOBIERNO BY FELIPE GUAMAN POMA DE AYALA, 1583–1613.)

base words mean a camelid hybrid (*wari*); from the crossing of a llama and an alpaca), and "folk" (*runa*). (The element *Wiracocha* is the name of the creator god – *VIRACOCHA* – but in this case was used by the chroniclers to refer to Europeans or Spaniards, who regarded these ancient pre-Incas as related to the people of Noah's ark.) These people were primitive, wore clothing of leaves, and ate only the wild plants that they could collect. They called their creator Ticci Viracocha, Caylla Viracocha or *PACHACAMAC*. It is unclear how the First Age ended.

The Second Age was more advanced, because its people practised rudimentary agriculture. They were called the *Wari Runa* (also hybrids), and they wore clothing of animal skins. They lived simply and peacefully, and recognized Viracocha as their creator. The age of the Second Sun ended in cataclysmic deluge.

The Third Age was inhabited by the *Purun Runa*, the "wild folk". Despite the name, civilization was increasing in complexity: people had learned to spin, dye and weave llama and alpaca wool; they practised more sophisticated agriculture, with a wider variety of crops; and they mined and worked metals to make jewellery. The population of the world increased, and people found it necessary to migrate from the Andes into the lowlands. They lived in towns, each with its own king, and there was conflict between towns and regions. The people generally called their creator Pachacamac in this age.

The Fourth Age was that of the *Auca Runa*, the "warlike folk". In some variations, this age included the beginnings of the Inca Empire, but more tidily, most versions excluded the Incas. At this time the world was divided into four parts. There was increased warfare, and people were forced to live in stone houses and in fortified towns. Like the land divisions, people were divided in this age into *AYLLU* lineages. Technology and standards of

living were more advanced and more complex. How the Third and Fourth Suns ended is not specified.

The Fifth Age was that of the Incas, and it came to an end when the Spaniards arrived. In their belief that a theoretical "Sixth Age" included the inauguration of true beliefs among the people of the Andes, the chroniclers refer to the *Guaca Bilcas*, or supernatural "demons of *CUZCO*", as the corrupters of the people during the Fifth Age – who, it was perceived, must have originally believed in the one true Christian God.

The notion of cyclicity was also endemic in the Inca post-colonial belief in the myth of the return of the Inca (see *INKARRÍ*).

PACHACUTI INCA YUPAN-QUI,

the tenth *INCA* ruler, emerges from legend into history as a real person and Inca leader, and as the

PACHACVTIC YNGA IX.

PACHACUTI INCA YUPANQUI is depicted here with the ceremonial axe-staff of office. ("CUZCO SCHOOL" GENEALOGY, 18TH-CENTURY.)

effective founder of the empire. It was he who began the Inca conquest of neighbouring cities within the Huantanay (Cuzco) Valley and expansion beyond the valley. The traditional dates of his reign are 1438 to 1471.

The rival city-state of *CHANCA*, to the west of *CUZCO*, attacked in the early 15th century during the reign of *VIRACOCHA INCA*. In one version of Inca history, Viracocha Inca repulsed the attack. But the stronger tradition declares Yupanqui to be the saviour of Cuzco, perhaps influenced by selective rewriting of Inca history by the latter. Viracocha Inca had already chosen as his successor his son *INCA URCO*, but when the Chanca

THE STONE TOMB at Kenko near Cuzco is claimed by some to be the tomb of Pachacuti Inca Yupanqui.

attacked the city, much of the populace and both father and son decided to flee into the hills to a distant redoubt. Yupanqui, a somewhat recalcitrant younger prince, stayed behind with a few companions, rallied those who remained and repulsed the first two Chanca assaults. In a third attack, when the fate of Cuzco seemed to hang in the balance, Yupanqui called upon the gods for help and received the assistance of the very rocks and stones, which arose transformed into Inca warriors. Thereafter, these *PURURAUCAS* became Inca objects of worship.

Yupanqui thus began his reign as Inca emperor by usurping his brother Urco and taking the name Pachacuti ("Earth-shaker King"). His subsequent mission of conquest was, as a result of these events, believed to have received divine sanction; and from this time Inca history becomes somewhat less legendary. The chronicles seem less mythical and more purely factual, simply recounting events in the history of Inca conquest. Yupanqui first won over the Valley of Cuzco and made all *QUECHUA*-speakers there honorary Inca citizens. (It is important, however, to bear in mind that, to date, archaeological evidence cannot corroborate any specific events in these Inca legendary histories.)

Pachacuti next turned his attention southeast, to the *TITICACA* Basin, where he conquered and incorporated the Lupaqa, Colla and other kingdoms around the lake. He then returned to Cuzco and turned his armies over to his son and chosen heir, *TUPAC INCA YUPANQUI*, to pursue further expansion of the empire while he devoted his own energies to developing the state and organizing the institutions and systems that would become the hallmarks of Inca rule: national taxation and labour levies, roadways and an imperial communication network, and extensive warehousing of food and other commodities for redistribution throughout the empire.

Pachacuti was further enshrined as an Inca legendary hero, and confirmed as receiving divine help and inspiration, by a legendary event that probably preceded the Chanca war. One day, as Yupanqui drew near to the spring called Susurpuquio near Cuzco, en route to visit his father Viracocha Inca, he saw a crystal tablet fall into it. At the spring, he peered into the waters and saw on the tablet the image of a man wearing a headdress (a *LLAUTO*), ear spools and a tunic like those worn by Inca men. From the headdress shone three sun rays, and snakes coiled around the figure's shoulders; from between his legs jutted the head of a puma, and another puma stood behind him with its paws on the man's shoulders, while a *SERPENT* stretched from the bottom of his back to the top of his head.

Pachacuti retrieved the tablet from the spring, and found that he could use it to see into the future. The Incas believed that he identified the image on the tablet with the creator god *VIRACOCHA PACHAYACHACHIC*, and that this inspiration prompted him to begin a programme of religious reform among the Inca peoples following the defeat of the Chanca and the commencement of his reign. He reorganized the main temple, the *CORICANCHA*, in Cuzco to accommodate and display six principal gods, ranged in the following hierarchy: first *VIRACOCHA* himself, then *INTI* the sun god, *QUILLA* the moon goddess, *CHASKA-QOYLOR* the god of Venus, *ILLAPA* the god of weather, and *CUICHU* the god of the rainbow. Because of his association of the crystal tablet's image with Viracocha, Pachacuti appears, in one interpretation of

PACHACUTI INCA YUPANQUI, the empire builder, was the first Inca emperor of historical credibility. Here he is seen brandishing a sun symbol and warrior's sling. (SKETCH BY FELIPE GUAMAN POMA DE AYALA FROM THE NUEVA CORÓNICA Y BUEN GOBIERNO, 1583–1613.)

these events, to have "promoted" the creator god to a position of superiority, above that of the sun god. On the other hand, this rearrangement of the Coricancha has also been interpreted as increasing the emphasis on Inti's status as a deity of near equal importance to Viracocha, and thus triggering the beginning of a "solarization" of Inca religion. Indeed, according to some sources, Inti also appeared to the young Pachacuti in visions, these apparitions inspiring him to perform great deeds and to strive for the betterment of humankind.

Despite a lack of specific corroborative archaeological evidence, its seems fair to credit Pachacuti with the beginning of the Inca Empire. It also appears justified to associate these myths and legends with the basic, and apparently correct, "facts" that are available involving the Inca state's rise to prominence in the Valley of Cuzco. The essential events of the war with the Chancas (disregarding the supernatural elements) might quite possibly represent the deep-seated oral history of the Incas, recording their overthrow of the final remnants of *HUARI* power in the valley – because the chronicled location of the Chanca state and the homeland of the Huari people coincide. Similarly, the reorganization of Inca religion and of the Coricancha might have been a practical way to record the effective usurpation of the throne by Yupanqui, defying his father, who bore the name of the creator god, and overthrowing his brother, whom his father had chosen as his heir.

There can be no doubt that it was Pachacuti's social manipulations, and his reorganization and formalization of the state religion, as well as his reconstruction of Cuzco, that formed the basis of the vast Inca Empire that was created by him and his successors over the next 90 years, until the arrival of Francisco Pizarro and his Spanish followers.

PACHAMAMA, or Pacha Mama, the *INCA* earth goddess, was a primeval deity responsible for the wellbeing of plants and animals. Her worship is thought to date back to the first constructions of sunken courts at Chavín de Huántar and other Andean sites, and continues to the present day in the form of offerings of *coca* (*Erythroxylon coca*) leaves, *chicha* corn (maize) beer and prayers on all major agricultural occasions. She is sometimes identified as the Virgin Mary of Christianity.

In one myth, the Inca ancestors (see *MANCO CAPAC*) sacrificed and offered a llama to Pachamama before they entered Cuzco to take it over. One of the sister/wives, *MAMA HUACO*, sliced open the animal's chest, extracted the lungs, inflated them with her own breath and carried them into the city alongside Manco Capac, who carried the golden emblem of the sun god *INTI*.

PACHATIRA was the *INCA* collective name used for the "dark cloud" constellations within *MAYU*, the Milky Way, particularly by the people of *MISMINAY*.

PAGE ABE ("Father Sun") was the name of the creator god of the Amazonian *TUKANO*.

According to Tukano cosmology, at the beginning of time there was Page Abe, the sun, and Nyami Abe, the moon (or "Night Sun"). Nyami Abe had no wife and was lonely, so he attempted to force himself on the wife of Page Abe. When Page Abe learned of this, he deprived the moon of his fancy feathered headdress and banished him from the family. Thus never again will the sun and the moon share the same quarter of the sky.

After this incident, Page Abe made the earth and all the plant life and creatures on it, including humans. He was helped in this creation, although not very usefully it seems, by the god *PAMURI-MAHSE*,

BELIEF IN PACHAMAMA, the primeval earth goddess, endures today. At time-honoured sites, traditional offerings of coca leaves and chicha (corn/maize beer) are made to her in modern containers.

and later by his daughter, *ABE MANGO*, who taught humankind many useful skills.

PAHMURI-MAHSE
see *PAMURI-MAHSE*.

PALLUTA was the third place of sojourn of the ancestors during their wanderings as recounted in the *INCA* state foundation myth (see *MANCO CAPAC*).

PAMPA GRANDE see *MOCHE*.

PAMURI-MAHSE was the name of the divine, but not particularly useful, helper of the *TUKANO* creator-god *PAGE ABE*.

According to the myth, among the animals being created, Pamuri-mahse brought down to earth the dangerous beasts, including the large snakes that live along the Amazon. One of these snakes, which had seven heads, fell in love with a young human girl and tried to carry her off with him, but a dog and a medicine man interceded. They fought a fierce battle with the snake, and succeeded in defeating all of the heads. The medicine man lit a fire and burned the snake's carcass, but the smoke and ashes rose into the sky and were blown by the wind out to sea. Over the sea the smoke and ashes fell as rain, and the fearsome snake was reborn.

A variant of the myth tells how the sun god ordered Pamuri-mahse to paddle a huge canoe, shaped like an anaconda snake, up river. At

every place where Pamuri-mahse stopped, a village was established, and the spirit beings taught the people of that village how they should conduct their lives, and instructed them in their customs.

PANACA was the term for the dozen or so royal *AYLLU* kin groups of the *INCA* imperial household. They were considered the direct descendants of the first ten kings of *CUZCO*, and complemented the original ten *ayllus* of the Tambos at *TAMBO TOCO*.

PAQCHA was a carved and painted wooden staff-like device with a bowl on one end, that was used in divination ceremonies by *INCA* priests.

PARACAS, a group of sites and a culture in the southern coastal region of Peru, was one of the first Early Horizon cultures to develop mummification and, probably, ancestor worship, a characteristic of virtually all later Andean and western coastal cultures. Mummies were "bundled" in tight, foetal positions, placed in baskets, and wrapped in multiple layers of high-quality woven and embroidered cotton and llama-wool textiles, displaying a wealth of natural imagery and supernatural mythological iconography that was clearly part of a rich mythology and associated with ritual practices. The burials were accompanied by richly decorated and plainer ceramic vessels, many in the shapes of animal effigies, and by sheet gold ornaments.

THE PARACAS CULTURE Oculate Being was the most prominent deity depicted on burial textiles – here it is depicted as a serpent-tongued, feline-faced anthropomorphic figure with staring eyes.

Among and between sprawling areas of habitation remains around the Paracas peninsula, special sites had been chosen as necropolises for hundreds of burials, each possibly the focus of a family cult. As the numbers of burials appear to exceed the requirements of the immediately adjacent settlements, it is thought that the Paracas necropolises might also have been pilgrimage centres, like the contemporary Chavín de Huántar and the later *PACHACAMAC* ceremonial centres farther north.

Because we lack written accounts for this early period, we can only surmise the names and details of any Paracas deities and ceremonial practices. The imagery shows strong influence from *CHAVÍN*, but soon developed its own regional flavour. Among the images depicted on the textiles, one is especially prominent and has been named the Oculate Being. This deity was portrayed horizontally (as if flying), upside down (perhaps looking down on humankind) and crouching.

THE PARACAS Oculate Being was often depicted repeatedly on textiles, as here, both upright and upside down on an embroidered burial mantle.

"He" has a characteristic, frontal face with large, circular, staring eyes. Long, streaming appendages originate from various parts of his body and end in trophy heads or small figures. The Oculate Being appears to have been a cult image that continued to form an important part of the succeeding NAZCA iconography in the same region. The face is often heart-shaped, and sometimes sprouts a smaller head from its top. On other figures, the Oculate Being wears a headband identical to actual sheet gold headbands found in some of the burials.

PARIACACA was the principal god of the pre-INCA *Checa Yauyos* of the Huarochirí region, in the western Andes of central Peru east of Lima, described in the *HUAROCHIRÍ MANUSCRIPT*. The *Checa* were pastoralist invaders or immigrants, who formed part of the *Lurin* (or "lower") *Yauyos* kinship group.

Pariacaca is described in the manuscript as a high mountain peak, regarded as a sacred HUACA whose spirit was able to move about the landscape in the simultaneous manifestation of a patron deity and culture hero. Among the Huarochirí *Lurin Yauyos*, his rival was the fierce, fire-breathing god *HUALLALLO CARHUINCHO*.

According to the myth, Huallallo Carhuincho had held sway over the people of Huarochirí for some time. Pariacaca was born on the mountain top of that name in the form of five eggs. Each egg became a falcon, and these were then transformed into five men, who became ancestors of the pastoralist *Yauyos*.

In this five-fold existence, Pariacaca arrived at Huarochirí and challenged Huallallo Carhuincho's supremacy. He prophesied that he would defeat Huallallo Carhuincho and drive him from the land. In the battle that ensued, each god used his most potent weapon – fire for Huallallo Carhuincho, and water for Pariacaca.

As five persons, Pariacaca rained down on Huallallo Carhuincho from five directions. He sent yellow rain and red rain, then flashes of lightning from all five directions. In his defence, Huallallo Carhuincho blazed up in the form of a gigantic fire across the countryside, thwarting Pariacaca's every effort to extinguish him. The battle continued from dawn to sunset. The waters of Pariacaca rushed down the mountainsides towards a lake called Ura Cocha. One of Pariacaca's five selves, called Llacsa Churapa, was too big to fit into the basin of the lake, so he swept away an entire mountain in order to block the waters from lower down and form a new, larger lake. As Llacsa Churapa's waters filled this lake, they rose up over the land and quenched Huallallo Carhuincho's fires. However, Huallallo Carhuincho refused to give up. Pariacaca continued to hurl lightning bolts at him from all directions, never allowing him a moment's rest, until

PUKU is the name of this typical Inca Pucara or hill fortification. It is situated near Cuzco.

finally Huallallo Carhuincho gave in and fled north to the lowlands of Antis (ANTISUYU).

Huallallo Carhuincho was not without allies, however, and the fight was not over. A female *huaca* called MAMA ÑAMCA attacked Pariacaca, and he was forced to defeat her as well, driving her west into the ocean.

These mythical battles appear to contain the historical kernel of a much telescoped history of the region. It can be argued that they strongly reflect what might have been a campaign of several battles, in which mountain pastoralist *Checa Yauyos* invaded Huarochirí, defeating the agriculturalist *Concha Yauyos* and driving at least some of them away. Perhaps allies of the latter arrived too late and were driven back into the sea. Nevertheless, there does not appear to have been a complete displacement of the peoples, since the Huarochirí Manuscript was written from the point of view of both of the *Lurin Yauyos* subgroups – pastoralists and agriculturalists.

More generally, the character and powers ascribed to Pariacaca in the manuscript reveal him to have been the god of rain, storms and floods, who was worshipped by the peoples of ancient western Peru (see also *HUATHIACURI*).

PERIBORIWA is the *YANOMAMI* moon spirit. The Yanomami call themselves "the fierce people", according to their belief that in the beginning the moon spirit spilled on to the earth and changed into

men as it touched the ground. Thus born of "blood", the Yanomami regard themselves as naturally fierce and aggressive, and must thus make continual war on one another.

A later descendant of Periboriwa gave birth to more docile men and to women.

PIKILLACTA was a Middle Horizon *HUARI* regional religious and political centre. It was established in about AD 650, and remained a ceremonial centre for the élite for about 300 years. Its vast complex of more than 700 rigidly planned structures with few doorways and corridors suggests a centre of special purpose and strictly controlled access and movement.

PILLAN, a deity of the *AUCA* peoples of northern Chile, was the god of sudden natural catastrophe, who sent storms, floods and volcanic eruptions to menace humankind.

PIPTADENIA SNUFF see *SHAMAN*.

PONCE STELA see under *TIAHUANACO*.

PONGMASSA see under *CHIMO CAPAC*.

PUCARA, or Pukara, was a general INCA term for a stone house or fortification in the mountains. The people of the Fourth Age, the *Auca Runa* (see *PACHACUTI*) had particular need of them in that period of increasing warfare.

THIS STONE *serpent carving is typical of the Early Intermediate Period site of Pukara near Lake Titicaca.*

PUKARA was an Early Intermediate Period ceremonial centre in the TITICACA Basin, a precursor to the rise of TIAHUANACO. It was occupied from *c.* 200 BC to *c.* AD 200 and displayed numerous stone stelae carved with FELINE, SERPENT, fish and lizard iconographic imagery. Its influence extended some 150 km (90 miles) to the north.

PUMAPUNKU TEMPLE see TIAHUANACO.

PURUN RUNA were the people of the Third Sun (see PACHACUTI).

PURURAUCAS were the stones miraculously metamorphosed by the gods into warriors at the eleventh hour during the siege of CUZCO. In INCA legendary history, PACHACUTI INCA YUPANQUI called upon divine help in the war against the CHANCAS, whereupon the stones in the fields rose up as armed men to fight beside the Incas. After the battle, Pachacuti ordered that the stones be gathered up and distributed among the city's shrines. As objects of worship the stones became HUACAS, sacred places.

Q'ERO was a town and people in the Valley of CUZCO (see ROAL).

QOCHA see MAMA COCA.

QORI KANCHA (literally "building of gold") see CORICANCHA.

QOYA, the INCA "queen" or "empress", was the principal wife of the SAPA INCA. In late imperial times and at the time of the Spanish arrival, she would also have been the Inca's sister. She was regarded as the earthly embodiment of the moon, QUILLA and, in that role, she regulated the tempo of ritual activity in CUZCO, in keeping with the lunar cycles.

QOYLOR was the general QUECHUA term for the stars (see, for example, CHASKA-QOYLOR).

QUAPAQ HUCHA see CAPACOCHA.

QUECHUA was the language of the INCA and, more generally, of central Peru. It served as the *lingua franca* of the Inca Empire, and is still spoken in Andean regions of Peru, Ecuador and Bolivia.

QUILLA was the INCA moon goddess. Just as the SAPA INCA, the emperor, was regarded as the earthly embodiment of the sun, his primary wife, the QOYA, was regarded as the embodiment of the moon on earth. One of the temples in the sacred CORICANCHA precinct in CUZCO was dedicated to her, and held her image, made of silver. The mummified bodies (MALLQUIS) of former Qoyas were kept in the temple and brought out on ritual occasions (for example, an October spring moon festival), when they were dressed in sumptuous clothes and jewellery, offered food and drink, and, like the mummies of the former emperors, carried on biers in processions.

QUILLA, *the moon goddess, was represented by the Qoya, principal wife of the Sapa Inca. As well as her temple in the Coricancha in Cuzco, she was also honoured with a temple at Machu Picchu (right).*

An eclipse of the moon was believed by the Inca to be an attempt by a huge celestial SERPENT or mountain lion to eat Quilla. During such events, they would gather in force in their sacred precincts and make as much noise as possible in order to scare off the creature.

QUIPUCAMAYOQS ("knot-makers") were the keepers of the QUIPUS. They were charged with recording official information of a statistical nature and also with tying the coded knots that served, in a manner not yet fully understood, as aids to recalling and narrating INCA myth, legend and history. Alongside their colleagues, the AMAUTAS, they were a principal source of Inca history, religious belief and social organization to Spanish chroniclers. Like the *amautas*, the *quipucamayoqs* must have struggled continually to keep the official state records straight

QOYA *was the Inca empress as well as being the representative of the moon on earth.* (ILLUSTRATION BY FELIPE GUAMAN POMA DE AYALA, FROM THE NUEVA CORÓNICA Y BUEN GOBIERNO, 1583–1613.)

and to reconcile the histories and beliefs of conquered peoples.

One document in particular, the *Relación de los Quipucamayoqs*, provides an example of their role. It was written in Spain in 1608, but was composed of materials assembled to support the claims of a hopeful late pretender to the Inca throne, one Melchior Carlos Inca. In his claim, he attempted to add depth and weight to his legitimacy by incorporating a version of the early foundation of CUZCO. His source was the manuscript of an inquest held in 1542, the informants at which were four elderly *quipucamayoqs* who had served the Inca before the Spanish conquest; their information provides some of the earliest known versions of the Inca state origins. Likewise, in his *Historia de los Incas* (1572) the Spaniard Sarmiento de Gamboa asserts that he interviewed more than 100 *quipucamayoqs*, and actually names 42 of them. This, too, is one of the earliest sources for Inca myth and legend.

QUIPUS (INCA), from the QUECHUA word for "knot", were linked bundles of knotted and dyed string, usually of twisted cotton, but sometimes also of wool. They were used to record, and served as

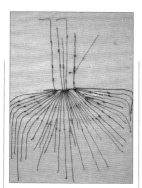

A QUIPU (above left) was a bundle of knotted string that a quipucamayoq (above right) used to record information and Inca narratives. (FELIPE GUAMAN POMA DE AYALA, THE NUEVA CORÓNICA Y BUEN GOBIERNO, 1583–1613.)

aide-mémoires for official Inca statistical information (for example, censuses and tribute accounts) and historical information, including their myths and legends.

QUIRIRMANTA

QUIRIRMANTA was the fifth place of sojourn of the Inca ancestors during their wanderings, as recounted in the state foundation myth (see MANCO CAPAC).

RAIMONDI STELA

RAIMONDI STELA see CHAVÍN.

RAUA

RAUA see MAMA RAUA.

ROAL

ROAL was a creator god of the Q'ero in the Valley of Cuzco. Their account of creation has elements in common with the creation story of VIRACOCHA and with the legend of MANCO CAPAC. The world was a dark place, unlit by the sun and inhabited by a race of powerful primeval beings. Roal, the creator, offered the gift of his power to these people, but they boasted that they were so mighty that they had no need of the god's power. This angered Roal, so to punish them he created the sun, which blinded the people and dried them up, but did not destroy them. The Q'ero believed that these beings still came out from their hiding places at sunset and at the time of the new moon.

According to the myth, the APUS (mountain spirits) then brought

forth a man and a woman, and named them Inkari and Collari. They gave Inkari a golden bar and instructed him to establish a city where the bar, when he hurled it into the sky, would come down and stand upright in the earth. The first time that Inkari threw the bar, it landed badly and did not stick. A second attempt ended with the bar lodged in the earth at an angle, but despite this Inkari built the town of Q'ero. The Apus regarded this as disobedience and attempted to punish Inkari by resurrecting the primeval men, who attempted to kill Inkari by rolling huge stone blocks at him. Inkari fled in terror to the TITICACA Basin.

Later he returned to the Valley of Cuzco and threw the golden bar into the air a third time, and this time it fell straight. So, at this site, Inkari founded CUZCO. He sent his eldest son to nearby Q'ero to re-populate that community, while the rest of his descendants became the INCAS. Along with Collari, Inkari then travelled throughout the Andes teaching the art of civilization until the two of them finally disappeared into the rain forest to the east.

SACSAHUAMAN

SACSAHUAMAN ("royal eagle") forms the northwestern end of the INCA imperial capital at CUZCO. The city was planned by PACHACUTI INCA YUPANQUI, and from an aerial perspective the outline of the Inca

SACSAHUAMAN, overlooking Cuzco, forms the head of the feline plan of the city, and was the sacred precinct built by Pachacuti Inca Yupanqui.

buildings and wall along the edge of the city forms the image of a puma in profile. The redoubt of Sacsahuaman forms the "head" of the cat, while the sacred CORICAN-CHA precinct forms the "tail".

One side of the Sacsahuaman complex runs along a cliff edge and overlooks the rest of the capital. The opposite side, sloping more gently, was encased in three successive tiers of zig-zag terracing. The huge polygonal stone blocks used in the walls were shaped and fitted together precisely; each one weighed between 90 and over 120 tonnes, and some came from as far as Rumiqolqa quarry 35 km (22 miles) southeast. The hilltop thus enclosed was flattened to accommodate a complex of ashlar buildings, including two huge towers, one circular and one rectangular, linked by alleys and staircases, incorporating a sophisticated system of stone channels and drainage chambers. The 16th-century Spanish chronicles record that 30,000 MIT'A workers were employed in its construction.

The imposing nature of Sacsahuaman has led some observers to conclude that it was built primarily as a fortress. The 16th-17th-century chronicler Garcilaso de la Vega said that it was a depository of "arms, clubs, lances, bows, arrows, axes, shields, heavy jackets of quilted cotton [armour] and other weapons of different types", but also declared that only Inca royalty and nobility were allowed to enter the precinct because it was the house of the sun,

INTI, a temple for priestly prayer and a place for sacrifice. The 16th-century Spanish conquistador and chronicler, Pedro de Cieza de León, however, stated in his *Crónica del Peru* (Seville, 1550–3) that from the start of its construction Pachacuti Inca Yupanqui planned it as a temple complex.

This information, written not long after its construction in the mid- to late 15th century, seems to support both interpretations. The manner in which Pachacuti gained his throne – by usurping his half-brother INCA URCO, who had been the chosen successor of his father VIRACOCHA INCA – also tends to support both arguments: the position of the complex would certainly have been advantageous for defence; equally, the site was ideal for the observation of the Milky Way (see MAYU) and other celestial bodies so important in Inca cosmology, calendrical calculations and the confirmation of mythological concepts. A wide esplanade forms a levelled space between the terraces or ramparts and a large, carved stone outcrop opposite. It has been suggested that this was a venue for staged ritual battles similar to those recorded by the chroniclers to have taken place in the capital's square below. Finally, the elaborate system constructed for channelling water through the precinct suggests its ritual manipulation, which appears to have been an ancient and common Andean practice (see CHAVÍN, MACHU PICCHU, TIAHUANACO).

HUMAN SACRIFICE
& CANNIBALISM

HUMAN SACRIFICE was widespread in ancient Andean culture. It was regarded as a sacred ritual to secure the favour of the gods, and appears to have been practised from the earliest of times. Evidence for strangulation, throat-slitting, clubbing to death and trepanning (penetrating the skull) has been found in the burials at Cahuachi, Moche Sipán and in the high mountain *capacocha* (child-sacrifice) sites, apparently often used, of Ampato, Llullaillaco and others. The Incas held annual ritual sacrifices of children and adults from all over their empire.

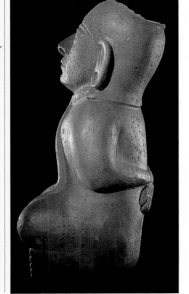

Among the tribes of the rain forest, ritual cannibalism was, until fairly recently, practised as a form of ancestor reverence: preserving the powers and character of an ancestor through "endo-cannibalism" or, through head-hunting and "exo-cannibalism", of capturing and holding, out of fear, the power of enemies.

THE MOCHE were particularly graphic and prolific in their representations of human sacrifice. Scenes were painted on pottery and on temple and tomb murals, frequently featuring the Decapitator God. Portable objects served as constant reminders of the practice, as in this redware (with traces of white paint) figurine (left and above) showing a sacrificial prisoner with his hands bound behind his back, while a second cord is tied around his neck and to his penis.

THE FRIGHTENING SCENE of a sacrifice in progress is shown on this Moche stirrup-spout ceramic bottle (above). Gripping the victim's hair to yank the head back, the priest/executioner, wearing a fierce-looking stag helmet, is about to slit the victim's throat – one of several common methods of execution. It is impossible to tell whether the victim's visage represents fear, resignation or a drugged state.

THE WEAPON normally used in execution by slitting the throat was the sacrificial tumi knife (left). Their characteristic, workman-like crescent-shaped copper blades were frequently elaborately decorated with exquisite gold handles, particularly in the Late Intermediate Period (c. AD 1000–1400) Sicán culture. This example has the large earspools, elaborate headdress and winged shoulders of the Sipán Lord.

SEVERED HEADS, a public reminder of sacrifice, were displayed in many ancient Andean cultures. For example, decapitated heads feature in early Chavín low-relief stone wall decoration and as stone heads tenoned into temple walls at Tiahuanaco. Portable examples are also found, such as this otherwise unprovenanced ceramic example (above), made as a container, from Peru.

SAPA INCA ("sole" or "unique" Inca) was the title of the ruling *INCA* emperor. He was believed to be the direct descendant of the founder of the dynasty, *MANCO CAPAC*, and the manifestation on earth of the sun, *INTI*. In this capacity, his presence brought light and warmth to make the world habitable.

SEMI-SUBTERRANEAN TEMPLE see *TIAHUANACO*.

SERPENTS, like *FELINES*, *JAGUARS* and fanged beasts, were a pan-Andean source of religious iconography. They figure frequently in all media: wall painting, stone carving, ceramic decoration, textiles and metalwork. They were a frequent element in the imagery of the deities of almost all the major cultures of the Andes and western coast, from Early Horizon *CHAVÍN* and *PARACAS*, via Early Intermediate Period *MOCHE*, *NAZCA* and *PACHACAMAC*, and Middle Horizon *HUARI* and *TIAHUANACO*, to the empires of *CHIMÚ* and the *INCA*.

SHAMAN (plural: shamans) is the anthropological term for a person who is in possession of special powers, usually aided by the use of hallucinatory plant drugs, which enable the shaman to gain access to the spirit world.

A YANOMAMI SHAMAN is seen taking hallucinogenic snuff in order to induce a trance and to enter the spirit world.

The tropical rain forest tribes of Central and South America believe that everything that happens on earth has a spirit-world cause and/or consequence. But the spirits are ambivalent, even fickle, in their relationships with humankind, and their powers must therefore be harnessed and channelled, even if only temporarily, and interpreted by an intermediary or medium. Thus the shaman is a combination

SERPENTINE and fanged figures pervaded Andean and coastal religious imagery in all media, such as this serpent-man figure from the coastal site of La Tolita, Ecuador.

of sorcerer, curer, spiritual interpreter and diviner, and also the upholder of the codes of the social moral order and the dispenser of justice.

Through the use of hallucinatory plant drugs – for example *ayahuasca*, *vihoo* or *Piptadenia* snuff mixed with tobacco or in drink – the shaman can temporarily enter the spirit world on behalf of the tribe and negotiate with the spirits on equal terms. Through this "window", he is able to understand the true nature of things, to explain events past and present, and even to divine the future and suggest appropriate courses of action. He can rid the village of pestilence and illness or send such ailments to enemies; or ensure the success of the hunt.

Entering of the spirit world is frequently done at night, when the shaman is believed to become transformed into another body. Those who become a *JAGUAR* are the most feared of all; to accomplish this feat, the shaman dons a jaguar skin and necklace of jaguar teeth or claws – often from animals he has slain himself – and in a trance growls and howls like a jaguar. Among the northwestern Amazon and Orinoco tribes, the shaman's drugs are sometimes referred to as "the jaguar's drug", or even "the jaguar's sperm", and are kept in a hollowed-out jaguar bone.

The shaman's visions are imbued with religious significance and give the tribe knowledge of the "mythological" past of "the ancestors". Connection with the past is believed by many to continue after the death of the shaman, who then becomes one of the ancestors, and whose powers continue to protect the village and tribe from the malevolent spirits and from the malicious intentions of shamans from other villages or tribes.

SI was the *MOCHE* and (later) *CHIMÚ* moon goddess, or god, and overlord of the Moche and Chimú pantheons. S/he was the supreme deity, omnipresent, and held sway over the gods and humankind due to her/his control of the seasons, natural elements and storms, and therefore agricultural fertility. Her/his origins have been traced to an earlier unnamed radiant and armoured goddess/god of war, who was related to or replaced *AI APAEC* in importance. One source refers to Si-an, a Chimú temple dedicated to Si, interpreted as Huaca Singan in the Jequetepeque Valley, possibly the structure known today as Huaca del Dragón.

The Moche and Chimú peoples became aware that the tides and other motions of the sea, as well as the arrival of the annual rains, were linked to the phases of the moon. For these reasons they allocated great power to Si, because their food supply and the wellbeing of their flocks were dependent upon her/his beneficence; in contrast, the sun was considered by them to be a relatively minor deity. Si was also regarded as more powerful than the sun because s/he could be seen by both night and day. Eclipses were believed by them to be battles between the moon and sun. An eclipse of the moon was considered a disastrous augury to be regarded with fear, while an eclipse of the sun was treated as a joyful occasion.

Si was also regarded as the protector of public property, for s/he could reveal thieves in the night. Given the tightly controlled redistribution mechanisms of Chimú society, revealed in the organization of the royal compounds at their capital Chan Chan, the importance of property and a protector thereof is understandable.

SICÁN was a later Middle Horizon-Late Intermediate Period culture in the *LAMBAYEQUE* Valley (see *BATÁN GRANDE* and *TÚCUME*).

upturned mouth has fangs, but whether it was a distinct deity or one of the many manifestations of the *FANGED GOD* is difficult to say.

SINAA is the *FELINE* ancestor of the people of the Brazilian Juruna tribe in the *XINGU RIVER* region. He was born of a huge jaguar father and a human mother. Although very old, Sinaa regains his youth every time he bathes, when he is said to "pull his skin over his head like a sack". Another of his traits is that, like his father, his eyes are in the back of his head. The Juruna believe that the end of the world will come when Sinaa decides to remove an enormous forked stick that they believe holds up the sky (see also *UAICA*).

SINCHI ROCA was the son of *MANCO CAPAC* and *MAMA OCLLO*, and the legendary second ruler of *CUZCO*. According to different versions of the myth of *INCA* state foundation he was born at the ancestors' second stopping place after leaving *PACARITAMBO*, before reaching the town of *PALLUTA*, or in Cuzco itself. With his father, mother and aunts, he established and organized the construction of the capital. He was also credited with having commanded the people of the Valley of Cuzco to cultivate potatoes – the staple crop when the Spaniards arrived.

SIPÁN is an Early Intermediate Period site in the *LAMBAYEQUE VALLEY*, with rich burials of *MOCHE* lords (see *DECAPITATOR GOD*).

SMILING GOD is an epithet sometimes applied to a deity of the Early Horizon. Like many other images of the *CHAVÍN* culture, its

THE STAFF DEITY was a pan-Andean deity of either gender portrayed as a frontal figure with outstretched arms holding staffs. The image originated in the Early Horizon *CHAVÍN* cult and endured through to the Late Horizon.

SUNKEN COURTYARD TEMPLES see under *CHAVÍN*, *FANGED GOD* and *PACHAMAMA*.

SUSURPUQUIO was the name of the spring outside *CUZCO* where *PACHACUTI INCA YUPANQUI* found a crystal tablet bearing the image of *VIRACOCHA*.

SUTIC TOCO, *INCA*, was one of the caves of *TAMBO TOCO* (see *MANCO CAPAC*).

SUYU was the *INCA* word for a "quarter" in terms of a division of territory. The Inca Empire was divided into four *suyus* (see *TAHUANTINSUYU*).

TAHUANTINSUYU, or Tawantinsuyu, was the *INCA* name for their empire, and literally means "land of the four united quarters". *CUZCO*, the capital, was the focal point from which the four, unequal, quarters were oriented. The four quarters were Antisuyu (northeast), Chinchasuyu (northwest), Cuntisuyu (southwest) and Collasuyu (southeast). Their boundaries were linked to sacred *CEQUE* lines radiating from the *CORICANCHA* in Cuzco, and were thus also associated with four great highways to the provinces, each of which departed from Cuzco along a route approximating an intercardinal axes of *MAYU*, the Milky Way.

Encompassing a vast territory, from modern Ecuador to central Chile north to south, and from the Pacific coast to the eastern flank of the Andes mountain chain west to east, it was inhabited by a great variety peoples and languages. In Inca myth, this diversity was explained by the deliberate actions of *VIRACOCHA*: when he had created the second world of humans from clay, he dispersed them after imbuing them with the accoutrements and languages of the different tribes and nations.

The division of the empire into the four quarters was as such virtually ignored in Inca mythology. One myth, however, recounted in Garcilaso de la Vega's *Commentarios Reales de los Incas*, described this

division as being the work of an *UN-NAMED MAN* who appeared at *TIAHUANACO* after the destruction of a previous world by deluge. This dearth of explanation is especially curious given the emphasis in Inca legendary history on the progress of state creation from Lake *TITICACA* (near the actual geographical centre of the empire) to the north and west. The direction of this progression makes sense for Antisuyu, Chinchasuyu and Cuntisuyu, but not for Collasuyu, which lies almost entirely to the south of Lake Titicaca. One explanation might be that the Incas recast the origin mythology of the peoples of this quarter in order to bolster their own claims to have originated from the Titicaca Basin and to legitimize their right to rule the region, for the ruins of Tiahuanaco and of other great cities of the region must have been recognized as an existing and former power base.

TAMBOCHACAY ("Tambo entrance-bearer") accompanied Ayar Cachi on his return to the *TAMBO TOCO* cave (see *MANCO CAPAC*).

THE TAMBOS were allies of the Inca ancestors (see *MANCO CAPAC*).

TAMBO TOCO ("window house") was the mountain with three caves, from the central one of which the *INCA* ancestors emerged; see *MANCO CAPAC, MAUQALLQTA.*

TAMBO TOCO, the mountain in Pacaritambo with three windows, is mirrored by the Temple of Three Windows at Machu Picchu (above).

TARAPACA was one of many names for *VIRACOCHA.*

TAWANTINSUYU see *TAHUANTINSUYU.*

TAYCANAMU was the founder of a new *CHIMÚ* dynasty in the *MOCHE* Valley in the 14th century. Like so many pre-*INCA* rulers in the kingdoms eventually subjugated by the Incas, knowledge of him is meagre and cloaked in legend. He was said to have arrived at Moche on a balsawood raft, "sent" from afar with the express mission of governing the valley peoples. Several unnamed kings succeeded him until the conquest of the valley, then under the rulership of *MIN-CHANÇAMAN,* by the Incas.

TEMAUKEL is the supreme being worshipped by the *ONA* of Tierra del Fuego. He is the all-powerful creator, and is believed to be without body, wife or child. Prayer and initiation rites to him are the preserve of men, who take the dominant role on earth now, after an initial period when women dominated.

TEMPLE OF THE SUN see *CORICANCHA, INTI, MACHU PICCHU, PACHACAMAC, TIAHUANACO.*

TEMPLE OF THE THREE WINDOWS see *MACHU PICCHU.*

THE THREE-CORNERED IDOL was a common deity, or *ZEMÍ,* of the prehistoric *ARAWAK* of the Greater Antilles, the giver of *MANIOC* to humankind. Carved of stone or conch shell, he is thought by archaeologists to derive from the observed form of the volcanic cone.

THE THREE VIRACOCHAS see *CON TICCI VIRACOCHA.*

THUNUPA VIRACOCHA was ostensibly one of many names for the *INCA* creator god *VIRACOCHA,* but it seems to be more ancient. The central figure on the Gateway of the Sun at *TIAHUANACO* has been interpreted as portraying Thunupa, a sky god and weather deity worshipped in the *TITICACA* Basin. He brought rain, thunder and lightning, but the rays projecting from the head of the figure are likely to represent the rays of the sun. Written sources for him are few and come from much later chroniclers, making it hard to imagine exactly how the Tiahuanacos perceived him. But it is known that the Incas acknowledged the ancient power of Tiahuanaco and revered its very ruins. The most ancient Andean myths emanated from Titicaca, and the world itself was believed to have been created there by Viracocha. Thus, according to the mid-17th-century Jesuit priest Bernabé Cobo, the Incas modelled their own god of weather, *ILLAPA,* on Thunupa.

The 16th-century Inca chronicler Juan de Santa Cruz Pachacuti Yamqui also relates the legend of Thunupa Viracocha, portraying him as a white man with a long grey beard and hair. Thunupa travelled about the land preaching and teaching, even performing miracles to impart moral behaviour to the people. In the enthusiasm of his own conversion to Christianity, and probably to please his new Spanish masters, Pachacuti Yamqui was convinced that Thunupa was the apostle St Thomas. According to Pachacuti Yamqui, the Incas, by forcing their official state cult of the sun (*INTI*) on their subjects, corrupted them and turned them away from the true God of Christianity.

TIAHUANACO, or Tiwanaku, an ancient site and kingdom in the *TITICACA* Basin, dominated the southern Andes in the Middle Horizon. It lies near the southern shore of Lake Titicaca and, in its heyday, occupied 445 hectares (1,100 acres). The earliest major constructions at the site were begun by AD 200 and, by AD 500, Tiahuanaco was the capital of a considerable empire, stretching to the Bolivian lowlands, the Peruvian coast, and into northern Chile. Its cultural and religious influence extended even farther. Its chief rival to the north was the *HUARI* Empire, and the two empires "met" at the La Raya pass, south of *CUZCO,* which became a sort of buffer zone between them. The prosperity of Tiahuanaco endured for roughly a millennium, matching the 1,000-year periods of the five "Ages" or Suns of Andean cosmology (see *PACHACUTI*).

The core of the city was formed by ceremonial-religious-civic structures, displaying religious motifs and gods whose iconography shows affinities to earlier *CHAVÍN* imagery

THE MONOLITHIC Gateway of the Sun at Tiahuanaco focuses on the central figure of the Staff Deity, probably Thunupa or Thunupa Viracocha, also called the "Weeping God", flanked by running "angels".

and indicates the continuity or resurgence of ancient religious beliefs. This core was aligned east–west, was confined within a moat, and was surrounded by residential compounds built of *adobe* bricks.

Tiahuanaco was a culmination of religious and mythological antecedents that appear to have united the peoples of the Titicaca Basin from as early as 1000 BC; ceremonial architecture at earlier sites such as *PUKARA* herald that at Tiahuanaco. The site chosen for the capital was in the midst of fertile land, enhanced by a sophisticated system of dykes, canals, causeways and aqueducts. The choice of location seems to have been deliberate, within a landscape itself perceived as sacred, in which natural features were worshipped: the sacred waters of Lake Titicaca to the west and the snow-capped mountain peaks to the east. The ceremonial centre was planned on a grid pattern, with all structures oriented on cardinal directions. The moat segregated it from the residential sections of the city, and reflected the sacred *HUACAS* of the *ISLAND OF THE SUN* and the *ISLAND OF THE MOON* in the lake.

Construction of the major elements of the religious centre had begun by *c.* AD 300. It comprised an area of stone temples, sunken courts, gateways and architraves. Some buildings were probably residential palaces, but the gateways and sculptures were the focuses of

open spaces clearly meant for civic participation in ritual and ceremony. Traces of gold pins within the stone blocks and remains of paint show that the sculptures were decorated and/or clothed.

At the island's core was the Akapana Temple, an artificial mound 17 m (56 ft) high, created from the excavation of the moat. It is roughly T-shaped (with a double bar across the top, one bar shorter than the other), about 200 m (650 ft) each side, composed of seven tiers clad in sandstone slabs. At the top is a sunken court in the shape of a quadrate cruciform, of an andesite base paved with sandstone slabs. Two staircases climb the east and west sides of the terraces, either side of which were rooms that might have been priests' quarters. Stone-lined channels and subterranean canals drained water down the terraces into the Tiahuanaco River, indicating ritual use of the sounds of rushing water (see also CHAVÍN, MACHU PICCHU, and SACSAHUAMAN). Lake Titicaca and Mount Illimani are visible from the top of Akapana.

Near the Akapana Temple are other monuments, principally the Semi-subterranean Temple to the north. This comprises a sunken court 28.5 x 26 m (94 x 85 ft), entered by a staircase on its south side. Its surrounding interior walls are adorned with carved stone heads, and at its centre stand several carved stone stelae, originally

THE FITTED stone block walls of the Semi-subterranean Temple at Tiahuanaco are adorned with carved stone heads.

including the "Bennett Stela" (after its discoverer, Wendell Bennett; now in the plaza of La Paz). The largest stone sculpture discovered in the Andes to date (7.3 m/24 ft tall), it portrays a richly dressed human thought to be one of Tiahuanaco's rulers or a divine ruler. In his/her hands are a *kero* beaker and a staff-like object, perhaps a snuff tablet.

Also north of the Akapana Temple, and west of the Semi-subterranean Temple, is the Kalasasaya, a low-lying rectangular platform 130 x 120 m (427 x 394 ft). It defines a large ceremonial precinct for public ritual, whose walls are made up of sandstone pillars alternating with smaller ashlar blocks. It is ascended by a stairway carved from stones set between two gigantic stone pillars.

At the northwest corner of the Kalasasaya stands the Gateway of the Sun. It seems to comprise two monolithic stone slabs supporting a third, carved, slab across the top, but is a single huge block of andesite whose top section is a panel completely covered with carving. The central figure portrays the "Gateway God", an anthropomorphic figure standing on a stepped platform resembling the tiered mounds of the sacred precinct. The figure has a squarish head adorned in a headdress with sun rays radiating from the top and sides; the eyes have large drops below them, giving rise to the name "Weeping God". Its outstretched arms hold two "staffs" – one has been interpreted as a spear-thrower and the other a quiver for spears, a clear resemblance to the STAFF DEITY of Chavín times. Flanking it are three rows, each of eight smaller winged figures in profile – sometimes called "angels" – running towards it, each of which also bears a staff. Below it is a row of carved heads.

The Gateway God is most likely a portrayal of THUNUPA, the god of thunder, lightning and rain. His sun-ray headdress also fits the character of a weather god, as do his spear-thrower and cluster of

spears, common metaphors for thunder and lightning.

Just within the Kalasasaya is the giant Ponce Stela (after archaeologist Carlos Ponce), 3.5 m (11 ft 6 in) tall. It portrays a ruler or deity, richly clothed, and with a mask-like face and staring eyes, thin trapezoidal nose, rectangular mouth and cheek panels. His/her hands hold a *kero* beaker and a staff-like object or snuff tablet.

Southeast of the Akapana Temple is the separate, much lower mound of the Pumapunku Temple, and ceremonial area. This is a T-shaped mound 5 m (16 ft) high, covering 150 sq m (179 sq yds), made up of three sandstone slab-covered tiers. The sunken courtyard at its summit, with carved stone doorways and lintels, was possibly the original site of the Gateway of the Sun.

The shared religious iconography of Tiahuanaco and Huari demonstrates that religious continuity prevailed from the Early Horizon through the Early Intermediate Period, despite political fragmentation in the Early Intermediate. Similarities include the Staff Deity image, winged and running falcon- and condor-headed creatures, often wielding clubs, and also decapitated heads. Priests might have kept contacts in the two capitals.

The Incas held the ruins at Tiahuanaco in reverence and regarded the Titicaca Basin as the place of the origin of the world. So great was their regard for the primacy of

A MONUMENTAL staircase leads up to the western entrance of the Kalasasaya at Tiahuanaco, a monumental compound with monolithic sculptures, including the Ponce Stela just within the arched gateway.

the site that they linked their own state foundations myth to it (see MANCO CAPAC) and regarded the huge stone statues at Tiahuanaco to be an ancient race of giants. In one variation of the deluge myth, the UN-NAMED MAN at Tiahuanaco divided the world into the four SUYUS and designated their rulers.

Despite such similarities, however, religious imagery at Tiahuanaco concentrated on stone sculpture at the ceremonial capital, which was built for public ceremony and with a preconceived plan. At Huari, by contrast, structures were private, more intimate, and development appears to have been haphazard. Also, religious imagery was concentrated on ceramics, textiles and other portable objects, and was therefore personal and perhaps more widespread.

IN COMMON with other Andean cultures, Tiahuanacan imagery includes bird, serpent, feline and other animal motifs, as exemplified in this painted ceramic drinking cup.

TIAHUANACO GIANTS
see *TIAHUANACO* stone figures.

TICCI, or Tiqsi, ("the beginning of things") was one of the many epithets used by the *INCAS* to refer to *VIRACOCHA*.

TICCI VIRACOCHA was the *INCA* name for a creator worshipped by the *Wari Wiracocharuna* of the First "Age" and one of many name variations for *VIRACOCHA* (see *MANCO CAPAC, PACHACUTI, CON TICCI VIRACOCHA*).

TIQSI see *TICCI*.

TITICACA, the lake in the central Andes on the borders of modern Peru and Bolivia, was the centre of the Titicaca Basin and the location of the ancient city of *TIAHUANACO*. Both the lake and the city maintained a pan-Andean importance during the dominance of the region by Tiahuanaco and afterwards as the legendary place of the origin of the cosmos, including the sun, moon, stars and humankind.

Peoples throughout the Andes created myths and legendary historical links to establish their origin at Titicaca/Tiahuanaco, including (and especially) the *INCAS*. The creator was invariably *VIRACOCHA*

ON LAKE TITICACA, Aymará fishermen continue to use reed boats like those made by the inhabitants of ancient Tiahuanaco more than 1,200 years ago.

who, in the episodic story of creation, was believed to have called forth the sun, moon and stars from islands in the lake, specifically the *ISLAND OF THE SUN* and the *ISLAND OF THE MOON*. The waters of the lake were said to be the tears of the creator, that he shed in acknowledgement of the sufferings of the beings he created.

Lake Titicaca also plays an important role in several versions of the origins of the Inca state. In these versions, *MANCO CAPAC* and his sister/wife *MAMA OCLLO* were associated with the Island of the Sun, and after their creation the "ancestors" were said to have made their way underground from Lake Titicaca to the

THE TOBA PEOPLE of Paraguay and northern Argentina believed that humans once dwelt in the sky.

cave of *PACARITAMBO*. Similarly, a strong link between Titicaca and the Inca capital at Cuzco was established by the travels of Viracocha. Temples dedicated to him were established at *CACHA* and *URCOS*, in the Vilcanota (or Urubamba) Valley to the northwest of the Basin, shortly after the creation.

TIWANAKU see *TIAHUANACO*.

THE TOBA, a tribe of the Gran *CHACO* of Paraguay and northern Argentina, believed that humans once dwelt in the sky. When they came down to earth to hunt animals, however, they became trapped here and have had to remain for ever (see also *KONONATOO*).

TOCAPO VIRACOCHA was the younger son or special aide of *CON TICCI VIRACOCHA* in different versions of the central Andean creation myth. After the creation of the world by *VIRACOCHA*, Tocapo Viracocha travelled northwards along a coastal route from Lake *TITICACA*, calling forth the clay models of people made by his father, naming the trees and plants, allocating their flowering and fruiting seasons and instructing the people in their uses

for food or medicinal purposes. He rejoined his father and brother, *IMAYMANA VIRACOCHA*, at *MANTA* on the Ecuadorian coast, and disappeared out to sea by walking across the waters.

TONAPA, or Conapa, was the divine assistant of the creator god *VIRACOCHA*. In one of many myths about Viracocha, Tonapa disobeyed Viracocha, and for this was set adrift on Lake *TITICACA*. His symbol was a cross, which over-enthusiastic Spanish priests took to be clear evidence of a pre-Spanish-conquest Christian connection.

TOPA YUPANQUI, almost certainly *TUPAC INCA YUPANQUI*, was a name for the conquering *INCA* lord cited in the histories of the dynasty of *TAYCANAMU* and *MINCHANÇAMAN* at *MOCHE*.

TOPACUSI was a golden cup alleged by *MANCO CAPAC* to have been left behind unintentionally in the cave of *TAMBO TOCO*.

TORREÓN SUN TEMPLE see *MACHU PICCHU*.

TOVAPOD see *AROTEH*.

TUPAC AMARU was the last claimant to the Inca throne in 1572.

TUPAC INCA YUPANQUI, probably the same as *TOPA YUPAN-QUI*, was the 11th *INCA* emperor, succeeding his father *PACHACUTI INCA YUPANQUI*, and ruling from 1471 to 1493. Like his father, he is less a legendary ruler and more a known historical figure. Less interested in developing the state than his father, he was mainly responsible for the second great wave of Inca imperial expansion, extending beyond the Valley of Cuzco and the *TITICACA* Basin, to encompass some 4,000 km (2,500 miles) of land north to south between modern central Ecuador and central Chile. The Inca manner of dealing with local kingdoms after conquest, incorporating local rulers and religious beliefs into their own systems, is demonstrated in the legendary account of the conquest of the *CHIMÚ* in the *MOCHE* Valley ruled by *MINCHANÇAMAN*.

THE TUPI are a rain forest tribe of southeastern Brazil (see *AROTEH, CEUCY, JURUPARI* and *VALEJDAD*).

TUPAC INCA YUPANQUI, the 11th emperor, continued the expansion of the Inca Empire after his father Pachacuti Inca Yupanqui. (SKETCH BY FELIPE GUAMAN POMA DE AYALA FROM THE NUEVA CORÓNICA Y BUEN GOBIERNO, 1583–1613.)

TRIAD see *ANDEAN TRIAD*.

TÚCUME, a late *SICÁN* site, was successor to *BATÁN GRANDE* in the *LAMBAYEQUE VALLEY* of northern coastal Peru. The largest concentration of monumental and ceremonial architecture ever constructed in the Andes, it covered some 150 hectares (370 acres). It served as the regional religious centre until the arrival of *CHIMÚ* conquerors in the 14th century.

THE TUKANO are a rain forest tribe from the upper reaches of the Colombian and Brazilian Amazon (for their myths, see *ABE MANGO, BORARO, PAGE ABE, PAMURI-MAHSE, VAI-MAHSE, YAJE WOMAN*).

TUMI knife, see *DECAPITATOR GOD*.

TUPAC AMARU, who was the last claimant to the *INCA* throne after the Spanish conquest, "ruled" from 1571 to 1572. His place in continuing post-Spanish-conquest Inca myth, discovered by anthropologists in the 1950s, derived from the fact that he was beheaded after leading a revolt against Spanish rule, and was/is therefore a candidate for the Inca millenarian belief in the *INKARRÍ*, or revival of the king.

TUPAC CUSI HUALPA is an alternative name for the *INCA* ruler *HUASCAR*.

SACRED SKIES

EVERY ANCIENT CULTURE OF the Andes worshipped the sun; most also worshipped the moon; and a few, for example the Chimú, considered the moon to be superior to the sun (*Inti*). It was the Incas who institutionalized worship of the sun, above almost all other deities, in their promotion of *Inti* throughout their empire. Their founding ancestor, Manco Capac, was regarded as having been the sun's representative on earth, and this epithet was applied to each emperor in the line of succession that

THE IMPORTANCE *of the sun in ancient Andean cultures is manifest from the earliest times. Temples and gold sun discs are obvious representations of this. Less evident is this stylized sun symbol woven into a cotton mantle from the desert Nazca culture of southern coastal Peru.*

followed. Observation and recording of the sun's movements were considered to be vital to the health of the empire, and were performed from distinctive carved stone platforms called *intihuatana*.

As well as the recognition of the importance of solar and lunar cycles, and their effects on the weather and seasons, the night sky – and in particular *Mayu*, the Milky Way – was regarded as a vast source of inspiration and mythological meaning. *Mayu* was seen as the celestial river, and its progression of positions through the night sky, tallied with the seasons, was the starting point for all calendrical correlations. In this vast galactic body, the Incas recognized not just points and regions of light, but also the dark bodies of stellar voids, the "dark-cloud constellations" which, to them, were just as important.

As with other major themes in Andean civilization, imagery and iconography reveal the antiquity of sun worship, from deities with haloed radiations emanating from their heads (for example, on the Gateway of the Sun at Tiahuanaco) to the sheet-gold sun masks of the Incas.

NORTHWEST *of Cuzco, in Antisuyu – in the area first brought under Inca rule – the fortress and sacred retreat of Machu Picchu (above) includes the massive Sun Tower, carved from solid granite and used for astronomical observation.*

AT SACSAHUAMAN *(top left), Emperor Pachacuti Inca Yupanqui's fortress-like sacred precinct on a prominent hill just northwest of Cuzco, massive polygonal monumental masonry required intensive labour, and undoubtedly served to impress upon his subjects the fullness of his power and the supremacy of Inti and the state religion.*

AT THE CONFLUENCE *of the Urubamba and Patakancha rivers, the ceremonial centre and administrative seat of Ollantaytambo (centre left), built for more than 1,000 residents, includes the Sun Temple, which was still under construction when the Spanish invasion began.*

AT THE FARTHEST *northerly provinces of the empire, the administrative centre and Temple of Inti at Ingapirca (bottom left) in Ecuador underscored Inca power and control.*

THE HEAVENS *at night and the movements of celestial bodies, star groups and the entire Milky Way (right) were equally important in Inca religion and cosmography, and were carefully charted. Without the "light pollution" of modern cities it is easier to imagine the immensity of the night sky and to see the dark bodies between stars, as well as the star clusters.*

U

THE TUPINAMBÁ are a coastal rain forest tribe located in south-eastern Brazil (see *MONAN*).

TUTUJANAWIN, a general and somewhat enigmatic pan-Andean deity, was an all-embracing concept of "the beginning and end of all things". He/she/it was a supreme power that gave life and energy to everything in the cosmos.

UAICA was a culture hero of the Juruna rain forest tribe of the *XINGU RIVER* region of Brazil, and a famous medicine man and teacher.

One day, when out hunting in the forest, he came upon a large number of dead animals piled beneath a tree. As he approached the heap of animals, he became dizzy and collapsed into a deep sleep. In his sleep he dreamed about the Juruna *JAGUAR* ancestor *SINAA*, who spoke to him. This dream occurred several times, until finally Sinaa ordered Uaica to stay away from him, a command that Uaica obeyed.

As the tribal medicine man, Uaica made a drink from the bark of a certain tree, which gave him special knowledge and powers. For example, Uaica could take away a disease simply with the touch of his hands. In his dreams, Sinaa gave him answers and instructions to supply all the needs of the Juruna people.

The Juruna urged Uaica to take a wife, but when he finally consented, the wife proved to be unfaithful to him. The lover even attempted to kill Uaica with a club, but, as Uaica had eyes in the back of his head (like the jaguar ancestor), he was able to dodge the blow, and subsequently disappeared down the hole made when the club struck the ground. Thus, through these events, the Juruna lost their medicine man, who declared, "I will not return. You will have to use arrows and clubs. I tried to teach you the wishes of Sinaa, but now I go." The Juruna claim that Uaica

A TUPINAMBÁ ceremonial dance.
(ILLUSTRATION BY JEAN DE LÉRY, 1556.)

beckoned them to follow him beneath the ground but, in their grief, they were too confused and afraid to follow him.

UCHU see *AYAR UCHU*.

UGWVU-CUENGO was the *KUIKURU* vulture king; see *KANASSA*.

THE "UNNAMED MAN", who appeared at *TIAHUANACO* after the waters of the great world deluge receded, is the principal character in the only substantial account in *INCA* myth of the division of the four *SUYUS*. His great power enabled him to create the four quarters of *TAHUANTINSUYU* and to designate a king for each, although the quarters assigned do not quite conform to the actual directional distribution around *CUZCO*, nor are three of the four kings otherwise known. To the northern quarter (*CHINCHASUYU*?) he appointed *MANCO CAPAC*; to the southern quarter (*COLLASUYU*?), Colla; to the

eastern quarter (*ANTISUYU*?), Tocay; and to the western quarter (*CUNTISUYU*?), Pinahua. He commanded each king to conquer the lands assigned and govern the people who lived there.

URA COCHA was the lake that figured in the battle between *PARIACACA* and *HUALLALLO CARHUINCHO*, as described in the *HUAROCHIRÍ MANUSCRIPT*.

URCO, or Urcon, see *INCA URCO*.

URCOS, a pre-Inca and *INCA* city and ceremonial centre about 35 km (22 miles) southeast of *CUZCO* in the Vilcanota (or Urubamba) Valley, was the setting for the second significant encounter between *VIRACOCHA* and the peoples north-west of the *TITICACA* Basin, shortly after the creation of the world.

According to the myth told to and related by the 16th-century Spanish chronicler Juan de Betanzos, Viracocha arrived at the site and immediately ascended to the

top of a nearby mountain. He sat down there and called upon the ancestors of the Urcos people, whose spirits were believed to inhabit the mountain (were buried there), to come out. The summit where Viracocha sat became a sacred *HUACA* to the people of Urcos and, on that spot, they set up a bench of gold upon which they placed a statue of the god. The contemporary chronicler Cristobal de Molina describes the image of Viracocha as that of a white man dressed in a white robe that hung down to his feet (see also *CACHA*).

The people of Urcos gave Viracocha the name Atun-Viracocha, meaning "great creator".

URPAY HUACHAC was the wife of *PACHACAMAC*, with whom she had two daughters. She was also the creator of fish, which she bred in a pond at Pachacamac, the site. As recounted in the text of the *HUARO-*

V

CHIRÍ MANUSCRIPT, CONIRAYA VIRA-COCHA seduced one daughter, and tried to seduce the other. When she escaped his clutches by transforming herself into a dove and flying away, he smashed the pond in rage, thus releasing fish into the oceans.

URUBUTSIN was the KAMAIURA vulture king (see KUAT).

U-SHAPED CEREMONIAL CENTRES see under CHAVÍN and FANGED GOD.

USHNUO see CAPAC USNU.

USNU PILLAR see under CAPAC USNU.

VAB see VALEJDAD.

VAI-MAHSE ("the master of animals") is the TUKANO tribal spirit of the forest and of the hunt. He is perceived to be a dwarf, with his body

painted red, and certain hills within the forest are sacred to him. His weapon is a highly polished stick, also painted red. He controls all of the game of the forest and all of the

fishes in the rivers, and even the herbs that grow around the bases of trees. Great care must therefore be taken not to offend him, lest in his displeasure he were to bring disaster on the people by withholding the game and the catch or by curtailing the fertility of the animals. He is a jealous god, and his concern with fertility extends to women, to whom he gives sickness and pain in pregnancy because he was not the cause of their condition.

VALEJDAD, and his brother Vab, were the first men according to the TUPI of southeastern Brazil. At the beginning of time, the brothers were born or created from a large rock, which was female. Valejdad was the wicked one of the two and, because of this, was banished to the north. When he becomes angry he sends torrential rains down south, where the Tupi live. (See also AROTEH)

VEGACHAYOQ MOQO TEMPLE see HUARI.

URCOS became a sacred site after being visited by Viracocha on his travels from Lake Titicaca. This is the Temple of Viracocha at Rachi in the Vilcanota Valley, southeast of Cuzco.

VILCAS WAMAN, like Cuzco, had an Usnu platform for making astronomical observations and to ensure cosmic order.

VENTILLA see under CAHUACHI and NAZCA.

VICHAMA see under PACHACAMAC.

VILCA, a HUAROCHIRÍ term, was a general name for the powerful male deities who play a role in the myth of the young virgin CAVILLACA and CONIRAYA VIRACOCHA, who seduced and impregnated her by concealing his semen in the fruit of a lúcuma tree.

VILCAS WAMAN, located about 50 miles (80 km) southeast of Ayacucho, Peru, was one of the Incas' earliest conquests as they began to expand beyond Cuzco. In common with the Inca capital it had an Usnu platform (see CAPAC USNU) and a Sun Temple of finely fitted monumental masonry architecture that rivalled those at the capital. The Sun Temple sits upon a three-tiered platform with trapezoidal doorways and niches for idols.

VILLAMA see under PACHACAMAC.

VIRACOCHA, or Wira Qocha, the supreme god of the INCAS, was the creator of the universe, of the human race and of all things on earth. In concept he became a rather remote and inaccessible deity, although his presence was ubiquitous and inescapable. Nevertheless, he was often represented as an old man with a long beard or as a man wearing a sun crown, holding thunderbolts in his hands and shedding tears from his eyes to represent rain. In the Inca capital at CUZCO, Viracocha was represented in his own shrine by a golden statue about three-quarters of the height of a grown man. He was white-skinned, bearded and wore a long tunic, as described by the Spaniards who first saw him there. In legend, Viracocha travelled south to CACHA, about 100 km (62 miles) south of Cuzco, where a statue was erected and a temple dedicated to his worship was built. URCOS was another important place of worship where a shrine and statue of Viracocha was erected.

In practice, Viracocha, as an immanent but primordial creator, remained nameless to the Incas. Instead, he was referred to by descriptive terms befitting his role in the various permutations of the creation myth. Thus he was known as Ilya (meaning "light") and as Ticci ("the beginning of things"), as Viracocha Pachayachachic or Wira-qoca Pacayacaciq ("great lord, instructor of the world"), and as Tarapaca. Spanish chroniclers, perhaps perplexed by this seeming confusion, gave him the general title of Viracocha. Possible meanings, or glosses, of the name Viracocha itself were "the lake of creation", "sea fat" and "sea foam".

Many Andean cultures, especially in the central Andes, believed that Lake TITICACA on the Peruvian–Bolivian border was the site of the creation of the sun, moon and stars, and that the waters of the lake were the tears of the creator god acknowledging the sufferings of the

beings he had created. Viracocha first created a world of darkness, which he populated with humans fashioned from stone. In one version, these beings were giants. These people, however, disobeyed Viracocha, and he had to punish them, destroying them by a flood, or by transforming them back into stones, which could be seen, it was believed, at ruined cities such as TIAHUANACO and PUKARA. Only one man and one woman survived, and were magically transported to Tiahuanaco, where the gods dwelt. Next Viracocha created the present race of humans, and animals, out of clay. On the humans he painted distinctive clothes and gave them customs, languages, songs, arts and crafts and the gift of agriculture to distinguish the different peoples and nations. Having breathed life into these humans, Viracocha instructed them to descend into the earth and disperse, then to

re-emerge on to the earth through caves and from lakes and hills. These places became sacred, and shrines were established at them in honour of the gods. The world was still dark, so Viracocha next ordered the sun, moon and stars to rise into the sky from the islands in Lake Titicaca.

It was thus from the Titicaca Basin that, in legend, Viracocha set out to preach and to spread civilization to the people, but he did so as a mendicant beggar dressed in rags, and under many names, such as ATUN-VIRACOCHA, CON TICCI VIRACOCHA and CONTITI VIRACO-CHA PACHAYACHACHIC. In certain other accounts, he was described as a tall white man. Many of those he encountered reviled him, but Viracocha taught humankind the ways of civilization, as well as working miracles among them. This initial active role with the earth and people gave Viracocha affinities in

common with the other preacher heroes so prominent in Andean theology, and he is therefore sometimes confused with similar heroes/deities such as NEMTEREQUETEBA and Thunupa (see THUNUPA VIRA-COCHA). To the Incas, however, he remained remote and only interacted with humans through other gods, particularly through INTI, the god of the sun, and ILLAPA, the god of thunder, lightning and rain.

The supreme Inca deity Viracocha was the final title for an ancient creator god who figured in the pantheons of many pre-Inca cultures in the central Andes (see also CONIRAYA VIRACOCHA). As with many other Andean religious concepts, he was partly adopted by the Incas from the cultures they conquered. For example, his portrayal with weeping eyes was a characteristic almost certainly adopted from the WEEPING GOD of Tiahuanaco. In the Inca legend of the creation of their people, Viracocha called out to them as the sun and moon rose at his command. He bestowed a special headdress and stone battle axe upon MANCO CAPAC, the Inca leader, and prophesied that they would become great lords and conquer many other nations. Manco Capac led his people back into the earth, from which they re-emerged at the cave of PACARITAMBO. A further connection with pre-Inca traditions was provided when Viracocha entered the Valley of Cuzco during his wanderings and created Lord ALCAVICÇA, also the name of a people living in the valley when the Incas entered it.

Although he later lost popularity, Viracocha was never neglected by the Incas, in spite of their elevation of Inti to near-equal status in their pantheon. He was accorded

his own temple in Cuzco, and human sacrifices were offered to him on the most important and solemn occasions, such as the investiture of a new emperor. He was especially honoured with child sacrifices, CAPACOCHAS, before which the Inca priests recited a specific prayer to him. Several such sacrifices have been discovered high up on Andean peaks and volcanoes, believed to be the abodes of the gods, and where the dry and frozen conditions have preserved the bodies and artefacts in a near pristine state at several sites.

A late Inca cosmology comprised a five-fold sequence of the creation of the Inca world (see PACHACUTI). The First "Age" was ruled by Viracocha and the other gods, and death was unknown. The Second Age was that of the giants, created by Viracocha, who worshipped him, but who displeased him and were destroyed by flood. The Third Age was inhabited by the first humans, again created by Viracocha, but they lived on a primitive level and lacked even the rudiments of civilization. The Fourth Age was that of the *Auca Runa* ("the warriors"), to whom Viracocha presumably imparted the arts of civilization, for these were creators of the early civilizations, such as the MOCHE. The Fifth Age was that of the Incas themselves, who spread civilization far and wide through conquest. Vira-

cocha himself ended his travels and teachings when he reached MANTA in modern Ecuador, from which he departed to the west, across the Pacific Ocean, "walking across the waters as if they were land", or on a raft, or by walking on his cape, in various versions. The Fifth Age ended with the coming of the Spaniards and with the downfall of the Inca Empire, but upon their arrival, the Spaniards were hailed as the returning emissaries of the creator and were referred to as *viracochas*, a term still used as one of respect among QUECHUA speakers.

The only serious rival for the title of creator was the coastal deity PACHACAMAC. After their conquest of the central Peruvian coastal peoples, the Incas went out of their way to reconcile this potential conflict. The ancient site and shrine of Pachacamac was included in the itinerary of Viracocha, which included the seduction and attempted seduction of Pachacamac's daughters. In a general way, the "rivalry" constituted a mythical manifestation of the distinctions and links between the two worlds of the highlands, represented by Viracocha, and the coastal lowlands, represented by Pachacamac.

Viracocha was also the name of the eighth Inca ruler (see VIRACOCHA INCA).

VIRACOCHA INCA was the

eighth, semi-legendary, INCA ruler, who traditionally ruled in the early 15th century. At this time, CUZCO was a small city among several

THE DEITY represented on the Gateway of the Sun at Tiahuanaco represents a combination of pan-Andean beliefs. Clearly in the tradition of the Staff Deity, he is variously assumed to represent Viracocha, Thunupa or the Weeping God.

in the Huantanay (Cuzco) Valley. This is a case where the shared name has caused blurring and confusion concerning the relationship between the god and the man, which has vexed scholars and remains unresolved. In one legend, the Inca (Viracocha the man) claimed that Viracocha the god appeared to him one night during troubled times. The creator calmed his fears. When the Inca reported this event to his people the next morning, he was unanimously proclaimed the creator and renamed Viracocha Inca. The troubled times were undoubtedly the result of the rivalries that existed among the various cities of the valley. In the war against the CHANCAS, a significant milestone in the beginning of Inca empire-building, some versions of Inca history record Viracocha Inca as the saviour of Cuzco. More traditionally, however – and no doubt owing to his recasting of Inca history during his reign – the saviour of Cuzco from the Chanca onslaught was Viracocha's son PACHACUTI INCA YUPANQUI, who became tenth ruler following on from the brief reign of another son, INCA URCO.

The person, kingship and divinity of Viracocha Inca provide a fascinating Andean parallel with the interlinked figures of Mixcóatl, Quetzalcóatl/Ce Ácatl Topiltzin Quetzalcóatl and Kukulkán in Mesoamerica, in whom mythology and historicity are also seen to overlap and become blurred. Mixcóatl was the founder of the Toltec nation, and was later deified; his son was the deity and legendary Toltec ruler, and founder, of the city of Tollán in central Mesoamerica; Kukulkán was the god and legendary leader of the Maya-Toltec city of Chichén Itzá in Yucatán, Kukulkán being the Maya translation of the name Quetzalcóatl. In all four cases, scholars are challenged with trying to separate the god from the man, although in Viracocha's case, the two are more distinct because, in the Inca example, the ruler assumed the divine name after his vision of the god.

VIRACOCHA PACHAYACHA-

CHIC, or Wiraqoca Pacayacaciq, (meaning "great lord and instructor of the world") was one of several terms that were used by the INCAS to refer to VIRACOCHA.

SACRED PLACES
& RITUAL LINES

AN INTEGRAL PART OF ancient Andean religion was the designation of features and objects throughout the landscape as sacred sites. Known as *huacas*, such locations could be as large as a mountain or as small as a boulder; or a cave, spring, field or other place in which an important event had occurred, or an artificial object such as a stone pillar.

Sacred places were individually significant and collectively linked by ritual lines, one elaborate system of which – the *ceques* – was used by the Incas. Ritual lines could be conventional terrestrial routes between *huacas*, or virtual networks – for example, lines of sight from one *huaca* to another on the horizon for astronomical observations. The cardinal *ceques* radiating from the Inca capital at Cuzco were the four great highways of the empire, leading to the four quarters, the *Tahuantinsuyu*. In addition to their practical purpose, they metaphorically bound the parts of the empire, and

SACRED PLACES and the sacred skies were intimately linked through natural and deliberately erected sacred stones, sited on prominent horizons for use in astronomical observations, as here at Horca del Inca in Bolivia.

served as ritual routes for the progression of sacrificial victims. Similarly, in earlier cultures among the coastal valleys from Nazca in the south to Moche in the north, lines marked out in the desert landscape to form anthropomorphic animal, plant and geometric figures – called geoglyphs – were used as ritual pathways for ceremonial progressions. They appear to be lineage or kinship routes, some used for a single occasion, others over generations.

Pilgrimage sites – some of them used for hundreds, even thousands, of years – were also important, and demonstrate the continuity of religious belief. Two of the most important were Pachacamac and Tiahuanaco.

VIRTUALLY THE ENTIRE landscape (above) was sacred in one way or another to ancient Andean cultures. Entire mountains were designated apus, as was Mount Ausangate in the central Peruvian cordillera near Cuzco.

PROMINENT ROCKS (huancas) in the landscape were named and regarded as sacred (huaca). The antiquity of their status as sacred places can only be guessed at in most cases, but when carved and well worn, as at Nusta Ispana, Yuruk Rumi in the Vilcabamba Mountains (above), it must have been great.

THE LANDSCAPE of the desert in southern coastal Peru has the greatest concentration of sacred lines (above) of anywhere in ancient South America. With long-distance straight lines, cleared areas and animal images, these geoglyphs knit together several aspects of ancient American religion: the sacredness of the landscape itself, the use of ritual pathways in the experience of religious ceremony and the expression of animal imagery to envision the deities. This example depicts a monkey, an animal of the Amazonian rain forest, far to the east of the Nazca culture whose people made the sacred pathway.

THE LONG-STANDING use of the desert for individual ritual pathways and cleared spaces for ceremonial gatherings (above) is emphasized by the density of crossing and overlapping lines.

LAKE TITICACA (above) was perhaps the most sacred site of all, and one of the most famous places of pilgrimage for ancient Andean peoples, for it was here that Viracocha created the world, caused the sun and moon to rise, and created humankind.

Y

THE WARAO of the Orinoco River delta (left) believe that they had originally dwelt in the sky with their creator Kononatoo.

WATAUINEIWA was the benevolent sky god of the Yahgan people of Tierra del Fuego (below).

WANADI is the sun god of the Yekuana, a Venezuelan rain forest tribe. The architectural details of the Yekuana's houses reflect the structure of their cosmological beliefs. The central support post links the underworld of lost souls with the earth of humans and the heavens above. At the top of it sits a carved crimson-crested woodpecker, the animal reincarnation of Wanadi. The main entrance faces east, to permit the rising equinoctial sun to shine on the central post, while the two crossbeams supporting the roof are oriented north–south, mimicking the way the Milky Way supports the "roof" of the sky.

THE WARAO, or Warau, are a tribe of the Venezuelan–Guianan Orinoco River (see *KONONATOO*).

WARI see *HUARI*.

THE WARI RUNA were the people of the *INCA* Second Sun (see *PACHACUTI*).

THE WARI WIRACOCHA-RUNA were the *INCA* people of the First Sun (see *PACHACUTI*).

WARRIOR PRIEST see *DECAPITATOR GOD*.

WATAUINEIWA (meaning "the most ancient one") is the benevolent sky god of the *YAHGAN* people of Tierra del Fuego, who they believe created and continues to sustain the world. Initiation rites and prayer to Watauineiwa are the sole preserve of men, who now

dominate the affairs of the earth after an initial period when women were dominant.

WAYNA CAPAC see *HUAYNA CAPAC*.

WEEPING GOD was an epithet applied to the god portrayed on the Gateway of the Sun at *TIAHUANACO*, possibly a manifestation of *VIRACOCHA*.

WICHAMA see *PACHACAMAC*.

WINGED BEINGS/CREATURES see under *HUARI* and *TIAHUANACO*.

WIRA QOCHA see *VIRACOCHA*.

WIRAQOCA PACAYACACIQ see *VIRACOCHA PACHAYACHACHIC*.

THE XINGU RIVER, which runs through central Brazil, is the homeland of a group of tribes, including the Juruna, Kamaiura and

Kuikuru, who share similar beliefs and deities and who have been studied extensively by anthropologists (see *ARAVATURA, IAMURICUMA WOMEN, KANASSA, KUAMUCUCA, KUARUP, KUAT, MAVUTSINIM, MINATA-KARAIA, OI, SINAA, UAICA*).

YACANA, the llama, was one of the "dark cloud" constellations that the *INCA* recognized within *MAYU*, the Milky Way. In myth, when the llama disappeared at midnight it was believed to have descended to earth to drink and thereby prevent flooding during the rainy season.

THE YAHGAN are a tribe of Tierra del Fuego (see *EL-LAL* and *WATAUINEIWA*).

YAHUAR HUACAC, or Inca Yupanqui, was the legendary seventh Inca ruler of *CUZCO*, probably reigning sometime in the 14th century. Like all *INCA* rulers, he was considered to be a direct descendant of the ancestors, *MANCO CAPAC* and *MAMA OCLLO*.

YAJE WOMAN, according to *TUKANO* belief, was the person indirectly responsible for providing the

IN THE SECOND AGE of Pachacuti or cycle of creation, the Wari Runa (left) were created. They wore only animal skins but recognized Viracocha, their creator.

THE NUMEROUS rain forest tribes of the Xingu River (above) of central Brazil have been some of the most intensely studied by anthropologists.

Z

YAHUAR HUACAC, the seventh Inca ruler, is shown holding a ceremonial axe-staff of office. (ILLUSTRATION FROM THE 18TH-CENTURY "CUZCO SCHOOL" GENEALOGY.)

rain forest tribes with the hallucinatory plants that they use to gain visions and knowledge. She was impregnated by the sun and, when her baby boy was born, she rubbed him with leaves taken from special plants until he shone bright red. Then she took him to the first men, each of whom claimed fatherhood and tore a piece from the child. In this way, each tribe acquired the distinctive plant used by its SHAMANS to gain access to the spirit world.

YAMPALLEC was the green stone idol in his own image brought by NAYAMLAP to the LAMBAYEQUE VALLEY when he invaded it.

THE YANOMAMI are a rain forest tribe of the Venezuelan Amazon who call themselves "the fierce people" (see OMAM, PERIBORIWA).

YAUYOS see HUAROCHIRÍ MANUSCRIPT.

THE YEKUANA are a Venezuelan rain forest tribe (see WANADI).

YURUPARY brought fire to the human race by stealing it from the underworld, but killed both himself and his brother with it in the process.

YLLAPA see ILLAPA.

YUPANQUI see PACHACUTI INCA YUPANQUI, TUPAC INCA YUPANQUI.

YURUPARY is the principal character in the Colombian Barasana tribal myth about how humans acquired fire. According to this myth, Yurupary – in some versions known as "Manioc Stick Anaconda" – obtained fire from the underworld and brought it back to humankind on earth.

Yurupary used the fire to kill his own brother, Macaw, but was himself also burned to death. His bones are the charred logs that are the result of the slash-and-burn method of creating a garden plots in the rain forest, and provide nourishment for the cultivated plants grown there by humans.

YUTU-YUTU the tinamou (the name of a partridge-like bird), was one of the "dark cloud" constellations or stellar voids that the INCA people recognized within MAYU, the Milky Way.

ZAPANA see CARI.

ZEMÍ was the general term used by the prehistoric ARAWAK of the Greater Antilles for their gods, and for anything else sacred. Spanish sources record that this term was applied to both the deity and to the idol representing it; to the concept of the idol's oracular powers; and

also to the powers of the sun, the moon, the earth, the sky, the wind and even the remains of the dead. Zemís were carved out of wood and stone, and were painted. In the conduct of rituals connected with the predictive abilities of such idols, SHAMANS would paint them-

selves in a similar fashion and were then granted visions by means of the use of an hallucinatory plant snuff. (See also THREE-CORNERED IDOL, HUACA.)

ZOLZOLOÑI was the wife of CIUM.

YANOMAMI WARRIORS relate their mythical origins by using the blood of Periboriwa, the moon spirit, and practise an elaborately graded system of intergroup violence.

ZUE was the name of the CHIBCHA sun god (see BOCHICA).

CHRONOLOGY

c. 15,000–3500 BC
ARCHAIC PERIOD
People migrated to South America in this period. Hunter-gatherer, stone-, bone-, wood- and shell-tool-using cultures reaching the tip of Tierra del Fuego by at least 9000 BC.

c. 3500–1800 BC
PRECERAMIC PERIOD
This term is applied to the first agricultural societies, which by 3000 BC had mastered the domestication of plants and animals – a process that had begun several millennia earlier – and constructed the first monumental architecture in the form of platform compounds.

c. 1800–900 BC
INITIAL PERIOD
During this period, irrigation agriculture was developed into a sophisticated technology. Constructions of monumental architecture included much more ambitious projects.

c. 900–200 BC
EARLY HORIZON
The earliest civilization of the central Andes, *CHAVÍN*, dominated much of the area, both artistically and religiously, if not politically. Meanwhile, the *PARACAS* culture also flourished on the southern Peruvian coast.

c. 200 BC–AD 500
EARLY INTERMEDIATE
The cohesion of *CHAVÍN* disintegrated, and several regional chiefdoms developed in the coastal and mountain valleys. Despite political fragmentation, some remarkable advances were made in urbanization and in political, social, economic and artistic expression. Most prominent among the kingdoms that developed were the *MOCHE* in the north Peruvian coastal valleys, and the *NAZCA* in the southern coastal valleys.

c. AD 500–1000
MIDDLE HORIZON
A wealth of cultures and political entities developed, but for the first half of this period two political centres built empires that unified the northern and southern Andes and adjacent western coastal regions. In the north was *HUARI* (or *WARI*) in the south-central Peruvian highlands. In the *TITICACA* Basin, the city of *TIAHUANACO* (or Tiwanaku) was built, and Tiahuanacan rulers expanded their state throughout the Basin and beyond.

c. AD 1000–1400
LATE INTERMEDIATE
This new era was characterized by political fragmentation. As before numerous local and regional city-states were established which, towards the end of the period, were united into larger kingdoms. The *CHIMÚ*, or Kingdom of Chimor, emerged (second only to the Incas in importance to Andean mythology). The Chimú capital Chan Chan was founded in *c.* AD 1000 and flourished until the Inca conquest in the 1470s.

c. AD 1400–1532
LATE HORIZON
The INCA capital of *CUZCO* was established, and in little more than 130 years the Incas built a huge empire, from Colombia to mid-Chile and from the rain forest to the Pacific. Part of their success is attributed to their practice of including the religious ceremonies and deities of subject peoples in their own religion to create a cohesive empire.

c. 1100 Incas and legendary first ruler, *MANCO CAPAC*, migrated into the Valley of Cuzco, founded *CUZCO* and established the Inca dynasty. Line of descent follows through sons – second to seventh rulers (*SINCHI ROCA*, *LLOQUE YUPANQUI*, *MAYTA CAPAC*, *CAPAC YUPANQUI*, *INCA ROCA*, *YAHUAR HUACAC*), through the 12th, 13th and 14th centuries, during which the Inca city was one among several city-states in Cuzco Valley.

c. 1425 *VIRACOCHA INCA*, eighth ruler, began Inca conquests and domination of Valley of Cuzco

1438–1471 After a brief reign of ninth ruler, *INCA URCO*, tenth ruler *PACHACUTI INCA YUPANQUI* continued his father Viracocha's conquests and began to expand the Inca Empire beyond the Valley of Cuzco. Built fortress of *SACSA-HUAMAN* at Cuzco and created the "puma" plan of the city.

1471–1493 The eleventh ruler, *TUPAC INCA YUPANQUI*, completed intense campaigns of expansion, including conquest of the Kingdom of Chimor in northern Peru. By the end of his reign, the Inca Empire had reached its greatest extents from north to south, and from the Pacific coast to the Amazon Basin.

1493–1526 The twelfth ruler, *HUAYNA CAPAC*, consolidated lands and built roads and fortresses throughout the Empire. He died of smallpox, brought to the New World (in Mesoamerica) by the Spanish.

1526–1532 Thirteenth ruler *HUASCAR* seized throne after father's death but this was disputed by his brother *ATAHUALPA*. The six-year civil war ended with the capture of Huascar. The arrival of Francisco Pizarro in 1532 began the conquest of the Inca Empire.

1532 Francisco Pizarro landed with a small army on the north coast, where he found the Incas involved in a civil war that had been raging for six years. Pizarro exploited this division and proceeded to conquer the Inca Empire and strip its wealth, both material and cultural.

POST-COLONIZATION
1533: Atahualpa captured and beheaded by Pizarro at Cajamarca. Out of these events grew the legend of the "future return of the king" known as *INKARRÍ*. The severed head was believed to be growing a new body for the rulers eventual return to overthrow the Spaniards and reinstate Inca world order.

1580s Merchant Antonio de Sepulveda cut a notch in the hills around Lake Guatavita in an attempt to drain it – so convinced was he by the Spanish legend of the treasure of *EL DORADO*, and the store of gold that was to be found at the bottom of the lake.

The 16th and the 17th centuries saw conflict of religions as Spanish conversion of the population to Catholicism was carried out. Ancient Inca religion survived into the 17th century.

BIBLIOGRAPHY

Alva, Walter, and Bill Ballenberg (1988) "Discovering the New World's Richest Unlooted Tomb", *National Geographic*, 174 (4), pp.510–49.

Alva, Walter, and Nathan Benn (1990) "The Moche of Ancient Peru: New Tomb of Royal Splendor", *National Geographic*, 177 (6), pp.2–15.

Alva, Walter, and Christopher B. Donnan (1993) *Royal Tombs of Sipán*. Fowler Museum of Cultural History, University of California.

Ascher, Marcia, and Robert Ascher (1981) *Code of the Quipu: A Study in Media, Mathematics, and Culture*. University of Michigan Press, Ann Arbor.

Aveni, Frank (ed.) (1990) *The Lines of Nasca*. American Philosophical Society, Philadelphia.

Aveni, Frank (2000) *Nasca: Eighth Wonder of the World?* British Museum Press, London.

Bonavia, Duccio (trans. P. J. Lyon) (1985) *Mural Painting in Ancient Peru*. University of Indiana Press.

Bray, Warwick (1978) *The Gold of El Dorado*. Times Newspapers, London.

Burger, Richard L. (1995) *Chavín and the Origins of Andean Civilization*. Thames and Hudson, London and New York.

Cobo, Bernabé de (transl. Roland Hamilton) (1653/1983) *History of the Inca Empire*. University of Texas Press.

Cobo, Bernabé de (transl. Roland Hamilton) (1653/1990) *Inca Religion and Customs*. University of Texas Press.

Conrad, Geoffrey W., and Arthur A. Demarest (1984) *Religion and Empire: The Dynamics of Aztec and Inca Expansionism*. Cambridge University Press.

Cordy-Collins, Alana (1992) "Archaism or Tradition: The Decapitation Theme in Cupisnique and Moche Iconography", *Latin American Antiquity*, 3 (3), pp.206–20.

Demarest, Arthur A. (1981) *Viracocha – The Nature and Antiquity of the Andean High God*. Peabody Museum Monographs, 6, Cambridge.

Donnan, Christopher B. (1976) *Moche Art and Iconography*. University of California at Los Angeles Latin American Center, Los Angeles.

Donnan, Christopher B. (1988) "Iconography of the Moche: Unravelling the Mystery of the Warrior Priest", *National Geographic*, 174 (4), pp.550–55.

Donnan, Christopher B. (1988) "Moche Funerary Practices", in *Tombs for the Living: Andean Mortuary Practices*, pp.111–59, Dumbaton Oaks, Washington, DC.

Donnan, Christopher B., and Nathan Benn (1990) "The Moche of Ancient Peru: Masterworks of Art Reveal a Remarkable Pre-Inca World", *National Geographic*, 177 (6), pp16–33.

Donnan, Christopher B., and Luis Jaime Castillo (1992) "Finding the Tomb of a Moche Priestess", *Archaeology*, 45 (6), pp38–42.

Donnan, Christopher B., and Carol J. Mackey (1978) *Ancient Burial Patterns of the Moche Valley, Peru*. University of Texas Press.

Hadingham, Evan (1987) *Lines to the Mountain Gods: Nazca and the Mysteries of Peru*. Random House, New York.

Harner, J. (1971) *The Jivaro*. University of California Press.

Hugh Jones, S. (1979) *The Palm and the Pleiades: Initiation and Cosmology in North West Amazonia*. Cambridge University Press.

Isbell, William (1997) *Mummies and Mortuary Monuments*. University of Texas Press.

Lumbreras, Luis G. (1969) (trans. Betty J. Meggers) (1974) *The Peoples and Cultures of Ancient Peru*. Smithsonian Institution Press, Washington, DC.

Kolata, Alan L. (1993) *Tiwanaku: Portrait of an Andean Civilization*. Blackwell, Oxford and Cambridge.

Kolata, Alan L. (1996) *Valley of the Spirits: A Journey into the Lost Realm of the Aymara*. John Wiley, New York.

Morrison, Tony (1979) *Pathways to the Gods*. Harper and Row, New York.

Morrison, Tony (1987) *The Mystery of the Nasca Lines*. Nonesuch Expeditions, Woodbridge, UK.

Moseley, Michael E. (1992) *The Incas and Their Ancestors: The Archaeology of Peru*. Thames and Hudson, London and New York.

Moseley, Michael E, and Kent C. Day (eds) (1982) *Chan Chan: Andean Desert City*. University of New Mexico Press.

Paul, Anne (1990) *Paracas Ritual Attire: Symbols of Authority in Ancient Peru*. University of Oklahoma Press.

Reichel-Dolmatoff, Gerardo (1971) *Amazonian Cosmos: the Sexual and Religious Symbolism of the Tukano Indians*, University of Chicago Press.

Reinhard, Johan (1985) "Chavín and Tiahuanaco: A New Look at Two Andean Ceremonial Centers", *National Geographic Research*, 1, pp.395–422.

Reinhard, Johan (1988) *The Nazca Lines: A New Perspective on their Origin and Meaning*. Editorial Los Pinos, Lima.

Reinhard, Johan (1992) "Sacred Peaks of the Andes", *National Geographic*, 181 (3), pp.84–111.

Reinhard, Johan (1996) "Peru's Ice Maidens: Unwrapping the Secrets", *National Geographic*, 190 (6), pp.62–81.

Rostworowksi de Diez Canseco, María, and Michael E. Moseley (eds) (1990) *The Northern Dynasties: Kingship and Statecraft in Chimor*. Dumbarton Oaks, Washington, DC.

Rowe, John H. (1946) "Inca Culture at the Time of the Spanish Conquest", in Julian H. Steward (ed.), *Handbook of South American Indians*, pp.183–330, Washington, DC.

Rowe, John H. (1979) "An Account of the Shrines of Ancient Cuzco", *Nawpa Pacha*, 17, pp.2–80, Berkeley, CA.

Salles-Reese, Verónica (1997) *From Viracocha to the Virgin of Copacabana: Representation of the Sacred at Lake Titicaca*. University of Texas Press.

Saunders, Nicholas J. (1993) "South America", in Roy Willis (ed.), *World Mythology: An Illustrated Guide*, pp.250–63. Duncan Baird, London.

Shobinger, Juan (1991) "Sacrifices of the High Andes", *Natural History*, 4, pp.63–9.

Shimada, Izumi (1994) *Pampa Grande and the Mochica Culture*. University of Texas Press.

Silverman, Helaine (1993) *Cahuachi in the Ancient Nasca World*. University of Iowa Press.

Urton, Gary (1981) *At the Crossroads of the Earth and the Sky*. University of Texas Press.

Urton, Gary (1990) *The History of a Myth: Pacariqtambo of the Origin of the Inkas*. University of Texas Press.

Urton, Gary (1999) *Inca Myths*. British Museum Press, London.

von Hagen, Adriana, and Craig Morris (1998) *The Cities of the Ancient Andes*. Thames and Hudson, London and New York.

Zuidema, R. Tom (1964) *The Ceque System of Cuzco: The Social Organization of the Capital of the Inca*. Leidenanford University Press, Stanford CA.

GENERAL READING

Brotherston, Gordon (1979) *Image of the New World: The American Continent Portrayed in Native Texts*. Thames and Hudson, London and New York.

Coe, Michael, Dean Snow and Elizabeth Benson (1986) *Atlas of Ancient America*. Facts on File, New York and Oxford.

Willis, Roy (ed.), *World Mythology: An Illustrated Guide*. Duncan Baird, London.

PICTURE ACKNOWLEDGEMENTS

The publishers are grateful to the agencies, museums and galleries listed below for kind permission to reproduce the following images in this book:

AKG:
36tc Linden-Museum, Stuttgart; 37tc Gold Museum, Bogotá; 37tr

Andes Press Agency:
51br; 53tl; 59tl

Bridgeman Art Library:
24br The Stapleton Collection; 45tr Phillips, The International Fine Art Auctioneers, UK; 49br Museo de America, Madrid; 49bl Museo Nacional de Anthropologia y Arqueologia, Lima; 58bl Freud Museum, London; 65tr Bolton Museum and Art Gallery, UK

Sylvia Cordaiy:
31br; 65tl

ET Archive:
11bc Archaeological Museum, Lima; 13tl, 18tc Larco Herrera Museum, Lima; 21tl Pedro de Osma Museum, Lima; 40br Bruning Museum, Lambayeque, Peru; 47tc Chavez Ballon Collection, Lima; 53br 54tc, 56tl Pedro de Osma Museum, Lima; 60br, 61tl Archaeological Museum, Lima; 68tr Pedro de Osma Museum, Lima; 81tl, 91tl Museo Nacional de Historia, Lima

Hutchison Library:
39br; 64tr

Panos Pictures:
18br; 29t; 42tcl; 91br

Nick Saunders:
60tc; 73br; 79t; 83tl; 89br

South American Pictures:
10tc; 12c; 14tr; 16 Tony Morrison; 19tc; 19br; 20tl; 20bc; 21bl; 22tr; 23br; 25tc; 25br; 26tc; 26br; 27tr; 27br; 29bl; 29cr; 30tc; 31tr; 31cl; 31bl; 32tc; 32cl; 32br; 33tc; 34tl; 34br; 35tc; 35bl; 35br; 36br; 37c; 38br; 39tl; 39cr; 41cr; 42br; 43tl; 43c; 43br; 44ct; 44br; 45br; 46tc; 47cl; 47br; 49cl; 50tc; 50cr; 50cl; 50bc; 51tr; 51c; 52tl; 52tc; 52cr; 52bc; 53tc; 53bl; 55tc; 55bl; 57tr; 59tr; 59bl; 61br; 62ct; 62br; 63br; 63tc; 65br; 66tc; 66br; 67cl; 68bl; 69tl; 69br; 70tc; 71tl; 71br; 72tr; 72tl; 72br; 73tc; 73tl; 76cl; 76bc; 77tl; 77tr; 77br; 78tl; 78br; 79bl; 79br; 80tr; 80bl; 81br; 83tr; 83cl; 83bl; 84tr; 85tr; 85bl; 86tc; 87tl; 87br; 88tr; 89bl; 89cr; 89tl; 89tr; 90tl; 90tr; 90bc; 90br; 91cr

Mireille Vautier: 41tl

Werner Forman Archive:
18cl Museum für Völkerkunde, Berlin; 21br; 28tr Museum für Völkerkunde; 30br British Museum, London; 39tr, 40tl Museum für Völkerkunde, Berlin; 49tl Dallas Museum of Art; 58tr Private Collection; 59br Museum für Völkerkunde, Berlin; 65cl Dallas Museum of Art; 65c Museum für Völkerkunde, Berlin; 70br David Bernstein Fine Art, NY; 74tr British Museum, London; 74bl British Museum, London; 75l, 75tr Museum für Völkerkunde, Berlin; 75br British Museum, London; 82tr David Bernstein Gallery, NY.

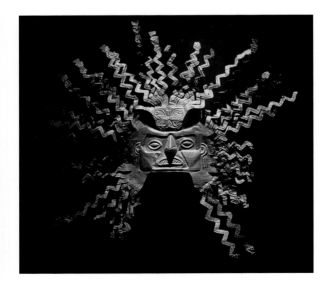

INDEX